# THE
# UNFORTUNATE
# EXPIRATION
## of MR. DAVID S. SPARKS

WILLIAM F. AICHER

# CLASSIFIED
# INFORMATION
# DO NOT DISTRIBUTE

**THIS DOCUMENT RECOVERED FROM LAST KNOWN
BASE OF COLONEL CALVIN SIMON AND
THE ASSOCIATED INSURGENT UPRISING
COMMONLY REFERRED TO AS
'THE CAUSE'**

**DOCUMENT DETAILS OUR LATEST INFORMATION
ON THEIR CONTINUED ATTEMPTS
TO RESCUSCITATE ONE MR. DAVID S. SPARKS**

## Memorandum

To: Colonel Simon
From: PFC Richards
Subject: The Unfortunate Expiration of Mr. David S. Sparks

I regret to inform you the most recent iteration of Project Sparks has resulted in a further repeated variation of the results from previous experiments. It is our hypothesis that a corrupted file remains the primary cause of failure for the resuscitation of the system's memory.

As per established protocol, the attached document follows, in detail, the collapse of this fourth revision of the project, and yet another unfortunate expiration of Mr. David S. Sparks.

Notes regarding this iteration, including variances leading to the failure as well as deviations between this and the previous three attempts are included. Should you wish to discuss the future of this project, I am available at your request.

# ONE
# OH, GREEN WORLD

A prickling at the tip of David's nose stirred him and the perfume of earthy grass, still damp from a recent shower, invaded his senses. Drops of water clung to thin blades of green, not yet dried by the throbbing sun. In the distance a faint hum, barely audible over the breeze, grew progressively louder. He hunted the expanse of emerald turf before him.

David rose to his feet. In every direction, as far as his eyes could see there was nothing but vacant pasture. No trees, no buildings, no people. Nothing but an open grassy arena rolling with hills.

The buzzing amplified, a constant thrum against his eardrums until, ultimately, he placed its source. A hundred yards to David's left, one earthen mound rose at an angle harsher than the others—a near-mountain birthed from the rolling hills. The source of the sound. It continued to swell, louder and louder until no longer a hum, nor a buzz, but an ear-splitting roar. David dashed toward the noise, the only hint of civilization in these damp fields. Up the loose rock of the innocuous mountain he scrambled, and, breaking its crest, he caught his first glimpse of The Preservationist.

Under normal circumstances the sight of the man in the valley below would have terrified him, but lost here in the wild, any fellow human was a welcome sight. Dressed in a pin-striped suit, professionally-tailored, but now tattered and frayed, the man stopped, stared at David and grinned. David, however, overlooked this toothy smile. He was too focused on the chainsaw buzzing idly in the man's grip.

The stranger opened his mouth and spoke, but the rattling of the chainsaw drowned it out.

"I can't hear you!" David yelled, pointing to his ear.

The man killed the blades.

"G'day my friend," the man said, over the slowing, rusty grind of the metal teeth.

The man stood tall—at least six-and-a-half feet—by David's estimate. But it wasn't the man's height that seized David's attention, rather his prominent forehead—a creased wall of loose flesh on top of an otherwise unremarkable face. The dusty gray bowler hat resting loosely on his head, propped in place by his ears, concealed the rest of his seemingly bald cranium. The man's only visible hair sprouted from his ears: wispy strands the same shade of cloudy gray as his hat.

Still clutched in his meaty hands, the chainsaw wound to a full stop. Orange rust spots dotted the chainsaw's body. All traces of paint were worn from the handle long ago, victims of time and heavy handling. A glint of breaking sunlight reflected off the polished grip. Grungy with clumps of dirt and grease, its teeth held bits of white lodged intermittently between them. The bar supporting its steel fangs was muddy and brown, not with rust but—from the way it peeled and flaked—with what appeared to be dried blood.

"Are you going to kill me?" David asked.

"Well sir, that depends on who you might be," the man replied, his voice a combination of Southern drawl and British Cockney. "Are you Progressive?"

His finger played with the saw's throttle trigger and he stepped forward, looking David in the eye. "I asked, are you Progressive? Do you have a chip?"

David's mind searched for an answer. "No ... No, I'm not progressive." Sensing the man's apprehension, he added, "I don't have any chip, if that's what you're asking."

The stranger lumbered toward David and excitedly slapped him on the back. "Then you're a friend! Well, shall we move on?" The man pointed in the direction David had just come from, back over the conspicuous hill marking the horizon.

"Who are you?" David asked as they walked.

"Those who know me call me Calvin. Those who fear me call me The Preservationist."

"Well then," David hesitated. "I'm still not sure what to call you."

"I recommend Calvin. If you were to call me The Preservationist, I'd have to prune off that pretty head of yours."

The man yanked the chainsaw's pullcord, accelerating its teeth to a frightful blur.

"Where exactly are you going?"

"To the sea!" Calvin replied. "Both of us of course, not only me. It's not safe here—at least for long visits."

"What do you mean?"

The man signaled toward the sky, waving his hands and the buzzing chainsaw in the air. "It's everywhere here. The air, the rain, the land... even the places we can't see. We spend too long here, we'll end up dead."

And so, the two walked on, trudging through the wet grass, silent beneath the leather soles of Calvin's loafers, squeaking with each step against the rubber of David's sneakers. Looking down at his clothes, he recognized them as the same he wore earlier in the day, when he phoned his wife in California and heard the shouts of love from his two children in the background.

Had that really been earlier today? If so, how did he come to be here? The blue of the sky suddenly seemed too blue. Electric. As he looked down at the grass, the blades snaked upwards, consuming his feet as they grew—reaching under the cuffs of his jeans, around his ankles and calves. Then they tugged as the roots began to retract, pulling him down into the muddy soil. Waist-deep, he reached up and realized Calvin had walked too far ahead to save him. He thrust his hand down to the ground, bracing himself to keep from sinking any further into the recesses of the earth below.

As his hand hit the ground a rush of cool air blew along his arm. Openness hit his hand as it dropped below the comfort of his bedsheets, to the side of the bed and into the open expanse of his bedroom. Upon realizing the vulnerability his hand suffered, dangling there ready for any old monster to seize from its hiding space under the bed, his arm convulsed reflexively, returning the hand back to the safety and warmth beneath his layers of sheets and blankets. Shifting his body, he drifted back to sleep.

# TWO
# SNEAKY SNAKES

A thousand icy bees stung at David's face. He swatted them away and opened his eyes. It was now night and a heavy rain fell. Finding himself again in the grassy field, the dirt now a soupy mud, he stood knee-deep, unable to move. A vast expanse of darkness spread infinitely in all directions. A flash of lightning in the distant clouds briefly illuminated his surroundings. He was alone.

Unsure which way Calvin had gone, and hesitant of which direction he, himself, had come from to find himself here in the first place, David searched the landscape, desperate for any indication of which way to go. Finding none, he continued forward.

Though he had managed to pull himself from the sucking mud, with each step he risked becoming stuck again. After some experimentation he learned he made better progress moving quickly rather than carefully. A few hundred yards of this slog, however, overwhelmed him and he paused for a quick breath, realizing all-too-soon his mistake. As he stood, bent over gasping for air, his feet began to descend into the muck, which now resembled a swamp more than virgin pasture. He tried to move forward but remained stuck, anchored deep in the ooze. There was no way he could pull free.

Fear struck like a lightning bolt from the storm overhead. Visions of sunrise filled his mind as the sun baked soil to stone, locking his feet in place like a pair of concrete shoes. In his imagination, birds descended on his trapped body, hungrily pecking at his exposed flesh.

The world around him exploded with light, and the loud crack of thunder brought him back to the storm, along with the realization that the stinging pecks were bits of ice falling from the sky. Still, the vision of himself trapped, feet cemented in scorched earth while crows gobbled his eyes, stuck with him. Straining with all his might, he gave one more attempt to wrench his feet free, and succeeded—well, mostly succeeded. His body lunged forward with the attempt, and he very nearly found himself once again face down in the mud. Regaining his balance, a strange sensation of wetness engulfed his feet. With a final push, he pulled his feet from his shoes, and now stood with nothing between himself and the ground but a pair of dirty socks. Deciding it better not to risk getting stuck again, David sprinted across the waterlogged countryside.

Soon David was no longer running across a field, but wading through knee-deep water. A new fear struck him. Am I going to drown out here? But that worry was immediately replaced with one much more rational—and much more real—when something massive churned in the flood near his feet.

He kept moving, as fast as the rising water would allow. This became progressively more difficult, however, as the water level lapped higher still.

Lightning struck again, brightening the sky for another flash of time, and David's heart leapt as he spied his destination.

In the distance, about twenty yards ahead, a hillside broke from the water. Rivers carved its banks, threatening a mudslide, but at this moment any land was better than the rising flood. A surge of adrenaline shot through his body at this sign of relief, only to be squashed when the thing in the water brushed against his shins, threatening to trip him.

He plunged forward, his nostrils filling with water. Reaching out, his hands could not find any bottom. Up and down lost all delineation and his lungs burned from the frigid water he already inhaled. The urge to cough—to breathe—to pull in any gasp of life-saving air wracked his body. But even as the burn tore through him, he resisted, for had he done so he was certain he would reflexively flood his lungs beyond repair.

Forcing himself to relax, he hung suspended in the rising water. His feet and lower body sank, and his sense of direction realigned through this simple expression of gravity. Once he determined which way was up, there was no question about what direction to swim.

As his head broke the water's surface another bolt of lightning hit, this time considerably closer than before, and the water tremored in its thunderous wake. He coughed the water he allowed to leach into his lungs and swam onward toward the shore, his chest burning with each inhalation.

With every stroke, the hillside drew closer. So close that even without the lightning strikes, he could see it through the downpour: a man-shaped mass crouched at the water's edge.

At first David thought it was a boulder or an overgrown bush, but as he drew closer the form rose to a standing position. He recognized it as the stranger in the suit. David's feet found purchase and he scrambled up the grassy incline, out of the water to the safety of land. As he clawed his way through the sloppy mess, he caught a glimpse of Calvin's widening eyes. The man reared his buzzing chainsaw into the air, sprung in David's direction and David dropped instinctively to the ground.

Calvin crashed into the water behind him in a momentous splash, slicing the chainsaw blade down as he hit. Surely Calvin intended to kill him. Lightning struck again, showering the scene in an explosion of light. Dark streaks painted Calvin's face and clothes and the storm surge before him blossomed in a sea of crimson. A rattling sound coughed from the chainsaw's motor, and it sputtered to a stop. Calvin trudged out of the water and stood next to David, the two of them staring as red faded to pink as another bolt rattled the hillside.

"Had an anaconda hunting you. Sizable bastard too," Calvin's shoulders slumped as he exhaled.

He dropped the chainsaw, blade-first, into the ground. The motor sizzled as drops of rain continued to fall on the cooling engine. Calvin sat down next to David and allowed his neck to relax, looking downward with his chin on his chest.

The two rested in silence for what must have been hours and waited for the rain to end. As the skies cleared and the sun began to peek its face over their hill, the path to the west showed nothing but slowly receding floods. Whereas to the east, the land continued to rise.

*I guess I know which direction we're going,* David thought as his eyes closed and he drifted off to sleep.

# THREE
# A COOL GLASS OF WATER

David rolled in his bed and peeled the sticky sheets from his skin. The bedside clock marked the time as 2:14 a.m. He smacked his tongue against the inside of his mouth, tasting dehydration, and stumbled to the master bathroom, half awake and half asleep. Choosing to avoid blindness from the light of the vanity and being woken further, he flicked on the dim bulb of the shower light. An ambient glow escaped the frosted glass of the tiled shower, filling the bathroom with enough light to effectively maneuver, but not enough to shake him from his daze.

The water from the tap was naturally cold, though the faucet handle was set to hot. It took a while for the hot water to make its way up the pipes, and though what poured from the tap had festered in the plumbing since morning, he twice filled his glass and gulped the water down. The drought in his mouth subsided, although his stomach now churned from drinking so much water in such short a time.

## FOUR
# A HEALTHY CROP

The world around David spun as his stomach churned. He opened his eyes to find somewhere to vomit—and was greeted with a view of a man's bottom in a soggy tailored, but tattered suit. A green sky rushed by above. He tried to straighten his body and heard a voice.

"Finally awake, eh boy?"

Calvin dropped David's body and he thudded face-first against the ground. David pushed himself upright and stood, rubbing his nose where it banged the sunbaked concrete of the ground.

"Looks like you busted your snout."

"Bleeding, but not broken," David replied, gingerly tapping the tip of his dripping nose. "Where are you taking me?"

"I'm not taking you anywhere. You're on your own now. Just didn't want to leave you at the side of the lake. You never can be certain what's lurking in there … almost got yourself killed last night."

David searched for an answer as to what this stranger was talking about. The only vision to surface was Calvin's demented face lunging at him, chainsaw raised. The man had tried to kill him.

David recoiled, putting distance between himself and this strange man.

"You said something about an anaconda?"

"Yes, last night. Not really an anaconda though—one of the field serpents," Calvin answered. "They made them," he added, nodding his head toward the East.

"They?"

"The Progressives. The ones in the plastic city."

David clearly had no idea what he was referring to and suspicion crept over Calvin's face

"Is that where you're headed? To the plastic city?" David asked.

"Yes sir. I have business there. I assumed that's where you were headed as well, since God knows there's nothing but death out here. You're welcome to travel with me, if you'd like."

And so, they traveled onward, Calvin in his dirty suit, chainsaw in hand, and David empty-handed and shoeless.

They walked, and hours passed in silence.

"Thanks, by the way."

"Of course," Calvin replied. "What for?"

"For helping me out back, with, what did you call it ... the field snake?"

"... field serpent. And I think you'd do well to ask yourself if you should be thanking me or fearing me."

"Trust me, I've asked. The trouble is, I don't have much of a choice here. Either I trust you or wander aimlessly. At least this way I'm wandering aimlessly with someone."

"It's not aimless if you've got somewhere to be. Do you have somewhere to be, David?"

"I ... I'm not sure yet," David couldn't remember sharing his name with the man. Then again, there was a lot he couldn't remember lately.

They both fell silent again and walked on. The field seemed to stretch on forever, although the air had taken on a new weight over the last hour. The dampness had brought with it a chill, and a steady breeze picked up against them from the East. David's stomach rumbled.

"The field serpent?" David asked. "What was that thing? You called it an anaconda at first."

Calvin stopped and stared at David with a look of surprise. "You honestly don't know? I wonder what happened to you, what happened to get you out into the middle of the Green Zone in the first place. They must have done something to you. That's what they do," Calvin's voice trailed off, his monologue turned inward. "They do things ..."

"So that thing was going to kill me?"

Calvin shrugged his shoulders. "Maybe. You never can tell. They spend most of their time underground. In the summer heat like this they're lucky if they move at all—at least when they come up to the surface. Traveling is usually safe to move this time of year; no one can see you. Well, at least not so deep in the Green Zone at least. Their ground patrols are useless."

"I'm afraid you lost me. I thought you said it was a snake," David hesitated, then added, "although I'm not quite sure what an anaconda would be doing this far north."

"It. Wasn't. A. Real. Snake." Calvin spoke each word deliberately, punctuated with agitation, while his right index finger nervously clawed the trigger of the dead chainsaw. "That's what we call them. Anacondas, field serpents, whatever you call them it makes no matter. They're all you're going to find out here, other than travelers like us of course. If you're lucky, the serpents don't see you before you see them."

"Well, lucky for me you were there to help," David replied cautiously.

"Lucky for you I suppose. You weren't dispatched. Regardless, they're aware you're here, which means they'll be ready for you. And with what I did, taking out one of their sentries, they'll be waiting for me too. Lucky for me they still have no idea when."

"What are you saying? These snakes are some sort of security system? Whatever you killed last night sure seemed alive to me—especially from the blood spray off your friend there." David pointed to the dangling chainsaw. "... and it most certainly didn't look like some sort of camera or machine."

"Serpents are SBS," said Calvin. David shrugged his shoulders unknowingly. "Symbiotic Biological Surveillance?"

"I have no idea what you're talking about."

"Of course, you don't," Calvin muttered. "After the chemicals made the Green Zone uninhabitable they set the serpents free here. At first, they were only genetic creations, but when the neural net went wireless they programmed it so the serpents' AI systems tapped directly in. In a way, the serpents are like the Eyefields, only these bastards are mobile. Since they're primarily bio they still have to spend most of their time below the surface due to the chemicals on the top layer. When it rains though the surface layers are safe for them; the chemicals dilute in water, and they can move about nicely—they're respectable swimmers. That's why I call them anacondas—like in the old days when the anacondas would swim through the South American marshes. They still haven't figured out a way to build an immunity to it for animals. Although I have heard talk of chimera research."

"Okay then," said David, oddly satisfied. "Any idea how much farther until we're there?"

"Not much more as far as distance, quite a bit further in time. We're going to have to stop at the top of this next hill."

As the duo reached the summit, David's eyes widened; the land stretching out before them was unlike anything David had ever seen. Separated into square parcels, it closely resembled farm fields, though there didn't appear to be any plants growing other than the grass in which they were currently standing. What made each parcel distinguishable from the surrounding field of grass were the tiny pinkish "things," accented in white, with flecks of blue, green and brown. And they were round. Whatever was growing out there, it seemed to be completely round—at least on top. To David's mind, they were like sparkling white marbles, flickering on and off like lights on a Christmas tree, all of them changing directions in unison, their movement made visible from the dark circles marking one side of the ball.

"Here we are, the Eyefields," Calvin said, matter-of-factly.

David blinked, attempting to bring his view into focus. "Wait.. Those are eyes?"

"What else would they be? We're at the edge of the prairies, after all."

David stepped forward to look closer, but Calvin reached his hand up and grabbed him at the shoulder, dragging him to the ground.

"Do you want them to catch us? I told you, we still have a bit of an advantage to us; they still have no idea when we're coming. I'd like to keep that secret to ourselves."

David examined the landscape. "Aren't you being paranoid? There's obviously no one around here."

Calvin put down the chainsaw, placed both hands on David's shoulders and studied him. "David, there are literally thousands of eyes down there. Each one of them is part of the network. If you want to walk through there and let them all see you, that's up to you. I do recommend, however, you keep your hands high and wave a white flag as you go through."

Understanding suddenly washed over David. "They really are eyes, aren't they ... growing there in the field. They're part of the same network those snake things are."

Nodding his head, Calvin added, "They grow them here in the fields for transplants, lab tests, spare parts. The salt from the sea on the far side of the fields helps keep their salinity more stable and if the levels go too low they fly over and salt-dust the bogs."

"So that's what all the blue is? They're growing in ponds?"

"Not ponds, bogs. Like cranberries. That's how the farmers keep the eyes and the simple muscle and bio-nutrition structure propagating beneath the surface moist. I've seen a dried-up field, once before. Farther south. The land there had gotten too arid from the encroaching deserts making it far too difficult to farm so they moved the bogs north toward the rain belts. They must have shut it down only a few weeks earlier because the smell of rot was overwhelming. The eyes had all been harvested, of course—the ones they could salvage anyway. The others had been long since pecked off by crow swarms. A cracking, drying, rotting heap of machine-flesh and the abandoned neurocables leading to the ocean. These were the early fields, the ones from before the network was able to handle that kind of bandwidth without some sort of land line. You could still see most of the nodules in the machine-flesh from where the eyes had been connected to the network, although quite a few shriveled up under the sun."

Calvin paused, his eyes searching the sky. "It smelt a bit of hamburger, actually, depending on where you were and how long the space had been baking," Calvin licked his lips. "I miss hamburgers."

"So, how do we sneak past them? What are they waiting for?"

"Eyefields are still grown primarily as a crop. The surveillance? A lucky side effect The Progressives stumbled upon in building them. When the sun goes down and the horizon starts to turn pink, it will trigger their eyelids to close and we'll be safe to move through. Provided we tread carefully, of course. There are still alarms around the area to ward of the poachers, and those are on all night."

"How do their eyelids close? They're just eyes—there is no lid."

"It's a preprogrammed system. When they engineered these replacements, they made a point to give them an internal shut-down mechanism to prevent them from adapting too well to the dark, and therefore avoid becoming overly sensitive to light. In the city it's never dark, and once these are transplanted to a city location they won't have much need for night vision. So instead of outer eyelids, there's a skin substitute that folds down, triggered by circadian rhythm."

"So, what do we do?"

"We wait for the sun to go down."

"Of course." David took a seat in the wet grass and Calvin took a seat beside him. "Hey Calvin?" he asked.

"What?"

"You have anything to eat? I'm starving."

Calvin reached into the pocket of his coat, retrieved a paper bag of granola and offered a handful to David. David thanked him, and the two talked while waiting for sunset to come.

"The fields ... you said they weren't habitable, but they're green with life. Plus, other than some hunger and the fact I'm exhausted, I feel reasonably well. What's the deal?"

Calvin shook his head. "I do wonder where it is you came from, David. Do you remember anything at all?"

The thought hadn't ever crossed his mind, but, now that he thought about it, David didn't have many memories. Not of this place, at least. When he thought back on his life he remembered a wife, two kids, a house and a job in security.

"Let's pretend I don't remember anything, okay? Can you give me a history lesson?"

"How far back would you like me to go?"

"For starters, the question I asked a minute ago—what's with the fields? I'd also like to find out where everyone is, where we're going, what the plastic city is, and who the hell you are."

"Well David, you do have an awful lot of questions," said Calvin. He turned his head to the west, noting the sun had nearly hit the horizon. "I'll answer what I can, but we don't have a lot of time until nightfall. Once the sun sets, we have to move."

"Tell me what you can."

"Okay then, I'll start with your first question. The fields we're in are more or less what they seem—fields of grass. There used to be a lot more here than grass, of course, before the migration. Before The Chemical Wars. The cities still stand where they did, but there's no one there other than people like me." Calvin considered David and added, "You, on the other hand, don't look like you came from one of the ancient territories, but you also don't look like you're from the city. If I'm to believe you, and for some reason I do, you claim you're not a Progressive, and I'll take you at your word.

"The fields, on the other hand, aren't the kind of place where anyone lives—at least not the place anyone can live for long. You said you were feeling fine, other than some exhaustion. Are you sure you're not experiencing a shortness of breath? Try inhaling—make it a deep one."

David took a deep breath and coughed as his chest constricted. It was as if his lungs were full; a memory flashed, reminding him of late nights spent in the bars as a college kid, in rooms full of too much smoke and too little oxygen.

"You see? That's what I'm talking about. It starts in the lungs, but it can seep in through the skin too. The eyes though, they suffer the worst of it." Calvin pointed at David's shoeless feet. "Really, osmosis is where most of the considerable damage comes from. You're going to want to wash those as soon as you find some water.

"The Organics had it right, even if they were a bunch of nutters themselves. Too much poison for the sake of mankind lead to near obliteration. The fields are green because they're alive, because of the chlorophyll in each individual blade of grass, but they thrive because there's nothing out here to harm them anymore. Life was fine, and we kept on multiplying, but the bigger problem was people weren't dying anymore. The scientists and doctors and technologists had basically beaten death, or at least most forms of it. For those who could afford it, of course. The ones who couldn't had already been forced from the city when homelessness was outlawed, and they built their communes out here, in the fields. They were the first to go. Couldn't fight in the war, even as it erupted in their own backyards.

"Some people blamed the farmers, but they were only doing what they had to do to survive. When it's kill or be killed, it's better to be the one holding the hatchet than to be the chicken on the chopping block. If there's one group of people who understands better than anyone else, it's the farmers. Anyway, they did what had to be done. The chemicals were the only way to protect the crops so they'd grow sizeable enough to feed the growing population. Sure, The Organics had their own crops, but those were for their own societies and there wasn't enough to share beyond their own borders ... caused them to have quite a few battles of their own," Calvin chuckled.

"So, without anyone realizing it, The Chemical Wars began ... but no one noticed until the homeless communes started to dwindle. The ones in the cities assumed it was an act of natural selection. These people didn't serve a purpose as far as the greater good of society was concerned, and without serving a purpose they had no real means as far as financial assets, which meant they didn't have any kind of healthcare or medicine other than what they could come up with on their own. All the technology was in the cities, and they certainly weren't welcome.

"When the city people started to turn sick, however, society did notice and did care. Their concern wasn't for the ruralites, mind you, but for their own well-being. At first they thought one of the homeless somehow snuck back into the city and brought a virus with them, but eventually it became clear whatever was killing people wasn't communicable. The doctors performed test after test while the citizens of the cities dropped like flies. No matter what tests they did, however, they couldn't find a virus and they couldn't find a bacterium. It didn't appear to be biological in nature at all and didn't match any recognizable chemical weapon. Finally, they came upon the answer. I've no idea how they came upon it, but they did. By then it was too late. Chicago was long gone, Milwaukee and St. Louis too. It spread from the Midwest out toward the coasts at a staggering rate, killing most of the population. It wasn't limited to the U.S. either. Most of Europe was already gone."

"What was it?" David asked. "What killed everybody?"

"Like I said, it was the farmers. They started The Chemical Wars without realizing it. Whatever it was they put on their crops to keep them growing was a poison, or at least acted as one once all the chemicals started to mix together. That's why it spread from the Midwest; right out of the corn belt, although California and Idaho were hot zones too. It's also why the grass out here is so green—still full of the chemicals. It killed their predators, but along with killing the predators it also killed off the animals and insects necessary for cross pollination of most of the crops. Sure, you'll come across a wild corn field once in a while, but that's mostly due to the wind carrying the pollen. Everything keeps getting choked out by the grass in the end though. The remaining progressives built the plastic cities on the sea to escape from the land and to allow it to heal. It wasn't safe here anymore, and the sea was the only refuge."

"So, am I going to die? If the land is poisoned, how are they safe growing the Eyefields?" David asked.

"Once the scientists realized what was happening, all chemicals were banned. The Chemical Wars raged on after this simply because what had been released was already out there, and there was nothing anyone could do to stop it. The land is healing, and some of us are starting to travel across it. As long as we don't linger, and we stick to the coasts, the effects are mostly temporary. You're safer the closer you travel to the oceans, except for California. The Progressives are aware of this too of course, and they're starting to venture back here as well. Some of us think the Eyefields are more than crops—that they're also experiments to see if our biological systems can survive here again. In the Eyefields they can test new treatments and manipulate genetic code to find a way to take back the land—all of it at once, rather than be forced to wait for what could be thousands of years before nature cleans up their mess."

"So why are you going there? Is that where we'll find shelter?"

"We can talk about me later. Right now, we have to prepare ourselves to move." Calvin pointed to the horizon, bright pink where the sun was about to meet the land. His hand changed direction and pointed to the Eyefields below. "Watch." His voice was commanding, yet David could hear a hint of awe behind it as well.

As the sun fell behind them, the sky changed from pink to crimson, and the Eyefields began to shift. The rapid movement of the eyes and their pupils slowed, eventually coming to a stop. As they stopped, David felt horribly exposed; the thousands of eyes stretching out before him all seemed to be looking directly at him.

"They turn west at sundown, so they won't be damaged when the sun rises in the morning," Calvin said, sensing David's question.

The crimson sky grew more vibrant as the sun fell, and the eyes began to change. It happened in waves, one row at a time, a rush of pink through the bogs as the eyes closed their inner lid, shutting down for the day to avoid any unnecessary night vision training.

When the sun disappeared and the last row of eyes turned its shade of fleshy pink, Calvin stood and yanked David to his feet by his collar.

"We have to hurry. Night might seem like a long time, but those fields are considerably more expansive than you'd think."

In the light of the moon, under a clear evening sky, they rushed down the hillside, onward to the fields of slumbering surveillance. Still, something nagged at David. And, despite the lack of trees, David suspected they weren't yet out of the woods.

## FIVE
# LIKE A GOD-DAMN OCEAN SPRAY COMMERCIAL

At the bottom of the hillside, level with the expanse of Eyefields, the air hung low and wet. A dense, knee high fog covered the landscape, rolling in and out of the bogs, like waves of dry ice. As they approached the perimeter a wire fence bordered the fields, humming with electricity. The entire area was, indeed, under additional surveillance— exactly as Calvin said. Crossing through here would be impossible.

"Damn it. I thought we hit farther south than where we are ... or is it north? Even I have a difficult time finding direction without a compass." Calvin licked his finger and held it up to the air, sensing the breeze. "We move south."

Calvin headed off and David quickly followed. The perimeter of unchanging fields of eyes glistened in the moonlight, their pupils casting grey circles under their thin, fleshy lids. About every thousand yards there would be a break where a grassy strip of land rose up, separating one bog from the next.

*Like a god-damn Ocean Spray commercial*, David thought.

A faint light appeared in the distance, shining increasingly brighter as they marched on. About a hundred yards out, Calvin stuck his hand in front of David. David stopped, concentrated on the light, and a tiny wooden shack materialized out of the darkness. A man sat in a chair in front directly under the lamp's glow, reading a book in the night.

"There's nothing wrong with us being out here," Calvin informed David. "This is public land, up to the fence. As long as we're casual and pose no apparent threat, we're nothing more than a curiosity. Follow me but keep your hands visible."

The two cautiously approached the man and his shack. The small building stood about ten feet high and covered only about a hundred square feet. It held no windows, and only had the one door accessible from outside the perimeter fence, in front of which the guard perched. He appeared in his mid-sixties, his crows' feet accented by the deep shadows cast from the light above his chair. His dress consisted of a dirty brown jacket and worn blue jeans, reminding David of cowboys from photos of the Old West. The man glanced in their direction at the sound of their footsteps but didn't rise from his seat.

"Preservationist? Is that you?" the man asked, with a gruff Irish accent.

Calvin stopped and bowed slightly. "Indeed, it is," he replied. "I didn't realize you had decided to up and join The Reconstruction," he added, more as a question than a statement.

"Aye. I figure I'll fare better on the winning side, if you catch my meaning."

"Oh, come off it, Finniman. You and I both know you wanted easier access to the crops."

"Right as always ... right as always. It's a lot easier than—" Finniman stopped suddenly, eyeing David. "Who's that with you?" he asked.

"This is Mr. Sparks, and to be honest, I'm not quite sure who he is. Then again, neither does he. I vouch for him though; you can speak freely."

"Hmph. Well, as I was saying, it's a lot easier than poaching, and the pay's not half bad either. I actually have a place of my own now. Not in the city, mind you, but in the coast village on the other side of the fields. And how about you? What are you doing here?"

"We're on our way back to the city. We were planning on cutting through the fields, but I see security's been upgraded. No more dogs, only miles of fence. It was easy to pass by the dogs."

"I reckon that's why they got rid of 'em."

"I hate to ask, but can you help us through?"

"Depends. What do ya plan on doin' once you're to the other side? They're not going to let you back in the city."

"I have some ideas. Is Applegate still around?"

"Listen, Calvin. I don't want ta get mixed up in whatever you've got planned. I have a hard enough time staying under the radar here, swiping and selling on the underground without getting caught. If I'm found out as sympathetic, that'll be the end."

"All we're asking for is passage and a reintroduction, friend. You'll have done a lot to help The Cause, without anyone being able to accuse you of such."

"I've no idea what you've got planned, Preservationist, but I trust ye. Come on then you two, we'll take the freight elevator."

The door to the cabin creaked as it opened, as was to be expected from the rustic shack it appeared to be. But, as David reminded himself, looks can be deceiving. Instead of dusty plank wood and a worn bearskin rug, they found a shiny metal room, devoid of any features other than brushed aluminum walls and a sleek obsidian floor. The three men entered, Calvin first, followed by David, with Finniman bringing up the rear. As Finniman entered, the door closed behind him and he reached into his pocket and pulled out a small key card. He waved the card in front of a small sensor affixed to the wall next to the sliding elevator doors and a panel opened.

"Ocular recognition required," announced a disembodied mechanical voice. David thought it sounded female.

Finniman stepped toward the blue circle of light on the wall and reached his hands up to his face. Using his right hand to hold the lower eyelid of his right eye in place, he stretched his upper eyelid up to expose the retina fully to the light.

"Commence scan," he said. The light flashed brightly with a sort of phosphorescent glow, like the black lights of discos and hippies' basements, and the elevator began to descend.

"Welcome to the freight elevators, my friends—the quickest way to travel through the Eyefields. If you two don't mind, I'd like to travel through here as quickly as possible, so I can return to my post without being missed."

"That's what we're looking for. This isn't a sightseeing venture," Calvin replied. David remained silent.

"Then we'll go straight through; avoid the stops up to the fields," said Finniman. "I wasn't sure if you were... here for some gathering," he added, speaking to Calvin.

"I'll pick up what I need at the other side."

"Very well then. Elevator: fast-forward." With those words the elevator lurched forward, having already come to a halt at the bottom of its descent below the fields. David's teeth gnashed, and he ground them as the elevator sped along. The initial movement nearly knocked him flat to the floor, but he soon regained his footing. He could feel the speed of their movement and it felt strange to him. It was obvious they were moving at extremely high speeds, likely in excess of a hundred miles an hour, but without any visual cues to reinforce this hypothesis he couldn't be certain. What he was certain about, was that between the movement and the lack of an outside marker for his brain to focus on, he quickly began to feel ill. Finniman took note but didn't say a word.

"Trip'll be done shortly. Only takes a minute or so to cross when we're traveling in fast-forward. This thing'll top out at almost two-hundred miles per hour when we're zipping through the fields, although you wouldn't ever guess we're moving at that kind of clip. Sure, you'll experience a jolt when we start moving, but after an initial shock the ride's a quick steady build and you hardly can tell you're moving."

David tumbled forward as the elevator came to a sudden stop. The air brakes hissed as the forward movement ceased and David had nearly regained his balance when the elevator started to rise back to the surface. Both Calvin and Finniman laughed as he crashed back down to the hard floor.

"Here we are, coastal side. Bandleshore's a few clicks from here, and the city's not much further."

"Finniman, could you open the back door?" Calvin asked.

"Sure…" Finniman hesitated. "But only take what you absolutely need. Anything more and it'll be noticed."

The metal doors through which Calvin and David had entered the elevator opened again, revealing direct access to the Eyefields. Calvin stepped through the doors and approached the nearest bog. There he reached into the water and plucked out a pair of sleeping eyes, like grapes from a vine. He put the eyes into his jacket pockets, one in the left and one in the right, turned on his heels and marched back to the elevator. The doors closed as he returned, and another set of doors opened on the metal room's opposite wall. Calvin stepped out of the elevator and David followed.

"Godspeed," said Finniman.

"Thank you, friend," Calvin replied. "Don't worry about us. Everything's already in motion. You've done more for The Cause than you realize. But trust me, you'll learn more soon enough."

The elevator doors closed, and Calvin shut the door to the wooden shack the elevator hid within. David heard the bolt of the electronic lock slide into place. There was no way back.

## SIX
# A ROUTINE OPERATION

In the distance, voices rang out in the air. Night had fallen less than an hour ago and it was still quite early. The moon shone brightly on the fields from its low perch and its full shape would soon light the entire hillside like a faded milky sun. Several buildings were visible about a half mile from where David and Calvin stood—the edges of a small town. David could make out lights in the town—flickering yellow and orange from gas lamps marking the streets and walkways to illuminate the night life. Bandleshore lay before them.

At first glance the town reminded David of a movie set representation of downtown London as it appeared in the late 1800s or early 1900s. Like something out of Tim Burton's *Sweeney Todd* or the Hughes' brothers *From Hell* or any of those other similar films where Johnny Depp always seemed to hold the lead role. Very little existed in terms of outlying areas. The town itself felt cramped, much like a city's downtown, and it was filthy and smelly like one as well. Definitely a blue-collar place: a place for the workers of the fields and those who couldn't afford to live in the city but were forced to commute in on the mag-trains each day. A few taverns dotted the streets, and judging by the sounds emanating from them, this was clearly where the townsfolk spent their evenings.

David and Calvin entered one of the taverns, a little place called Vonshine's. At least a dozen people crowded around the small bar, and two dozen more milled about, elbow to elbow in the open space between the bar and the entrance. No music played, and there wasn't even space for a band— the only sound was the murmur of patrons, almost all men, talking and arguing. The stink of alcohol and danger hung low in the air, like a fight was always brewing among these men, ready to erupt at a moment's notice. Calvin elbowed his way through the crowd, up to the bar, dragging David along by his hand. When they reached the bar he tapped on a man's shoulder.

The man turned around, anger welling up in his eyes, his fist clenched ready to strike out at whomever had interrupted his drinking. When his eyes registered Calvin, however, the man relaxed his fist and his eyes shrank from their look of anger to one of dread.

"Preservationist! What a pleasure to see you!" The man's voice quivered as he spoke.

"You may dispense with the pleasantries, Devon," Calvin replied. "I'm in need of your services," he continued, pointing subtly at his eyes as he did so.

"I'm sorry ... but I can't. I—I can't." Devon stuttered. "They've been watching me close—they suspect me! If I'm found out I'm going to be done. You're fully aware they're not holding trials on this. They'll call me a terrorist and that'll be it for me."

"Devon ..." Calvin's echoed a warning.

Devon stood from his bar stool and attempted to leave but was stopped when Calvin grabbed him by his shirt collar.

"I'm not a doctor anymore! I can't! I can't!" he shouted fearfully, his eyes twitching from place to place around the room, eager to find an exit.

"Come on David, we're leaving." Calvin tugged hard at Devon's shirt, dragging him toward the door. "Devon, you're going to help me."

Once outside the bar, Devon managed to calm down and Calvin released his grip on the man. Devon brushed his hands down his front, smoothing his shirt as best he could. "Have you got the, um, supplies?" he asked.

"I have the parts, but I need your tools and your hands."

"Very well," said Devon. "This guy with you?" he asked, tilting his head in David's direction.

Calvin nodded.

"Okay then. Both of you follow me."

The three men walked down the streets of Bandleshore, away from the noisy bustle of the taverns, clear across to the edge of town. Surf crashed nearby, its constant hum buzzing like a distant, muted beehive. He looked in the direction of the sound and met moonlight glimmering on cresting waves. A beach spread out in both directions here at the end of town, broken up by what appeared to be a massive train station, positioned on the ocean's edge.

An immense structure built of gleaming metal beams and massive glass windows, the station stuck out in contrast to the wooden shacks of Bandleshore. A single track stretched out from it, running out across the sea. David's eyes followed it until the night's lack of light hid it from view. Off in the distance he could make out a small glowing orb.

Calvin noted David's questioning gaze. "Plasticity. You honestly haven't been there?"

"No." David shook his head. "No—not that I can remember at least."

As they talked, Devon took his chance and darted off in the direction of the train station. A stone hurtled through the air, catching him in the back of the head, and he crumpled down into the sand.

"You know better than to run, Devon." Calvin hoisted him to his feet and slapped him on the back of the head where the rock had hit. "Let's keep moving, or next time I'll make it hurt."

---

A door creaked open and Devon ushered them into a room full of medical equipment. Much less a doctor's office than a disused morgue, a rusted gurney sat abandoned to one side and yellowed sinks stained with rust dripped sporadically in the back. It obviously had not seen active duty in quite some time. Either that, or it was one highly unsanitary doctor's office.

Calvin reached into his pockets and pulled out the pair of eyes he recently picked from the Eyefields. "I need a swap."

"You've done this too many times already!" Devon replied, his voice thick with exasperation. "I'm begging you, do not risk this again," he pleaded.

"Devon, I need to make it to the city and you and I both know there's no way I'm going to make it onto the mag-train without swapping my eyes. These eyes," he pointed forcefully to his face, "they're in the system. There's no way I'm going to make it through security with them."

David chewed at his lip. "How am I going to bypass security?" he asked. "I don't think I'm on file at all, they won't register me when they scan. Or, worse yet, maybe they will recognize me and I'll be arrested on the spot."

"Definitely a possibility. The thought had, of course, crossed my mind. I hadn't given it much credence though since. Now we're here though, I'm beginning to worry. Scan him, Devon," he commanded.

Reaching into a metal cabinet mounted to the wall, Devon retrieved a small white device with a screen in front. *Like my first iPhone*, David thought. Devon pressed the device's touchscreen a few times, then held it in front of David's face.

"Look at the circle."

David stared at the screen. It was blank except for a small black dot in the center. He focused on it and was blinded when the screen flashed a brilliant white.

"I can't see anything!" he exclaimed.

"Don't worry, it'll take a few minutes 'til you can see again. This baby here is a hack job, but it's all we've got. You'll be fine in a few minutes," said Devon, looking back to the device in his hand. "No file. He should be clear."

David stood in blind silence.

"You're clear for entry, David." David recognized the voice as Calvin's. "I, on the other hand, am not. I need Devon here to do a quick transplant or I'll be held at security. This far out they're not too concerned with safety measures. There're too many people traveling in and out of the city these days, what with the start of terrestrial repopulation. The only checks now are for red flags. All registration takes place in the city, so we'll be able to pass inspection without any questions."

"What happens once we're in?" David asked. "Are we going to have to register? I checked my pockets earlier and I don't have any kind of identification on me at all." He started to see the familiar outlines of the room begin to reappear.

"I don't think that'll be an issue," Calvin replied hastily. "Well then, Devon, shall we get on with it?"

"I keep telling you, Calvin, you've done this too many times. The nerve signals start to fade after too many swaps. I don't want to blind you."

"Do it Devon. This is my decision, and you'll have completed your debt. Besides, this is my last swap."

"Your eyesight back?" Devon grumbled.

"Me? Yeah, mostly anyway. Why?" asked David.

"I think you're gonna want to leave. You don't wanna see this."

## SEVEN
# A MAN ABOUT TOWN

David left the two of them to go about their surgery. They were right, he didn't want to see it, whatever it was they were doing. The makeshift surgical space was far from sanitary, and besides, David couldn't stand the sight of blood. Sure, fake blood in the movies was no big deal, but real blood— the kind flowing within him, pumping through his heart and arteries and veins, giving his body life, that was a different story. David could stomach it when he knew the red mess consisted of nothing other than corn syrup and food coloring. But the real deal, thick with platelets and swimming with unknown disease, that was a whole different story.

It was still fairly early in the evening—no later than ten o' clock by David's guess, so he headed back to the bar. As he made his way back down the street, he heard the clinking of glass and the raised, drunken voices filtering their way through the doors and onto the deserted streets and alleys.

The wet slap of David's feet against the pavement echoed in the night.

*First thing I'm going to do when we reach the city is buy a pair of shoes*, he thought. *Maybe I can rustle up a pair here before we leave in the morning—if we're waiting until morning to leave.*

Inside Vonshine's, bodies pressed tightly against one another and the stink of hot breath and bad beer permeated the atmosphere. He pushed his way through the crowd, back to the same spot at the bar Devon occupied earlier. A new patron now sat on Devon's stool and silently scrutinized David.

"You a friend of Devon's?" he asked.

"I guess you could say so. I'm actually here with Calvin."

"Shh!" the man hushed him. "You don't want to be talking about him too loudly. If people knew you was palling around with The Preservationist you'd be in a world of trouble. Even out here in the Edgelands not everyone is sympathetic to The Cause. You catch the ear of a Progressive and that'll be the end of you—and trust me, they do come out here once in a while. Business mostly, but they're here and you never can be sure who's who."

"Sorry," David replied. "Thanks for the tip."

"So, friend of Devon, what's your name?"

"David. David Sparks."

"Glad to meet you. I'm Conor. Let's have a drink."

"Love to, but I'm afraid I don't have any money."

"No need for money. Flaherty, the man tending the taps tonight, he recognized your ... *traveling companion* ... and I'm sure he'll take care of you." He waved his hand and hailed the bartender, who brought over two mugs of warm golden ale.

"On the house," the bartender muttered as he slid the beers across the bar, carefully avoiding eye contact with David.

"You'll get used to it, I'm afraid. People here are paranoid, and for good reason. Things have been getting hotter than ever lately; the tension between the Futurists and The Progressives is thick as a cut of New York strip and rumor has it something paramount is coming. Those of us who aren't involved at that kind of level keep our heads down at times like this," Conor said. "I'm sure you can fill me in a bit though, given the kind of company you've been keeping."

"You mean Ca—" David stopped short of saying his name. "You mean the man I came in here with earlier?" he corrected himself. "I actually don't know much about him, other than I think he might be crazy. When I first met him he was waving a chainsaw around like a madman."

"A chainsaw ... figures. Their weapon of choice. They think they're being clever."

"How so?"

"Irony, or something. Chainsaws are symbolic of the deforestation of the land back when everything was cleared to make room for more farm fields. If it weren't for the chainsaws, or at least the men who originally wielded them, none of this would have happened—or so the argument goes. People like your friend see the chainsaw as just desserts. It all would have happened anyway though, in my opinion at least."

"So, what are they ..." David stopped himself, realizing it in his best interest not to give away he knew nothing about what was going on. If he was going to find any answers,

Conor seemed to be his best bet. Right now, his best approach was to pretend. "I mean, what do you think about all this?"

"This war has been going on for too long, is what I think. It's an extension of The Chemical Wars, which themselves were extensions of The Class Wars—but no one ever talks about them."

"Maybe you can?" David prodded.

"Heh," Conor's lips curled into the hint of a smile. "It figures you'd ask. If there's any place better suited to discussing them than here, I haven't heard of it."

"Why's that?"

"Bandleshore's the epitome of what The Class Wars represented. The people who live here are at the edge of civilization, some of them by their own decision but most of us had this forced upon us. Displacement all over again."

"You mean like when homelessness was banned in the old cities?"

"It reeks of the memory, what's happening here." Conor nodded and scanned the room, double-checking no one had become keen to eavesdrop on their conversation. "The Class Wars started well before the banning of homelessness though. That was only one of the battles of the bigger war, albeit one of the key battles. No, The Class Wars went much farther back—back to the technology revolution—past that, even—although that's when it did start to become a real threat. Everyone thought we were past division by difference. Culture wars were a thing of the past. The field was levelling, and everything seemed right—or at least so we thought. But The Class Wars, the ones kids will read about in history books someday, those wars were the battles of The Futurists vs. The Organics and they didn't see color or race or sexuality. These were philosophies of what it meant to be human and what it meant to be the predominant species here on Earth. They were the precursors of The Chemical Wars and today's battles of Preservation vs. Progression—the same war drums your friend is beating, I might add."

"Sounds complicated."

"Of course, it's complicated! What in life isn't? When technology continued to grow at an exponential rate, the first space it expanded was in the availability of knowledge, something hailed by all the thought leaders as key to our future. Some called this spread of information through the network, with its availability to everyone regardless of their education, The Great Emancipator. Imagine that! Named after Honest Abe himself! What they ignored, the spark igniting The Class Wars, was though this knowledge was freely available, it was only available to those with the means to access it. Those with the means to purchase the technology to tap into the network were at an immense advantage over those who lacked such tools. Sure, government libraries and their declaration of basic network access as a public utility gave information and a voice to those who previously had none, but by then the gap between free technology and what those with deep pockets could afford had widened too far.

"Knowledge, of course, was not enough to start a war. The war started when it became clear those at the lower end of the social spectrum were unable to access the other opportunities new technology provided. By the middle of the

Twenty-First Century immortality was becoming a reality, to those who could afford it. As soon as the government stepped in and started regulating information-sharing, it was obvious there was no money in that part of the business. Along with this regulation came the government's plan to provide health care for all, but the capitalist system society was built around made sure not to add any additional regulation to the health care industry. With more money pouring into the system, it was clear medical technology was where the money was.

"As health technology grew, so did the costs of access. Soon it became clear the government's plan of universal health care was one of the lowest common denominator, and although everyone had access, those who had the means could access much more than those who could not. As the population swelled, and technology continued to grow, overpopulation plagued the planet and along with it, unemployment. There simply weren't enough jobs for everyone. The government kept raising taxes on those with the money, but soon realized if they went much farther with this plan there'd be no incentive for anyone to succeed.

"Feeding this massive population became the next major hurdle, with most funding spent on chemical engineering and genetic manipulation, but by then it was too late. The geeks knew this well ahead of time, of course, and they had wisely sided with technology. Others were not so lucky. The streets of every major city were swarming with the homeless, and the President granted all cities the option to purge. It wasn't long before all of them did. First Chicago, then LA … New York, Vegas, Atlanta. Then? Dominoes. They effectively banned homelessness and an entire class of society up and disappeared."

David's stomach churned as he contemplated this disregard for human life. "Doesn't sound like much of a war, more like a genocide," he said.

"True, although no one was actively killed. They kind of … died off. Especially as The Class Wars gave way to the Chemical ones."

"Ca—he mentioned those to me earlier—The Chemical Wars. They were what wiped out our ability to live on land right? What drove us to build the cities on the sea?"

"Exactly. The geeks were right."

"So then, what's The Cause?"

Conor's eyes widened, alarmed at the flippancy in which David posed the question. He made a calming motion with his hand, pressing his palm down into the air in an effort to silence David. "I told you," he whispered. "There are certain things you don't want to talk about in public." His focus switched from David to the space behind him. "Oh shit," he muttered.

A hefty, well-manicured hand grabbed David's shoulder firmly, pinching his nerves and causing him to wince in pain.

"Interesting company you keep, stranger," boomed a voice from behind. David tried to turn to face his assailant, but the man's strong hold prevented him from doing so. "We need to speak with you… outside."

Conor turned his attention away from David and now focused solely on the mug of beer in front of him. He ran his fingers nervously up and down its handle, avoiding any eye contact with either David or the group of men behind him.

"What's this all about?" David demanded. "Conor?" But Conor ignored his pleas, even as the men tore him from his seat and shoved him through the crowd out the bar's side door.

"Keep walking. We need to find some privacy."

David walked in silence, guided by the man behind him, still gripping his shoulder tightly. From the clack of the footfalls David guessed there were at least two men, possibly three, in the group besides himself. They led him to the edge of Vonshine's and turned left into an empty alley. The light from the gas lamps in the street had no chance of reaching this far into its recesses and the moon had not yet risen high enough to illuminate the space. The noises of the bar filled the backstreet, the shouts and laughter only slightly deadened by the thin wooden walls separating the alley from the bar's lively interior. As they reached the end of the alley, the man's grip tightened further, forcing David to his knees. The man released his hold and David turned around.

With what little light was available to him, it was impossible for David to make out the men's faces. From their silhouettes against the lights of the street's gas lamps, he could determine they were tall—not Calvin tall, but still well over David's own six feet. Their heads appeared to be shaved or bald, from the smooth round silhouettes. David tried to stand but was forced back down to the ground.

"We don't know who you are, but we know who you came here with and we have a message for you to deliver to him."

"I have no idea what you're talking about."

One of the other two men stepped forward. "Just give The Preservationist the message!" he screeched, before kicking David in the gut. David howled and buckled over from the pain. The third man stood back in silence, watching.

The first man spoke again, "Tell Calvin no one wants a war. We've seen enough pain already. Peace is near."

"Funny way of showing it," David bellowed, still clutching his stomach.

"Yes, I s'pose so," the man conceded.

The third man who had remained silent until now dropped down to David's level and put his mouth to David's ear. "We have something else for you to deliver," he hissed.

"What is it?" asked David.

The man righted himself and punted David square in the face. David's nose let out a wet crunch and he saw an explosion of stars. Then … nothing.

# EIGHT
# HAVE A NICE TRIP

The crack of thunder rang, shattering the room in unison with the flash of lightning and, from the way the picture rattled, it may very well have hit the house. David's eyes shot open from the scare, and he twisted to look at his alarm clock. Nothing. The power in the house was out.

David rose from his bed, stumbled sleepily out of his bedroom and down the two flights of stairs into his basement playroom. Along the way he tried a few light switches but none of them worked. In the basement he felt his way through the darkness, arms stretched and fingers splayed, probing the murk before him. *Thank God the kids aren't here and their toys are put away*, he thought. *If I tripped and broke my neck, there'd be no one to find me for days.*

He reached the door leading to the back storage and utility area of the basement. It was here he'd find the circuit breaker necessary to bring the house back to life, but there was no way to navigate through the mess of the space blindly. On the shelf next to the door, his hand found cold metal. He took it into his hands, weighing the military grade aluminum, and clicked the rubber button, bringing the half-dead flashlight to weary life.

The underpowered bulb did little to brighten the space, hardly putting forth enough light to illuminate the far wall. Swinging the dull beam across the floor, he maneuvered through a dim maze of storage boxes and outgrown toys. Aiden's dusty rocking horse creaked like death against the concrete floor as he brushed past. Besides his flashlight, the only source of light in the room came from the small flicker of the furnace pilot light, not nearly enough to provide any meaningful aid.

His journey through the gauntlet of forgotten toys and cardboard caged memories ended as his beam fell on the circuit breaker. Nothing appeared to be broken—no sparks or smoke or smells of torched wiring. Mouthing a silent prayer thanking God they didn't still live in the old house with the fuse box, David reset the main breaker and the fan on the furnace roared to life. The basement, however, remained shrouded in darkness.

He slithered back through the maze of boxes to the door separating the storage space from the rest of the basement and switched on the lights. Some escaped through the open door, casting the rest of the basement in a lifeless glow. After propping the door open with the flashlight, he bolted through the playroom and up two flights of stairs, turning on the lights as he passed. Screw the electric bill; he'd turn the lights off in the morning when the sun was up.

When he reached his bedroom, his eyes immediately explored the dark space beneath the bed. He flicked the light switch, then quickly off when he realized he'd be unable to sleep with the lights on and made a run for his bed. In the dark it was impossible to determine if he tripped on some clothes left on the floor, or if it was due to something reaching out from under the bed to grab his foot and pull him under. The split second of time while his body tumbled forward onto his bed was not enough to be certain, and the crack of his skull on the headboard knocked him unconscious before he could give it a second thought.

## NINE
# HAVE A NICE TRIP, PART 2

"Stand up," a voice commanded.

Opening his eyes, David made out the silhouette of Calvin kneeling before him. He was still in the alley, although the sun had risen since his altercation the night before. Busy voices echoed through the streets of Bandleshore as the people began their day. David tapped his nose gingerly, cringing at the prickle of broken bone and cartilage shifting under his touch.

"Put these on." Calvin handed David a pair of brown loafers. "Size twelve, right?"

David slipped on the shoes and stood, grasping Calvin's shoulder to retain his balance. His head still swam from the concussion and he expected to vomit but looking down to the ground where he spent the night, he realized that ship had already sailed. Beer and granola stained the pavement next to where his head had been, like a bowl of oatmeal tossed aside by a displeased toddler. He licked the inside of his teeth and spit, attempting to dispel the rancid taste.

"You look like hell," said Calvin.

"I figured as much. Nice eyes, by the way. Blue suits you—much better than the dingy gray you were sporting before."

"Thanks. What happened to you?"

"I had a run-in with some friends of yours. They wanted me to give you a message."

"Consider it delivered." Calvin waved his hand in dismissal and walked down the alley. "Come on. First train out leaves early. We need to be on it."

"Can't we stop and eat something first? We can catch one of the later ones."

"No. We're on this one. Let's go."

Despite the cacophony of voices echoing through the alley, the streets of Bandleshore displayed far less life than David expected. No cars traveled the narrow roadways yet the few people who were out stuck to the sidewalks. About half of them donned workingmen's clothes—dirty overalls and worn-out shoes—and appeared to be headed in the direction of the Eyefields. The other half wore freshly pressed but threadbare business suits and traveled in the opposite direction, presumably for the train to Plasticity.

"A border town if I ever saw one," said Calvin.

Vonshine's doors were closed, as were the doors to most shops on the way across town. One shop, however, attracted David's attention. The smell of fresh baked goods wafted through the front door and open windows out into the streets. As it hit David's nose, his stomach began to rumble.

"Seriously Calvin, I need to eat something."

"Have you got any money?"

David turned out his empty pockets. Nothing. Not a gum wrapper or a nickel. Not even a wad of lint.

"Here," Calvin handed David a roll of bills, none of which seemed familiar. "Buy me a scone while you're at it—and a cup of coffee—dark roast."

A few minutes later David returned with Calvin's scone and coffee, and a banana and cappuccino for himself. He thanked Calvin for the food, and they ate as they continued on their way.

In the daylight, the massive structure of the mag-train station was staggering—a proud immensity utterly unappreciable in the moonlight the night before. Gigantic beams of gleaming metal jutted from the sand like spears, acting as the main support for the structure. An illustrious expanse of stone stairs extended up from the beach to a wall of glass doors. As they climbed the staircase David realized the steps, rather than stone, appeared to be made of crushed and reformed concrete.

"What is this stuff?" he asked Calvin, tapping his new shoes on the steps.

"Recycled from the freeways. All the plants and quarries and construction industries are long gone. If you want to build now, you have to use what you can find."

"What about the train station? That doesn't seem to be recycled."

"The train station was first constructed when they built the city. It used to be attached to the second floor of a shopping mall, but it burned down. The Progressives suspected we were behind it, although I never heard any proof to that rumor. At least no one on our side has ever laid claim. Honestly, I wouldn't be surprised if those damn Progressives did it themselves to try to shut down access into Plasticity once they were all out there. The Cause was a handy scapegoat."

Calvin took a cigarette from a silver case he kept in his suit pocket, lit it with a match, and continued.

"Soon enough the city people realized they couldn't survive forever out there in their plastic island at sea and they were forced to send crews out to build a new entrance to the station, reopening it to the public in the process. Since most everything had already been destroyed, they had to make do with what they could find. Most of the freeways are gone now, you'll notice. Everything's been looted and reused, but the land still hasn't recovered to a point where anything growing is new or useful for us—especially not trees."

The climb up the stairs showed how out of shape David was. As if the run through the flooding fields and the beating in the alley weren't already enough, his calves burned like fire from this latest leg of their journey. The pain, along with the steep stone-like stairs, brought back stinging memories of climbing the stairs of the Sun Pyramid in Teotihuacan on his honeymoon.

David stopped suddenly as realization of this memory washed over him. He turned to Calvin. "I had a wife. I have a wife," he paused. "Have or had, I'm not sure."

"Finally starting to remember?" Calvin arched his right eyebrow.

"Yeah—the climb now—it triggered something. We had our honeymoon in Mexico." He stopped, forced his mind to relax, and continued, "It was winter—January I think. I remember thinking about the rest of my family and friends, stuck back at home in the cold while we were tramping through jungles in 80-degree heat."

"Be careful of what memories you call your own. Just because you remember it doesn't mean it happened. Your mind's mixed up, David. There are no jungles anymore—and no one's been out vacationing on the land for almost 100 years. I think your memories are getting garbled with videos you've seen of the old world. A little too much time watching holofilms."

As quickly as it had come, David's surge of excitement vanished. Calvin was right. There was no way he had been to Mexico. The world was inhospitable to man now. Whatever he remembered, it hadn't actually happened—or at least he hadn't been there. It must have been something recalled from his subconscious.

"Maybe I am from the city. How else would I have seen a holofilm?"

"Excellent point—maybe once we're back you'll start to remember more," Calvin conceded. "But if somehow your memories start to return, and you discover you're the head of the Progressive army, I'll have to kill you."

From the look on his face, David could tell the man wasn't joking.

The inside of the station was far busier than Vonshine's had been the night before. Hundreds of people milled about the interior, most of them dressed in business suits, but some wore less formal clothing. Jeans, t-shirts … stupid hats.

Who're they?" asked David, nodding his head in the direction of a family.

"Vacationers. The city's self-enclosed and a few hundred feet above sea level. Now that the shore has been declared safe, Bandleshore's a popular travel destination for city-dwellers looking for a cheap getaway. They're probably on their way home from a little trip to whatever nature we can still safely enjoy. At this end of the tracks they have access to beaches and can swim in the ocean—though they advise against it due to the poison level in the water from land runoff. But still, they come."

David's eyes strayed from the family to take in the station's substantial size. From the inside it stretched further than he imagined when he first saw it from the exterior. The metal beams from the sand continued to run up the sides of the building at various angles, with smaller supporting beams interjected throughout, crisscrossing in a geometric firework display of angles. Between the beams, vast sheets of salt-caked glass provided the only separation between the inside and the air blowing in off the sea. The whole thing reminded David of a greenhouse—an architecturally fantastic greenhouse.

On the far side of the station a stretch of what appeared to be some sort of rail or track ran out into the sea. People lingered along the side of it, waiting for the next train to arrive. A security gate separated David and Calvin from this area.

"Time to put Finniman's work to the test," said Calvin, walking toward the turnstiles.

"What am I supposed to do if something happens?"

"Like what?"

"I don't know, like an alarm or something."

"Are you kidding? There won't be any alarm—not in a place this busy. They're trying to avoid admitting there's a war brewing. As far as most people are concerned, life is finally improving. The government is fixing everything. Soon they'll be back on land ... and soon they'll be able to destroy it all again," Calvin replied. "No, there won't be an alarm—you won't realize you've set off the system until you're too late. If something goes wrong here, it will go very wrong. Wrong as in they'll shut you down wrong.

"Get this clear—if you're ever found out as an undesirable and they have a DNA match in a closed area like this, you're done for. They'll send out a swarm of nanobots and those bots will hone in on your DNA structure and invade. In a matter of seconds, they'll shut down your muscular system—and all it will look like to onlookers is like you've fainted. A medical crew will rush out, strap you to a gurney, wheel you away and place you under arrest. And if you're on the terror list, like I am, there will be no trial and you'll never be heard of or seen from again."

David swallowed. *God, please don't let me be a terrorist,* he thought, and proceeded to walk towards the turnstiles.

"Here, you'll need this. Swipe it through the scanner." Calvin handed David a paper ticket. "See you on the other side."

The turnstiles looked no different from those in a subway, or at least those in a video of a subway. After swiping his card, the turnstile unlocked and he walked through, following Calvin. As he did so, a row of blue lights flickered on the ceiling and he averted his eyes instinctively.

"Sir, you need to be scanned," said a female voice.

David's heart raced as panic set in. "Who, me?" His eyes searched for an exit and caught Calvin. "Stay calm," Calvin mouthed.

"Sir—look up sir."

David's eyes continued to search, now for the source of the voice.

"You need to be scanned, sir."

The voice came from overhead. He scanned the ceiling and found a strip of electric blue lights.

"Thank you, sir. You may proceed." The voice was a recording, spouted from a small speaker above David's turnstile.

Sweat dripped down David's forehead and he scurried across back to Calvin's side.

"Looks to me like Finniman's still got the gift, regardless of what he thinks," said Calvin.

After a short wait, an electronic bell rang out. At first David thought it was a clock, marking the hour, but soon realized it was an alarm announcing the arrival of the morning mag-train. A set of lights began to flash, orange and yellow, and the train pulled into the station. The doors opened, and a few people strode out. Not many visitors came into the town in the morning—it seemed traffic worked in the opposite direction this time of day.

"Go find someplace to sit. We may have gotten through the scanners, but that doesn't mean no one's going to recognize me. We'll be safer splitting up for now." Calvin moved down the train toward the front, exiting their current car and moving on to the next.

Alone in a metal tube full of strangers, David's breath quickened as he realized once again he was alone and oblivious to the world around him. He took a seat on the nearest bench. The man next to him was familiar—a patron from Vonshine's the night before, now barely recognizable in his shabby business suit. David considered striking up a conversation, but after further consideration decided against it. His mind was on overload already with all he learned in the past few days. Anything more and it was liable to explode.

After a few minutes the train began to move. It was a smooth ride, with the train riding on a cushion of air from its opposing pole magnetic flotation system. David marveled at how quickly the train gained speed, and at how quiet the whole thing operated. *This is nothing like riding the subway*, he thought. *Well, except for the stink of people.*

As the train sped out across the ocean the travelers inside moved about, the first-timers forced their way to the windows to take in the view of the wide expanse of water spread out before them. Several pointed excitedly at a pod of whales rising and falling in the distant waves, water spraying high into the air when they exhaled as they broke the water's surface. This kept David's attention for part of the ride as well; he marveled at the beauty of nature when it was left to its own devices, uninhibited by man's overbearing hand. His attention diverted, however, when the door to the next car opened and someone new stepped in.

Tall and pale, the man stood on a pair of thin white legs and boasted a disproportionately massive, bald head—like a cross-breed between a regular human and one of the aliens from classic sci-fi movies, or an old X-Files episode. An air of reverence surrounded him, as did a group of admiring women, like an old Persian harem. But unlike the harems, these women dressed professionally, in suits like those worn by the business men commuting into the city from Bandleshore. David was amazed at this, these women were surely accomplished members of society, yet they attached themselves to this tall geek with adoration and a look of lust in their eyes. Surely this must be one of The Progressives Calvin had mentioned.

Rather than speculate, David thought it best to confirm his suspicions. He turned to the man in the seat next to him and asked directly, "Is he a Progressive?"

The man regarded David with shock and disgust. "Heathen!" he said, accusingly.

"Excuse me?" David asked, confused.

"How dare you call someone that?"

"I-I'm sorry," David apologized. "I didn't know. I didn't mean to offend."

"Well, one can't help one's upbringing," the man replied. "But if you're planning on spending any time in civilized society, you should realize that name is not a word to be bandied about. They're above offense, of course, but their idolizers are not. They'd gladly kill you and face the legal consequence rather than allow someone—" he paused to look David up and down with a withering glare, "especially someone of your ilk—to speak poorly of their darlings."

"Thanks for the tip. Again, I didn't mean to offend."

"As I said, one can't be blamed for one's nature," the man replied. "And to answer your question, yes, he's one of your so-called 'Progressives.'" He sneered as he said the word. "Henry Johnson, I believe. One of the young diplomats in the New Society. I've heard fine things about him, and terrible things as well. You'd do best to keep your mouth shut and your wits about you in his presence."

Deciding it in his health's best interest, David remained silent the rest of the train ride. Off and on he stole clandestine glances at the man and the women gathered around him. He couldn't see what the fuss was all about; the man was unremarkable, his skin wax-like and his musculature almost nonexistent. If David hadn't been told otherwise, and had the man not been surrounded by a gaggle of gooey-eyed women, he would have dismissed him as a weak, socially inept geek.

About twenty minutes into the ride, the attention of the first-timers moved from the sea and they craned their necks to look forward toward the front of the train.

"Arriving in Plasticity in two minutes. Please take your seats and secure your belongings," a voice rang out through the train's speaker system.

David scooted over in his seat and pressed his face against the window in hopes of catching a glimpse of this plastic city on the sea from the outside. What he saw took his breath away. Situated on a series of metal beams, like those supporting the structure of the station at Bandleshore, was what resembled a gigantic glass ball. The entire sphere was clear, and the train track disappeared into it at ground level, about a third of the way up. In the area below street-level, David discovered a complex system of immense gears, turning mechanisms and color-coded electronic systems. This secondary sublevel separated into numerous distinct levels of its own with human engineers and robots alike scurrying about like ants in a child's toy farm.

Each level became smaller and more crowded as the ball narrowed and neared sea level, making it increasingly difficult to make out the area inside. The windows there at the bottom were crusted over with sea salt and long-dead barnacles. Waves rolled gently about fifty more feet below. The water must have been higher at some point, David thought, or else the barnacles never would have grown—not that high up. When the city was built it must have rested at sea level, like a fish bowl floating on the ocean's surface, ironically filled with people for all the fish to come and see.

Above ground level, a city thrust up as high as the round walls would allow. In the center of the city the buildings stood the tallest, their peaks almost scraping the top of the globe. At the edges the buildings curved in a warped sync with the rounded edges of the glass walls surrounding the city. Space was obviously limited, and the city had been engineered for maximum three-dimensional efficiency. Nearly all of the buildings reached to the top of the globe, becoming shorter the farther from the city's center they stood.

The train slowed, and a glass panel slid open in the side of the globe where the tracks met its edge. The train rolled in and David's jaw dropped as he caught his first glimpse of the actual city of Plasticity—a split-second before a thunderous explosion tore through the train.

His first glimpse of future society was stolen instantly— replaced with a flash of light, a searing pain, and blackness.

## TEN
# HOME SWEET HOME

"David! Oh God, David, wake up!" Alice's voice shook with fear as she urged David back to consciousness. One hand gripped his arm like a fearful vice, while her other rested gently against his forehead, fingertips gently stroking his hair. She resisted the urge to shake him, not knowing if it would cause more harm.

"The ambulance is on its way. Don't worry honey, everything will be okay."

David groggily opened his eyes, the sunlight in the room sending sharp pains through his head as he did so.

"Alice? Is that you?" His vision wavered, unable to focus. But as he touched her face, his fingertips found the same familiar curves and laugh lines of the woman he loved. "Are you crying?" he asked.

"Of course I'm crying!" Tears flowed freely down her face, dripping onto the duvet. She rubbed her eyes, smearing her mascara. "How long have you been like this? I tried calling and you didn't answer, but I didn't think much of it." Globules of snot bubbled from her nose

"You're back already?" he asked as the fog of sleep began to lift from his mind.

"Today's Sunday, David. We came back early when we didn't hear from you. How long have you been out? What happened?"

David attempted to sit, the mattress damp and squishy beneath him. However long he had been out, it was long enough to soil himself. As he leaned forward, his stomach lurched, and he vomited. Alice gently pushed him back down onto his bed.

"I'll find some towels and help you clean up."

Slowly and deliberately, Alice worked to clean David and to change his clothes, all the while fighting back tears as she urged him to lay still. Any movement, she feared, could only exacerbate any damage already done. After a few minutes, sirens sounded in the distance, their piercing wail intensifying through the cool Sunday air as they approached the house. Alice ran downstairs at the ring of the doorbell and David heard the soft, anxious voices of his children in the hall outside his room.

"Is Daddy going to be okay?" Aiden asked as Missy began to cry.

He needed to run to them, to tell them everything would be fine. In his mind he pictured the two of them, his little darlings, huddled together in the hallway, comforting each other while they worried about what might happen to their

Daddy. But even though he wanted to, he found himself unable to move. "Daddy's fine," he whispered, though no one could hear him. "I promise you I'll…"

David faded in and out of consciousness, and soon sensed the presence of EMTs. Each bump as they carried his motionless body down the stairs shook through him, sending his head into fits of ravaging pain. He did his best to distance himself from the agony, pressing his eyes shut to avoid the stinging brilliance of the morning sun. Still, the combination of motion and pain took their toll, and he passed out before they lifted him into the ambulance.

Alice gathered her sobbing children and ushered them into her own car, remaining as stoic as she could amidst the chaos. The ambulance pulled out, sirens wailing, and the Sparks family followed the flashing lights as they rushed the Man of the House to Liberty Hospital.

## ELEVEN
# OPEN-APPLE-C

The steady beep of the monitors woke him. As he came out of his sleep, unfamiliar voices filled the room in a clamor of hushed conversation.

"The file system's repaired and network connections are fully restored," said a woman. "Everything's copied back to the way it was, or at least as close as the diagnostic repair system could manage. He spent quite some time in the FloatNet. Hopefully we got all the bits and pieces out of there and properly reverted back to the previous restore point."

"Exemplary work, Juliet," a man replied. "Ray, bring him out of stasis."

A second man spoke. Ray, David assumed. "It looks like he's coming out on his own, sir."

"Even better," said the first man. "The system's coming online on its own. A positive sign. Means everything's operational and eager to boot up."

David opened his eyes found himself in what appeared to be a hospital room. Three strangers in scrubs stood at the foot of his bed, their bodies stark against the colorless walls. The woman and one of the men wore uniforms of frigid blue, while the other man wore the same sterile white as the walls. They noticed his open eyes and ceased talking, David their sole focus.

"Mr. Sparks!" the man in white exclaimed. David recognized the man's voice as the one he assumed to be the others' superior. "Welcome back! How are you feeling?"

Having only been conscious for no more than a minute or two, David still couldn't comprehend the situation, nor where was. He blinked, stretched his arms, flexed the ache from his fingers and sat up.

"Don't—" the woman tried to stop him but was too late. As he leaned forward a sharp yank tugged at the base of his skull. He reached back and met a bundle of wires connected to a metal bracket newly implanted on the back of his head.

"Is this the Matrix?" he asked.

The man in white laughed. "Of course not! Although I suppose this does share some similarities to that silly relic."

The woman approached the left side of David's bed and directed the other man to his right. "Lie back, David," she said. "You woke before we had a chance to disconnect you. We have a bit more work to do and you'll be up on a FloatLink."

David sunk back down into the mattress, guided by the gentle cradle of the woman's hands. She nodded to the man in blue, and he jammed a needle straight into David's upper left arm.

## TWELVE
# LYING HERE IN MY HOSPITAL BED

"I'm afraid you've suffered a fairly severe concussion, Mr. Sparks. Nothing life-threatening, but concerning nonetheless."

All through the morning nurses, doctors and at least a dozen other people David assumed were hospital staff, due to their incessant measuring, note taking, muttering, poking and prodding rushed hurriedly in and out of David's room. Alice paced the room as the children occupied themselves in the play area down the hall. No one knew what caused the concussion, though the scene in David's bedroom lent several theories.

But what caused it wasn't what worried Alice. What worried her—what made her sick—was she had no idea how long he'd been like that, and what could have happened if she came home a day later like originally planned. After a week in California with her parents she was ready to go home. The kids missed their toys and their friends, and Alice missed her partner. After twelve years of marriage, they still loved each other … but work, life and two kids tended to put romance on the back burner. Nonetheless, they still knew they needed each other and time apart always reminded them of this simple truth.

She had called Saturday to give David a heads-up they were coming home so he'd have a chance to clean up any mess he made, but it wasn't until Sunday morning when they landed that she became concerned. Normally she wouldn't have worried about David's lack of a phone call, assuming he'd been busy with one project or another around the house and simply had lost track of time, as he was liable to do. But this, this total lack of response after several days, this worried her.

When she and the kids arrived home, the first thing she noticed was his car still in the garage. As they came in she and the kids called through the house, hopeful to hear David shout back a surprised hello in response. But when no one answered, she rushed from room to room, her heart dropping closer to her stomach as each stage of her search came up empty. Finally checking the bedroom, the scene of her husband splayed out and unresponsive almost gave her a heart attack. At first, she was certain he was dead. Then, upon a test of his pulse, found him thankfully alive, but still unconscious.

Her fear subsided somewhat when he stirred under her touch, but frantic confusion took its place as she ran through the various scenarios that could have led to what she found. A 911 call and fifteen minutes later, he was on his way to the hospital.

The first several hours of their visit, of course, were spent waiting in the emergency ward for space to open. The doctors figured he'd already been unconscious for a few days, so it was unlikely another few hours would make much of a difference, especially considering the more traumatic, life-threatening injuries. When they did finally see him, they attacked with a barrage of questions. Yes, he bumped his head on the bed. No, he couldn't name what day it was. Yes, he knew his name. Yes, it still hurt. These questions were followed by a CAT scan, and then more waiting.

"You'll be dispatched today, Mr. Sparks. I spoke to your wife, and she said she's on her way back to the hospital," said the doctor. "You're going to need to take things very slow for a while and get plenty of rest. Your brain has experienced a severe trauma, although it doesn't appear there is any permanent damage. There's very minimal bleeding, and from our tests it appears the worst of it is over."

David nodded in understanding, his brain splitting with each tilt of his head.

"This does mean no going to work—and absolutely no driving. You very likely will experience continued blackouts, so our suggestion—our prescription—is you sleep as much as you can. You should start to recover most of your faculties within the next several days, and within a week I expect you'll be back to normal. Push it, though, and you risk permanent brain damage."

"Thanks. I understand," David said, resisting the urge to nod. "I don't think I can accomplish much of anything right now anyway—I can't even stand up on my own."

"We'll be sending you home with a wheelchair, David, but it will be absolutely temporary. There's nothing wrong with your actual muscles. Your sense of balance and equilibrium is off. You could probably force yourself to walk, but at this early stage I strongly advise against it. Chances are you won't need the wheelchair after you've gotten back into your home and gotten some valuable rest. Bring it back when you come in for your check-up in a week."

David's eyes fluttered as the doctor spoke. He forced them to stay open, but it became harder and harder to focus on what the man was saying.

"You need to sleep, David. Your wife will be here soon and then you can go."

David mumbled something unintelligible as his eyes fell closed and he drifted back to dreamland.

## THIRTEEN
# SECRET AGENT MAN

A piercing clatter woke David and he bolted upright in his bed, searching for the source of the racket. The woman in blue, Juliet, knelt below him as she meticulously gathered a variety of medical instruments from the floor.

"I'm sorry if I woke you. So clumsy," she said, waggling her fingers. "How are you feeling?"

David twisted his head from side to side. Besides being a bit stiff, he felt healthy, well-rested and full of energy.

"I feel ... magnificent," he said. "Is it okay if I stand? Stretch a little?"

"If you're up to it, you can do anything you like."

David swung his legs over the side of the bed and let his feet alight upon the ground. Besides being strangely gummy, like the padding found in gyms, the floor radiated an odd heat. Rather than tile or linoleum, it consisted of a shiny plastic-like, spongy material. He turned his sights to the window at the left side of the room and peered out. He gazed absently through the window, taking in the wide expanse of sea, as he massaged the alien object embedded in his skull. The bundle of wires that tugged at him earlier were gone. In their place he discovered a metal plate, warm and buzzing with electricity.

"We've upgraded you to wireless. No need for cables anymore," the woman said. "Not that you're going to need any connection of course. Your files are updated and you're back to normal. We did leave a physical data port below your panel, however, should you need a firmware update or prophylactic backup in the future."

"Where am I?" David asked.

The woman frowned. "Hm. I guess we knocked out a few recent files when we cleared out your temporary memory."

"What?"

"You're in the Plasticity Federal Medical Facility– the NeuroReconstruction Unit, to be exact. I guess I could fill you in. It'd probably speed up your brain's file recreation processes after all."

David furrowed his eyebrows. A pinch tweaked the back of his neck.

"What's the last thing you can remember?" she asked.

"I was on a train, on my way across the ocean. I remember a city in a bubble, but after? I can't remember a thing."

"That's the last we could access too. You don't remember an explosion? Pain? Strange sounds?"

"No ... the train—then nothing."

"You're a lucky man, Mr. Sparks. What you've been through normally requires quite the series of invasive removals to delete. Lucky for you, your mind was already shut down."

"I—I'm afraid I don't understand."

"You were caught in a terrorist act, David. The train you were on was carrying explosives, and they detonated as the train pulled into Central Station. Most of the people on the train died, as did many who were in the station. We're fairly certain The Preservationist was behind it—he and his so-called "Cause.""

David's heart raced, he knew they caught him on surveillance with Calvin prior to entering the train—all it would take would be one look at the security footage and they'd assume he had something to do with it.

"So ... I'm free to go?" he asked, trying to act casual.

"Of course. There are a few things we'd like to discuss, however."

*Oh God, here it comes. Pretend you don't know anything.*

"When you came in here, you were in rough shape—we didn't think you'd make it, but after a quick retinal scan we saw who you were and moved your case to high priority. Your body was too badly burned to make a visual identity, you see. After the retinal we confirmed your connection with Calvin Simon—or, as he's more commonly referred to, The Preservationist."

Defeated and helpless, David slumped back in his bed.

"Don't worry, Mr. Sparks. You're not under any suspicion—not after the memory dump."

"Memory dump?"

"Yes. Beyond the external physical damage, your internal organs also sustained major injuries. Most of your neural system remained intact, however, so we transferred your neural system into the FloatNet. After that, we shut down your autonomic system and proceeded with a full rebuild, complete with reconstruction of all internal systems and external physical features."

David scratched at his metal plate.

"Your body was too far gone to repair while keeping your brain alive. We had to kill you, David, to rebuild your system. Growing organs takes time; no matter how much we advance the technology we're still operating under the laws of nature. So, we transferred your consciousness to the FloatNet, our neural staging network, where it remained stimulated in a position of stasis. Of course, it received regular exercise while exploring your subconscious, and should still be as healthy as it was before the accident—nothing more than a long dream, as far as your brain is concerned. Once your body was rebuilt, we transferred your mind system back from the FloatNet and into your newly revived, and updated, brain."

"Are you joking? You're telling me you killed me, and then went digging around in my head?" David asked, pounding his fists on the table. "This is science fiction. Stuff like this doesn't happen in real life! Besides aren't there laws against this? What about my right to privacy? You invaded the only place a man truly has for himself!"

"To answer your first question: no, David, we would never joke about a matter like this. Normally we would have let you die, but while we were exploring your neural system in the FloatNet, we did some prodding to determine your connection to The Preservationist," she answered. "Regarding your second question: the rule of law is suspended in instances where terrorism is suspected. We do what needs to be done to preserve the society, and this was clearly a case of terrorism. Still, as far as we were able to determine, you have no real connection to him other than trust—and trust is something we need in our organization."

David took a few deep breaths. "I'm not quite sure I follow ..."

"Our research indicates you had no prior association with The Preservationist, or, as you refer to him, Calvin, before the events in The Grasslands. Still, for some reason he placed his trust in you—and we need you to help us."

"Help you how?"

"Calvin Simon is a bad man, Mr. Sparks. He, and the war he is attempting to incite, are a threat to the continuation of the human species. We need you to reconnect with him and find out what you can about his next plan."

"Wait a minute—he survived the explosion?"

"Our sources indicate he abandoned the train seconds before detonation and is currently in hiding somewhere here in Plasticity. He's building an army, David—only we don't know where, who, or when they're going to strike. We need you to help us."

"Wait, wait, wait. You want me to spy?" David asked. The very idea was preposterous. "Why would you assume I want to help you? As far as you know, I'm working with him."

"Yes, and as far as he knows, you possess that capacity. You're not a leader, David. You're a follower—and you're loyal. Calvin has likely already figured this much out," she replied. "Besides, we have a way to pay you back."

"I don't need your money," David replied, defiantly.

"Of course you don't," said Juliet. "But what you do need is information. We were able to recover your files, David— the files from before The Grasslands. The problem is, they were extraordinarily damaged. They're still in your system, of course, but there's a low likelihood your body will be able to fully repair the connections on its own. We, on the other hand, are actively working to restore the full file system— but this will take time."

"You're saying you can give me back my memories?" David asked.

The spark of light in his eyes showed that her words had hit a soft spot—something she could use.

"I'm saying, we're already working on it—but I'm also saying this isn't a simple process. In the past, when we've seen damage like this, we've simply deleted the files—but our scans of your more recent memories indicate a desire, even within your recent memory, to fill in those missing gaps. Frankly we're concerned if we don't fill in those gaps— if we don't bring back those missing fragments—your brain will determine it is too damaged to continue to function."

"So, load in what you have then. Let me figure it out."

"That isn't how NeuroRestoration works, David. If we were to load in bits and pieces, it would cause your brain to suffer a time-subjectivity fracture. We need to load it all at once, otherwise you'll never be able to reintegrate."

"You're saying you want me to be a spy?"

"Not quite a spy, more like a double-agent. And only while we rebuild your memories. After that…"

"But after that, who knows what you'll uncover." David's face reddened, and he again slammed his fists on the table, knocking the medical instruments back onto the floor. "Who knows what you'll learn. What it'll mean or what you'll have to me do next."

"Calm down, David," she placed her hands on his shoulders and met his emerald eyes. "Yes, we want you to gather and share information, but part of your role also requires you work as a spy for Calvin and his Cause—a spy against us. He's going to know you were here—you've been missing for a few weeks already. His people are everywhere, including this building, and they've certainly told him you're here. We've kept security tight around you, but only as tight as we needed it to be. We do let a few pieces of information slip through the cracks, and our hope is once you contact The Cause, Mr. Simon will consider you a valuable resource.

"You've undergone major reconstructive surgery, both physical and neural, and federal law requires you come back for regular checkups, otherwise you'll be terminated remotely through wireless. Calvin is fully aware of this, and our sources tell us he's desperate for solid information about plans for the Reconstruction. We know his profile, and we know he's going to let you back into his fold—so long as you don't give him reason to distrust you. He'll enlist you as a spy—and if he doesn't, you need to volunteer yourself. He'll use your checkups as a means to bypass security, and he'll likely try to hack into FloatNet as well through your wireless node. All we ask is you report back to us and relay to him the information we give you as facts of your infiltration of our network."

"I'm not really the sneaking type," David confessed.

"Are you so sure? You don't have much knowledge about yourself at all, Mr. Sparks. And frankly, neither do we. This is a risk for all of us ... but one we feel worth saving your life for." she replied. "We'll learn more soon enough, of course. While we sit here chatting away, our analysts are developing a set of subroutines to detect and purge any garbage code from the data construct of your corrupted memories. It won't be long until we start to unravel exactly who you, Mr. Sparks, truly are. Surely you'd like us to share this information with you?"

David sighed. "So, do I get a gun or what?"

## FOURTEEN
# MAKE LOVE, NOT WAR

Unfortunately, the answer to David's question had been a resounding "no." No, he did not get a gun. No, he did not get super-secret spy training. No, he didn't get to learn to Kung Fu, and no they didn't download codes for ju-jitsu into his brain. What he did get was a warning.

"Be careful out there, David. We don't expect you to do anything other than observe—in fact, we require you do nothing but observe. You are not a superhero. If you ever sense you're in danger, do not try to attract our attention. Any attempt to do so will surely end up with you dead," Juliet said.

"Are you sure I'm okay to go? I mean, healthy enough?" He glanced around, uneasily—shaking his head as he returned to the window. In it, the city became lost in his own reflection—the vision of a man whose face had gone pale and was about to be sick.

"One of the first things they'll do is check to see if you're bugged, and then they'll shut down your main communication OS and upload their own hacked version. Even if you're not working for us, they're going to assume we've installed a back-end logger that will upload your memory. They also know it won't be a real-time feed, because there's no way we can disguise that much bandwidth. So, what you're going to do is give us a nightly dump of your files. You'll be uploading through a proxy, so those bastards will have a lot harder time tracing it. We'll also be intermittently sending packets through randomized secure nodes, kind of like a decentralized torrent to mask any abnormally large data transmissions. But all this extra security means each daily upload will take longer to transfer than would be normal for a data chunk that size. And, we'll obviously have to shut down your neural system to do this."

David tried his best to listen and make sense of it all, but all he could comprehend was Juliet's buttery yellow dress. Every other time she visited she wore the same moldy blue lab coat she had on the day he woke up. Normally this splash of color in the drably appointed room would have been a welcome change, possibly even given him a spiritual lift, but today that yellow simply reminded him of bile.

"Let me make it easy for you: at night, before you go to bed, think the code word: "Fenway" and you'll initiate the transfer. Be sure you're ready to go to sleep for the night though, because once you trigger the process you're going to lose all but your basic neural activity. In essence, you'll go to sleep."

"What if I accidentally think of Fenway? Like, what if the Red Sox are on or something?" asked David.

"I fail to understand why the color of your socks has anything to do with this," said Juliet. "And why would you accidentally think of Fenway?"

"Well, how do I not think of it now you've said it. Go on, think of a white bear. Now don't think of a white bear. Try to think of anything but a white bear. Impossible, right?"

"What is all this about white bears and red socks? You're worrying far too much. Just do it when the time is right and your body will take care of the rest," she said. "Oh, and whatever you do, do not drink alcohol or take any drugs. It is crucial you keep your neural connections in prime condition. The upload is a copy of a delta of all new connections and memories created or changed since the last sync—including any repairs your own brain may have made to your damaged memories. The introduction of foreign substances into your system can not only inhibit your judgement, but potentially lead to your neural system's failure to build a permanent connection—not to mention accidental deletion."

And so, with minimal training and no sense of duty whatsoever to those directing this mission, David Sparks set out into the world of tomorrow. He had no idea of the layout of the city, he knew no one, and he had not received any direction as to where to go.

"They'll find you," the woman insisted. "And if they don't, take this. It'll get you into an apartment we set up for you, in case you need it. Address is on the back of the card."

Although hesitant to leave, he didn't have any other choice. He surely couldn't stay at the medical center, that much was clear. The government run healthcare didn't cover reconstructive cosmetic surgery, and it surely didn't cover neural development, storage, and transfer. The services he received were reserved for VIPs only, and if he refused to cooperate they had made it clear he would be out on the street and denied any future support—not to mention they'd cancel the restoration of his damaged files and delete the whole damn folder. Maybe even shut him down.

He was found immediately after leaving the building. Either The Cause had tasked a team with surveillance on the building for the past several weeks, waiting for him to show, or they'd been tipped off by someone inside. From what David now knew of Calvin, both were likely.

"Excuse me sir, but can we bother you for a survey?" they asked, crowding uncomfortably close around him.

"Did Calvin send you?" he asked.

The man who spoke grabbed David by the back of his neck and scrutinized him, his eyes penetrated David's, digging for any twitch or signal of peril. His grip loosened, and the man's calloused fingers dragged coarsely up David's neck to the base of his skull, where they tapped casually on David's new metal plate. "Don't say his name," he whispered. "We don't recognize anyone by the name of Calvin. Preservation is near though."

"Not very subtle…" David mumbled.

"What was that?"

"Nothing." David said, straightening his collar. "I'd love to take part in your survey,"

"Come with us then, sir. Our polling center is down the street."

The rest of the men stepped aside as the first gestured for David to start walking. As he took his first step a firm pressure dug into his spine.

"There's a 2,000,000-volt energy blaster pushed against your spinal cord." The man's breath burned against his ear, each word a thousand degrees hotter than the last. "You try to move, or call in the Progressive Army, we'll light you up like a menorah."

David did his best to remain calm and remember his training. Realizing he'd received none, he opted to rely on his knowledge of spy films instead. The spies who lived always proceeded with caution, waiting for the right moment to make their move. Since David's next move would be quite some time off, this was easy for him to do.

"Take it easy guys. Are you with The Cause? How come you guys didn't break me out of that prison?"

"Break you out of Society grounds? Not worth it."

"If you're really a friend to The Cause—a friend to The Preservationist, then you understand your best interest is to keep moving," the second man said. With each hesitating step, the pressure on his spine intensified and David moved faster.

"Of course, I understand. But where are we going?" David asked.

"Keep walking," said the man behind him. "We'll tell you when to turn. You try anything, and you'll never realize the thought crossed your mind. We're taking a risk coming for you, and to be honest, we don't trust you."

"I'm going guys. Lead the way and I'm there."

The two men led David down an alley. Several dozen surveillance cameras and twice as many Society operatives followed their movement through the tracker in his port.

When they reached the end of the alley, the man with the gun said, "You're going to keep on walking, but first we need to shut down your recording system. Don't worry, the process won't hurt you and you'll stay awake, but you're also not going to remember anything that happens in the next two hours."

A sharp pain stabbed his right shoulder as the second man jammed the needle in. Enough with the shots already, he thought. It was his last thought for quite some time.

## FIFTEEN
# BUY ME SOME PEANUTS AND CRACKER JACK

To hell in a handbasket—that's where David's life was headed. Of course, he was being melodramatic, as he was prone to do. In High School his classmates voted him the Drama Queen. His Senior year yearbook confirmed this fact: there he was, on page 97, dressed in a gown, holding a skull like some sort of cross-dressing Hamlet. At the time he thought it funny, and Alice had found it embarrassingly endearing.

David hated that yearbook and intended on starting a collection encouraging all his former classmates to sell him back their copies, so he could have a massive book-burning to erase the memory. Alice voiced an inelastic "no" on this scheme.

The entire ride home from the hospital, David slept. Barely awake when Alice came to pick him up, the idea of taking him home scared her. And his lack of consciousness from the time the car started through the turn onto their drive worried her more. Still, the doctors insisted he was ready to go home. Spending time in his everyday life, around his wife, family, and usual surroundings would do more to help him back on his feet than any extended hospital stay. As she pulled into the garage, however, she became concerned with what to do if he didn't wake up. There was no way she would be able to carry his dead weight, and it was too cold out to leave him in the car. Thankfully, David's eyes crept open as the garage door closed.

"Home again, home again, jiggidy-jog," Alice chimed.

David forced his right eye open lazily. "Home? What about Calvin?"

"Who's Calvin, dear? One of your doctors? We need to get you inside. Hold on and I'll come help you out of the car."

David shook his head to scatter the cobwebs. "No—no I'll be fine," he insisted. "Need a second to clear my head."

Always strong-minded, David hated to have his abilities questioned. Enough of that went on at work, he always said. Slowly and deliberately, she gathered her purse and keys, shut her car door and strode the steps to the entry, pausing once more before entering, in case her husband did need her after all.

It took him a few minutes, but eventually David climbed out of the car on his own and hobbled back into his house. The kids were playing a board game in the family room;

David's mother had come over to watch them and help. *Ugh, as if my headache couldn't get any worse*, he thought.

He lumbered up to his room, aided by his wife and was soon back in the same bed that triggered his trip to the hospital in the first place. As he lay himself down on the welcoming mattress, he noticed a dent in the headboard where his melon cracked. The sight of it made him wince; though he couldn't recall the event, he was sure it had hurt like a son of a bitch.

"The doctors said you need as much rest as possible, so please, go to sleep," Alice said in a comforting, yet disciplinary voice. Under normal circumstances the tone would have given him a little tingle, but these were not normal circumstances.

"What about Aid and Missy? I'd like to say hi to them—let them see I'm okay."

"Sure –hold on a second and I'll fetch them." Alice withdrew from the room and he soon heard her call downstairs to their two children. Immediately after her shouts, he heard their footsteps on the stairs. The pictures on the wall rattled as they pounded down the hallway and they were about to jump onto the bed when Alice stuck out her arm to stop them. "Daddy has a headache, kids. Give him a kiss and tell him you love him," she directed. "Once he's feeling better you guys can all play."

"I missed you, Daddy," Missy wailed.

"We both missed you," Aiden countered. "Are you going to be okay?"

"Absolutely." Tears welled up in David's eyes. The sight of his entire family there before him was enough for him to thank God he was alive. "Daddy's a little sick and needs some sleep so he can feel better."

"Do you have a cold?" Missy asked. That little curl of his four-year-old's auburn bangs hung down past her eyes. As she wiped it away, David saw a hint of tears in her eyes as well.

"No, not a cold honey. I just bumped my head."

"Oh good, I hate colds!" she replied.

"Me too."

"Come on guys, time to let Daddy sleep," Alice said as she ushered the kids out of the room. "You need anything?"

"Actually, I don't know if I'm going to be able to fall asleep right away, and my head is killing me. Can you turn on the TV so I can have something to focus on?"

Alice turned on the TV and flipped through the channels, waiting for David to pick something he liked.

"Stop!" he commanded as she turned on ESPN Classic. "Leave this on. I love watching the Red Sox at home." His eyes fluttered with sleep. "There's just something about I love about the big green wall at Fenway."

## SIXTEEN
# FEELING LIKE
# A HUNDRED BUCKS

"Mr. Sparks!" a peacefully feminine voice resonated from the shadows. "How nice of you to join us."

David shook his head to clear the lingering clouds as the room emerged from his fog of sleep. How long he'd been cooped up here was anyone's guess, but at least the bed was comfy. His breath caught at the sight of thick velvet drapes drawn back against a three-paned picture window, the mahogany four-post bed cradling him in a nest of thick cotton, and the expansive buffet of fruits and bottled mineral waters spread on a polished wood table cut from a single slab of ancient oak. Far from the prison he expected to wake in, this room was a vision of opulence.

"Take your time. Brush away those cobwebs. You've been gone quite a while."

Dressed in a silk ivory gown suitable for a ball, the woman spoke with a kindness matching the smooth contours of her face. The soothing cadence of her voice held purpose yet kept David at ease—confident wherever he was, he was safe. No older than twenty-five, David found her quite beautiful, even with the few partially-hidden scars marring her left cheek and arm. They reminded David of knife wounds, and no matter how much makeup she applied over them, she would never hide them completely.

"I'm Bethany," she said as she curtsied. "Welcome to my home."

"This is your home? What is it you do?"

"I'm a woman of many persuasions, David, but above all I tend to the needs of The Cause. My home is a haven for its members, provided everyone who enters does so with caution and reverence."

"I see. Where are the men who brought me here?" his voice quavered at the memory of how they treated him.

"Them? They've been dispatched. I must apologize for the way they handled the situation. I had requested they simply invite you, but Calvin thought otherwise," she said. "And Calvin has final say in these matters."

"May I?' David asked, pointing to the food.

"Oh, but of course. You must be famished! A shot of Fenzolex always brings on the most dreadful appetite—or so I'm told."

David strolled nonchalantly to the table and its bounty of apples, pears, peaches and berries but once he began to eat, he dug in with voracity. The last time he ate anything even close to resembling food was the scone in Bandleshore and the portion of granola he had shared with Calvin, but that had been weeks ago.

"Eat up, David. You're not going to find fruits like this often. We're fairly limited here in the city for greenhouse space: most of this is smuggled in. Soon it will be back to nutrient paste though you may have grown accustomed to it by now, after such a long hospital stay. I hear it's an acquired taste—but not one I've personally developed."

David bit off a large chunk of a crimson red apple and turned as a man entered the room, dressed in the same threadbare suits the business men on the train wore. The formidable door, constructed of a dark rich wood, again likely mahogany, clicked quietly behind him. He whispered in Bethany's ear, and she nodded.

"I'm afraid I must be going David, but Calvin will be with you shortly. The news of your return has reached him, and I'm told he's eager to see you again."

Bethany and the man left the room and David was once again alone. While he waited, he enjoyed a few additional berries, followed by a bottle of water that smelled like seawater, although it was not salty. He walked across the room and gazed through the transparent glass wall across the empty sea and watched the swells of the ocean stretch out into the far horizon. A deafening boom panicked him, as Calvin marched in, slamming the door behind him.

"David! I can't believe you're alive!" Whether the fanatical look in his eyes expressed excitement or irritated disbelief was unclear. "I'm sorry I almost killed you back there on the train. I should have told you what was happening, but I didn't know if I could trust you. The last thing I needed was for you to somehow give away the game."

At this point, David realized in a roundabout way, Calvin had attempted to murder him. Or at the very least, he had been fine with idea of letting David perish in the explosion. That this man so flippantly determined David's life—along with the lives of everyone else on the train—as disposable, roiled his stomach. Still, he was in a bind and needed something he could not discover on his own—and his memories were worth leaving this particular past alone.

"Well, now you can see I'm trustworthy. I'm here, aren't I?"

"David, we kidnapped you and brought you here."

"Sure, but I didn't put up a fight. Didn't your goons tell you that? There was no reason to drug me, or whatever the hell your people did. I planned on finding you on my own."

"Oh really? And why might that be?" He slipped his hand into his coat pocket and formed a grip around whatever hid inside.

"Because I find you intriguing—you and The Cause, that is," David braced his expression, consuming every ounce of will not to break his composure in the face of this uncertain threat. "I'm not familiar with this place. After being here for a few weeks, I can honestly say I don't remember anything about Plasticity; I'm almost certain I've never been here before."

Calvin removed his hand from his pocket and took a seat on the couch. "Sit down, David. Tell me more."

"First: questions. How long has it been since the explosion?"

"Three weeks, four days, six hours and …" Calvin reached into his coat pocket and pulled out a brass pocket watch, "… seventeen minutes."

"So then, I've been in a hospital for almost the entire last month. I don't remember how I got there, and I have no memory of what happened for the first few weeks. I didn't wake up until a few days ago. What I do know, is whatever they did to me, even if it saved my life, it was wrong. A violation."

Calvin moved in closer, his eyes widening again. David swore drool seeped from the corners of his chapped lips.

"They dug around in my brain, Calvin. They told me they killed me and brought me back to life. I never gave them the right to do something like that, and I definitely didn't give them permission to invade my privacy. This place," David waved his hands outward, invoking the city itself. "This place is … not respectable."

"Oh, come now, David. You've hardly been outside the hospital. How would you know anything about Plasticity?"

"You're right. I haven't spent any time in the city, but I've seen what people consider normal here and what the government does. If they can do something like this to me, I would hate to see what they do to those who openly disagree with their systems."

"No, David, you definitely would not want to see that," Calvin agreed.

"I want to leave here, Calvin. I want to leave Plasticity."

"Leave? I suppose it's possible... but remember, there's nowhere else to go. The Grasslands are still inhospitable, and you do not want to live in the cities—they're overrun with horrible creatures. There's always Bandleshore, I suppose ... but you've seen what that place is like as well."

"Doesn't sound like there are many safe options."

"Because there aren't, unless ..."

"Unless what?"

"Well, David, there's a reason I had you brought here—and no, it wasn't to kill you."

"I figured that out."

"What do you know about The Cause?"

David shook his head. "Not much—primarily what you've told me. I heard some mention of it in the hospital, but when I inquired further, people shook it off as meaningless."

Calvin slammed his fist down on the plastic coffee table in front of them, cracking it. "Arrogance! That is their sin!"

David slunk back from Calvin.

"I'm sorry, David. I'm not easily frustrated, but when dealing with The Progressives I just can't handle their haughty attitude." Calvin folded his hands in front of his mouth, closed his eyes and bowed. After a few deep breaths, he continued, "I'd like to give you a lesson in civil liberty, David."

David relaxed. "Okay," he said.

"The Cause ... it can be difficult to explain The Cause to one who doesn't know the background and history. I suppose I should start with The Class Wars."

"Actually, I know about The Class Wars—the gist of them at least. Someone in Bandleshore filled me in."

"Oh really?" Calvin's eyebrows scrunched up. "Who?"

"Some guy named Conor."

"Ah yes, Conor. He's friendly, although a bit too open-mouthed at times," Calvin said, dismissing the issue. "Well then, I can skip the history and go right to the meat, as it were. In the simplest of terms, The Cause is an attempt to overthrow the government and to realign society with the Earth."

"I thought you said you weren't an Organic."

"No, I'm not an Organic, but those of them who stray outside pure pacifism do tend to side with us. The leaders of modern society are the same ones who got us into this mess in the first place—not the same people, they're long dead of course, but the same type of people. As you've seen, Plasticity is one of the last bastions of human life. There are other cities like it, but their numbers remain few, and though scattered, they are aligned in policy as to how to take back the planet.

"The Cause argues we should not take it back. Instead, we believe that we should become one with it. You've seen what's already happened out there. It's like a green desert. Alive, but lifeless. And the things you haven't seen—the death and the mutation and the sickness still plaguing the interior is horrifying. The Society still lives by the same moral standards as they did before: technology is their God, and through their worship, they abuse it.

"Do you know what happens when you abuse your God? When you beat him and cheat him and take him for granted? He strikes back. That's what's happened here—it's what's happened to mankind—and my cause—The Cause—is an effort to stop it from happening all over again."

"Surely The Progressives have learned their lesson."

"Oh, I'm quite certain they've learned some lessons. But their greed remains. They are elite, in their own minds, and most of society agrees with that assumption. Technology got them into this mess, and they expect technology to save them. Out there," Calvin pointed toward the shore, "they're experimenting with ways to rid the planet of the mess they made. But, in the case that isn't possible, they're also working on ways we can live there again—primarily by manipulating humans themselves. That's part of what the Eyefields are for. Eyes are highly sensitive and easily absorb chemicals and air pollutants—it's why you'll find so many blind people wandering about the cities ... well, the ones who don't get eaten ..."

Calvin's voice trailed off; he appeared deep in thought. David remained silent, waiting for him to continue. A clock on the bedside table ticked away the seconds.

"The eyes are being continually engineered to be resistant to the poisons out there, and they're using the same technologies on individuals here—grafting, gene therapy, cloning. These biological aberrations, as well as integration with the new Singularity are their plan for bringing us back to land."

"So, what's your plan?"

"I trust you David, but I don't trust you that much," Calvin chuckled. "You're part of it though, if you want to be."

Exactly the opening David hoped for. Like the woman in the hospital predicted, Calvin would invite him back, even if only to further his own best interests.

"I understand you feel violated by what The Society has done to you, David, but in an ironic way, that's what will bring them down. You said you had some work done on your brain. Do you know much more about it?"

"I do remember them saying something about a FloatNet. They also mentioned something about having to kill me to do it?"

"That's wonderful, David!" Calvin said. "You were treated under Federal Health, meaning you must follow Federal Health Guidelines, which also means you are required to go in for regular checkups. Part of those checkups will require connecting you to the diagnostic network—and that's our way into the system. If we upload a Trojan into your head, we can insert it on the network and break into the FloatNet core. You in?"

"This Trojan.. Is it dangerous?"

"Of course not! It's a simple procedure—you won't feel a thing. Just a small file upload. It'll be like a twitch in your brain, then it'll be over. As for when you're back in the Federal network, you'll be sleeping anyway. And if they catch you, we'll be sure to leave a few tracers on the Trojan to have the fingerprints point to some hacker kids."

David pondered this for a while, or at least pretended to. If he appeared to eager to join in, he'd blow his cover. Then again, he didn't want to come off as too sheepish and risk losing whatever little trust he had so far acquired.

"So, like I asked, are you in?"

David reached over and shook Calvin's hand.

"Excellent. Let's go see Sage."

## SEVENTEEN
# BOTTOM OF THE BOWL

"Most day-to-day operations of the city are powered primarily by ocean waves," Calvin explained as they took a glass freight elevator down from the surface through the multiple sublevels beneath the city.

"What you see there is the main plant, set up here beneath the city, built to capture the power of the ocean's movement and convert motion to energy. The problem is for it to function, you need waves. This is all well and good during hurricane season, but at times when the ocean is at peace, like today, the wave generators are insufficient for the needs of a city the size of Plasticity—even with the battery reserves.

"The citizens started complaining about the brownouts, and so city officials agreed the only solution was an additional power source. Those same officials also didn't trust the track record of nuclear power, and with good reason—especially after what happened in San Diego. But even aside from the obvious dangers, they feared the risks of a buildup of nuclear waste in a city with nowhere to dispose of it. Simply dumping into the ocean wouldn't do. The ocean, as tainted as it is, was now their last refuge. Dumping it on land had been an option, but rather than continue to spoil the land they'd already destroyed, not to mention the logistics of transporting so much waste, they opted for a cleaner, more renewable solution."

As the elevator slowed to a stop, David saw that, unlike the other sublevels, sublevel fourteen consisted of a singular wide-open space, free of partitions, rooms and corridors. A pool of water lay placid in the center, directly on the bottom sphere in which Plasticity itself was housed. Stretching several thousand yards across, the amount of space the pool occupied would have allowed for at least two or three additional sublevels to have been built below the fourteenth. But instead of using the space for people, machinery or housing, this bottom quarter of the globe housing Plasticity held nothing but a massive volume of water.

The air stank of salt and seaweed, and the atmosphere hung low and heavy from the tremendous amount of moisture. Even though sunlight poured in through the mirrored windows surrounding the massive expanse, David couldn't see out of them due to the accumulated condensation. A plastic grid of catwalk surrounded the perimeter, crisscrossing throughout to allow access to the tens of thousands of square feet of surface.

David stepped forward to the edge of the catwalk, his toes peeking over the edge, and stared down into the water below.

"Why is it so green?" he asked.

"This is where the algae blooms. It's where Plasticity grows its energy. Sage can explain it better than I can. Let's see if he's around."

The wide-open space of sublevel fourteen appeared empty, sans the catwalks and water below. Calvin walked forward, searching.

"Keep your eyes open. If you see anyone, tell me."

The two walked about the space for several minutes, the sound of their footsteps ringing a wet echo against the pool's surface and the glass walls. Water dripped steadily from the walkways and ran down the walls in long streaks. David nearly lost his footing once or twice but managed to catch himself before he could fall into the soupy, emerald pool below.

"Is there anyone down here?" Calvin shouted. "Sage?"

"Calvin, is that you?" a gravelly voice rang out, the ensuing echo masking its source.

"Yes, it's me." Calvin yelled back to the emptiness. "Where are you?"

Several hundred feet away, two walkways over, a body rose from the ground. The man had been lying prone on the catwalk's slippery surface. In his hands, he held a test tube full of the green water. A pair of nerdy glasses perched on the tip of his nose, and he slid them up as he stood. Dressed in a white lab coat that was smeared with green stains, the man was the most normal-looking individual David had yet encountered while in the city.

"Calvin, what are you doing down here? It's so unwise of you to be" he looked around, "in the open," Sage spoke rapidly. "The sublevels are under security now—so much more security than ever before, what, with that unfortunate mess you made up top."

"What are you implying?" Calvin grinned as he spoke.

"Now Calvin, you mustn't be so cavalier!" Sage scolded. "You're so very important. So very important. So very, very important ..." Sage's voice trailed off and he fell silent, staring into the pools of water below.

"Sage!" Calvin shouted, and the man snapped back to attention.

"Calvin! What are you doing down here? It's dangerous for you to be here. You mustn't be out in the open like this!"

"Sage," Calvin rested his hand on Sage's shoulder, much like he'd done earlier with David, although David detected a hint of sadness in Calvin's eyes as he did so. "This is David, Sage."

Sage twitched with a bit of shock when he noticed David and nearly hurtled himself into the water. Like a striking cobra, Calvin reached and caught his arm.

"David has access, Sage. He can get in."

Sage sneered. "We don't need another hacker. You know they'll trace any hacks we try; their security bots are too damn reliable! Besides, if I can't get in, no one else will be able to either."

"Not a hacker, Sage. A patient." Calvin lowered his voice to a whisper and Sage leaned in. "A patient. And a friend to The Cause. He's not going to hack in, they're going to plug him in to the network on their own. We just need you to help us in."

"Ah!" Sage pointed his finger into the air, dropping his test tube into the pea soup below, and marched off. "Come with me!" he shouted, as they scrambled to follow. "I have just the thing."

## EIGHTEEN
# HAMMERING IN MY HEAD

Sage dragged a banker's box out from under his bed and plopped it on the mattress. David and Calvin stepped to the side, squeezing uncomfortably close in the cramped confines of Sage's quarters on sublevel nine.

"So…" David started, as Sage began to rifle through the box. "What's with all the water and the seaweed downstairs? Calvin said something about growing electricity."

"Yup," Sage replied. He tossed aside the first box and reached back under the bed. "For the hydrogen plant on sublevel four."

"David's never been to Plasticity, Sage. He's not from around here."

Sage eyeballed David, his glasses again sliding down to the end of his nose. "Organic?" he asked.

"Not quite sure, actually. I'm here to help though," David replied.

"So then, you don't know anything about our little city. No idea about how we continue to exist, even though we've been out here for decades now. The answer's in sustainable energy!"

"I already filled him in about the waves, Sage. He wants to learn more about your little greenies."

"Ahhhh." Sage smiled as he dropped another box onto the bed. "They're what keeps the city going. We figured out how to make them break water down into hydrogen and oxygen. That's what the fields are there for downstairs. With the ocean, we have a hugely abundant supply of water, and the algae separates the molecules into hydrogen and oxygen. We capture the two gases through reclamation units near the water's surface and use the hydrogen to power the electric plant on four, The O-two is used to keep the air here in Plasticity at healthy levels—and free of pollutants. Quick and dirty explanation, of course. It's obviously much more complicated."

Sage stood up, a small green pill pinched between his index finger and thumb. "A-ha! Here's what I was looking for."

David shook his head furiously. "I'm not taking any more drugs. I've had enough of them lately."

"This is no drug! It's an ingestible NanoSwarm. Just swallow this, and thousands of nanobots will enter your system, allowing me to insert a Trojan into your cerebral cortex without having to bypass the security of the I/O port they installed on the back of your noggin."

David studied Calvin. "You trust this guy?"

Calvin nodded. "Absolutely."

"If you're serious about kicking the Soldiers of the Reconstruction right where it hurts, we're going to need to know more about them. Take the pill and I'll reprogram you—it won't take more than a few minutes."

"Soldiers of the—?"

"The official name of The Progressives," Calvin answered. "They claim they're not interested in a war, yet they subtly threaten to start one even in the names they choose. They know this is a war, whether they publicly admit it or not, and they're positioning themselves as the heroes."

"Oh, okay," David didn't like the sound of this. "What happens to the nanobots after you're done? Won't they be detected somehow?"

"Oh, don't worry about them. You'll just poop 'em out!" Sage nudged David's shoulder. "Make sure you eat plenty of fiber before you go in for your next checkup," he whispered.

David swallowed the pill and waited.

"That swarm was programmed to respond only to reprogramming from my own personal wavelength—a security measure I added. I already have the code figured out in my head, so for this particular virus, I'll just need to send the instructions over into the swarm mentally. It will, of course, take some time for them to build the program."

"Will it hurt?"

"Oh, God yes!" Sage replied, his face filled with gleeful enthusiasm.

A flood of anxious energy coursed through David's body. He considered spitting up the pill, but from the warm sensation spreading in his gut, he knew the Nanos were already starting to disperse.

"Isn't there something you can give me?"

"You said no drugs," Sage replied, matter-of-factly.

The swarm rushed up through his neck, into his head and the base of his skull screamed with a searing pain.

"I changed my mind!"

"Well, I'm quite certain I don't have any painkillers here," Sage replied, digging back into his box. "I suppose I could go up to the surface and procure some morphine."

Tears began to pour down David's cheeks, the pain stabbing like hot knives through his head. He frantically searched the room for anything to rid him of the agony. Seeing nothing, he leapt from the bed, leaned back, and slammed his forehead against the wall. His skull made a bang like the crack of a bat and, with green memories of sublevel fourteen, one thought entered his mind before he went unconscious: Fenway.

## NINETEEN
# SOMEWHERE BETWEEN WAKING AND DREAMING

David lingered at Aiden's door and stared at the dark space below his bed. Watching for movement, he scanned for anything peculiar: a moving shadow, a glint of eyes reflecting the hall light. Frozen in place, he stood terrified at the prospect of investigating what could lie beneath, but there was no way he could expose this fear to his son.

"Please Dad, please just look under the bed. I swear I heard something."

"Aiden, you're six years old and we've done this every night since you were two. Don't you think we would have found something by now?"

Aiden and he had been through this countless times before, and usually it was a quick look, a confirmation that nothing was there, and lights out. But tonight? Tonight felt different.

*David, you're a grown-up. Just look under the bed and everything will be fine.*

He repeated this mantra three times, then slowly dropped to his knees. He imagined reaching into the abyss, only to feel the cold, leathery claws of some kind of gremlin latching on, tearing into his skin, scraping its nails across his bone. Still several feet away from the bed, he couldn't really see anything without moving closer. He tilted his head and leaned forward, looking sideways at the dark expanse. To his right, the night light cast a faded glow, brightening the room much more than when he first entered, now that his eyes had since adjusted to the light.

He turned his gaze to the side of the bed, the shadowy area falling into his peripheral vision.

Then he saw it.

A flash of light, like cat's eyes, in the blackness beneath Aiden's bed. He blinked and took a double-take, only to realize it was just one of Aiden's toy robots. A little pair of cameras on a set of wheels. *Probably something he got from Grandma and Grandpa,* he thought.

----

"I said, do you want any cereal?"

David's eyes scanned the kitchen. Missy and Aiden sat at the table with him, Missy munched on a bowl of blueberries while Aiden prodded at a mountain of scrambled eggs with his fork.

"David? Are you alright?" Alice slowed her speech, pronouncing each word deliberately. "Can ... you ... hear ... me?" she asked.

"Yeah, yeah I hear you. Sorry, I must have been daydreaming," he answered. "To tell you the truth, I'm not hungry, but I figure I should eat something. Sure, I'll have some breakfast."

Alice grabbed a bowl and spoon from the dishwasher and placed them in front of David. He poured a bowl of cereal and splashed some almond milk on top. Outside the sun shimmered, and the ancient oak tree, now stripped of leaves, creaked heavily in the wind.

"Thanks, honey."

"Of course, baby. I just want you to start feeling better. Tell me if there's anything I can do for you."

David turned his attention to his two children. "How are you two doing today?"

Aiden groaned. "I wish I was hurt—then I wouldn't have to go to school—"

"I wish I could go to school!" said Missy. "Mommy's boring."

David laughed, and Alice, despite being the butt of the joke, managed to let out a chuckle of her own.

"Well you're in luck, little lady," David said. "I'm going to be home with you all week too."

"Can we go to the zoo?"

"Honey, the zoo's closed for the winter," said Alice. "And your Daddy needs as much rest as he can manage, so he feels better."

Missy's lips curled into a pout.

"Don't worry. I won't be sleeping all the time. We'll play too."

"David, please eat your berries," said Alice.

"I'm not having berries, I'm having cereal." David scooped his spoon into his bowl and retrieved a spoonful of blueberries.

"You need to eat more. Those antioxidants will help eliminate any stray Nanos."

David blinked his eyes in confusion. "What are you talking about, Alice?"

"Who's Alice? Are you sure you're okay to do this?"

David blinked again, and upon opening his eyes found he was no longer in his kitchen, but instead back in the safe house with Bethany. A small silver platter of blueberries, cherries, dried plums and strawberries lay in his lap.

"You don't have to go in for this checkup if you don't want to. We have access to our own medical units—some of them better than anything you'll find at a Federal facility."

"No, I'm fine. Daydreaming, I guess."

David swore sparks lit up Bethany's eyes. "Oh really? What about?"

"I'm not quite sure. I think my memory might be starting to come back. I was in a kitchen with my wife and kids. It was sunny and the tree in the yard was—"

"Yard? You must have been dreaming. So, are you still ready to do this?"

"Do what?"

"Your checkup? …Well, and to upload the Trojan too—but that won't require any actual work on your part."

"Isn't it a little soon to be going back? They're going to expect me to have some kind of malfunction if I'm back so soon, won't they?"

"It's been a week, David. Federal Regulations require you go back for your checkup after a week."

The last memory David had was the cracking sound of his forehead smacking the wall while the NanoSwarm attacked his brain. Still, no lingering discomfort pained his head, and looking at his reflection staring back from the silver of the fruit platter, he could see only a few faint yellow remainders where the bruise would have been.

"Yeah, I'm ready. Let's do this."

## TWENTY
# LET THE MEMORY LIVE AGAIN

"We only received one uplink while you were gone, David. Is there some issue we should be made aware of?" The woman, Juliet, wore the same blue lab gear she wore the first time he saw her. David missed the sunny dress.

"I'm not quite sure, to be honest. Things have been a little cloudy while I've been gone. I can't remember all the time I've been absent. Then again, I've been knocked unconscious more often than I can count in the last few weeks—so I'm sure that might have something to do with it. You might want to check for me, while you're in there."

"According to your last uplink, you're carrying a virus in your mind. Is that correct?"

David rubbed the wireless device implanted in the base of his skull. "That uplink of yours really works, doesn't it."

"Of course, it does," she said, as she tapped at her touchscreen. "Why would we risk such a procedure if it wouldn't?"

David shrugged. "What else have you learned?"

"We've learned everything you've learned, of course. We've learned about the safe house, and about Bethany. We couldn't track the location of the safe house, of course, since they certainly would have detected the trace. Besides a place like that is surely protected by GeoScramblers."

"So you haven't learned much of anything then?"

"I didn't say we haven't learned anything. We were able to find a match to Bethany in the Federal records. Her real name is Samantha Helkamp, and the woman you've met, Bethany, as she calls herself, has undergone major cosmetic surgery. The only way we were able to track her down in the system was through an ocular scan. Thank you for looking her in the eye when you spoke to her, by the way. Try to do that more often—it's a tremendous help."

David hadn't realized that he looked her in the eye, but made a mental note to do so in the future.

"And even though we couldn't track it, we're fairly certain we've discovered the location of the Safe House. Samantha Helkamp still has a house registered in her name over on Wozniak and we've had eyes on it since Sunday."

"So, what's next? When do you attack?"

"We won't be attacking, David. From what we've learned, the safe house is merely a temporary shelter. People come and go, and even though sometimes those people include Calvin Simon, a small hit like that would do little to stop this so-called Cause. What we're looking to do is to take out their main base of operation, and so far, you have not been taken there, nor been informed of its location. So, for now, we continue as usual."

"How do you know they'll ever take me there?" David asked.

"We don't," the woman looked up from her touchpad and directly at David. "But so far our hypotheses have been correct. Calvin trusts you. A big point in your favor, and a big point in favor of this entire operation. If you can determine the location, or if you can find out when and where they plan to attack next, we'll be able to deal them a potentially lethal blow."

David thought about this, and about the people he met recently. None of them seemed to be particularly evil, although every time he thought of the train station bombing, he remembered what they were capable of. Still, even though their methods were despicable, he couldn't help but think they had reason for what they were doing.

"My memories, I think they're starting to come back," he said.

"That's wonderful news, David! What can you remember?"

"I remember a house, a wife, and two children. I remember having a family."

The excitement on the woman's face shrank as her smile turned to a frown. "I'm sorry, David. I don't know how to tell you this … but we've had some luck here as well, restoring your old memory files."

"That's nothing to be sorry about. Sounds like great news!"

"Well yes, it is. But even though we haven't rebuilt much of the file system, there's been no mention of a family. What else can you tell me? When do the memories come? Are there any other details you can recall?"

"Well, now that you mention it, the memories only seem to resurface when I'm dreaming. But they're the same memories each time—or at least they take place in the same time and setting. In the latest one I was eating breakfast with my family, and I just got over a head injury, so everything was a bit fuzzy."

"A head injury. Like your real life," she interjected.

"Yes, although these take place in a very different time and place. It seems to be back on the mainland; there are trees in the yard, for example."

"This is quite odd, David, but it does confirm that some concerns we've had are viable."

"What concerns?"

She hesitated, looking around the room. Her eyes paused on each of the four security cameras. "You mentioned gaps in your memory, even since the restoration. We're seeing them as well—and they all seem to occur while you're sleeping."

"Well that makes sense though, doesn't it? If I'm sleeping, there's nothing to record."

"Not exactly true, David. As you fall asleep, your brain does tend to shut down somewhat, but once someone enters R.E.M. sleep and starts to dream, their mind is quite active. For many individuals, a dreaming state is nearly indistinguishable from a waking state—and in some instances can be even more vivid and realistic than waking life."

"You're telling me I don't dream? I know I have dreams. I just told you about them."

"What I'm saying is we don't see your dreams. When you are sleeping, it's like your brain is shut down. When we first analyzed your files our systems thought you had actually died, David, but we knew that couldn't be right, since you can't upload after you're dead; the uploads operate as a subroutine of your regular brain function—it's why you can't upload when you're sleeping either. The trigger has to be set consciously, otherwise if you were compromised, or were suspected of spying, The Cause could start sending in a string of keywords to your subconscious just to crack your system and see if they can trigger an upload."

"Then what happens when I dream? Is there something wrong with me?"

"We have some theories, but nothing concrete. Rest assured we're working on it. Now if you could lay back on the bed, we'll do that routine checkup."

"Don't you need to delete the Trojan?"

"No, we're going to let it in… but we're going to be selective about what information it relays, and which bits of information we let out are true and which are false."

David eased back onto the bed and closed his eyes. Within a few minutes the I/O port began to hum, and a gentle warmth spread through the base of his skull. Once again, David's world faded to black.

# TWENTY-ONE
# SPY GAME

"—that's unfortunately the way things are now. You're going to have to find yourself a new path from here."

David's grip on the phone tightened, the involuntary contraction of his arm muscles slipping the handset down his sweaty cheek. He pulled the phone back to his ear and cleared his throat, his mind swimming.

"I—I don't understand. Who is this?" David asked.

"David, I said I was sorry for this, so please don't shut down on me. We're going to have to close the whole firm down—there isn't enough demand anymore with the way the economy is. You're not alone."

David squeezed his eyes shut and focused on the voice on the other end of the line.

"I understand, Fred," he said, but the line was already dead.

----

"Welcome back, David."

David's eyes shot open and he was greeted with the sight of Juliet. The warmth of his I/O port faded, replaced by a small release of pressure at the base of his skull as the port hissed, disengaging his cortex from the input mechanism.

"What happened? Are you done already?"

The woman nodded. "At this point we're only running deltas to grab anything new. The comparator function is quite efficient, especially given the high-speed data transfers we can achieve on a hard link; but in order to keep costs down we only fetch new data. You would have been out even sooner if we didn't have to allow extra time to ensure the upload of that Trojan you were carrying."

"It's in then?"

"Of course, but we'll keep it isolated. We have a mirror environment set up for this kind of thing. It'll share information, but only some things. Obviously our highly-classified files won't even exist there."

"What do I do now?"

"Why, you return to Calvin, of course."

David rose from the I/O chair and stretched, rubbing the spot where the transfer cable had recently been inserted. His finger caught on a snarl of hair.

"So that's it? Business as usual?" He continued to work the snarl loose. "I'm happy to help and all—but ..."

"But what, David? We restored you to life. I don't believe we're asking too much in return for what we've done for you."

"No—no, that's not it. I guess I hoped you'd have a little more information for me about who I am. If what you've said is true, and the memories or visions or experiences or ...

whatever is in my head isn't real, then I would love to find out what's missing. Or better yet, where these hallucinations are coming from."

"As I said, David, we're working on it. We've recovered some information, but a neural reconstruction like this isn't as easy as you might think. We're starting to build a picture of who you are, or rather, were ... but to share that information with you in such a fragmented state could be potentially fatal to your already damaged network." She paused, biting her lip surreptitiously. "I'm sorry. I can't divulge anything to you yet. You're too important."

"Important? For you and your spy game?"

"David, trust me." She motioned to the door. "You'll learn more soon. I promise."

---

The walk from the medical center back to the train station gave David time to ponder what Juliet said. In his mind, he knew who he was, even if he couldn't put it into words. He could sense his intuition and the direction of his moral compass. He had no doubt about the kind of person he'd be in a tough situation. His soul, the thing that defined him, was clear. What he couldn't figure out was who he was previously. Who he had been. His past remained clouded and any attempt to try to bring the memories forward, back from whatever dark corner they hunkered down in, was met with nothing but failed frustration.

The most significant nagging point in all of this was the discomforting thought he might have been wrong about himself. Deep in the thick marrow of his bones it seemed unquestionable that he was a virtuous person and that his recent decisions matched this theory. Still, doubt tugged the tendrils of his mind. Perhaps he wasn't as virtuous as his limited conscience let on.

After a fifteen-minute walk, David entered the door of the small apartment the Reconstruction set up for him following his initial stay at the medical center. The 500-square-foot unit didn't provide a lot of space, but it was suitable enough. At only five minutes from the city center, he was able to quickly travel to the places he needed to—which in most instances had been Beverly's home / headquarters. In fact, he couldn't recall a single night in the bed tucked in the corner of the room, only a few stops to grab a quick bite or take a quick rest on the couch. The sheets were still crisply made, aside from the occasional wrinkle where he had taken a temporary seat.

The biggest inconvenience of the space, to David at least, was the position it held within the building. Considering ground level of the city only managed to take up about ten square miles, travel time from one end to the other was quite minimal. But, since Plasticity's ground level was well below the widest space of the sphere in which it was situated, vertical space was the more highly prized commodity.

All the way up on the 102nd floor, David was afforded a rather spectacular view of the ocean and its receding horizon. The problem was, David didn't care a single iota about the view—he was more concerned with the ridiculously long elevator ride from the ground floor up to his apartment.

Traveling across Plasticity was a breeze—traveling up and down much less so.

----

David had no sooner laid down to rest, when an incessant buzzing began to ring in his ears. He lifted his head from his pillow, confused, and realized someone was at the door.

The man at the door stood short, no more than five feet tall, and was wearing a finely tailored suit. His dark hair was slicked back, and a pair of wire-rimmed glasses perched daintily on his nose.

"Your presence, sir," the man said in a high pitched, nasally voice, "is requested downtown."

"Where? I already am downtown."

The man contemplated David, scrunching his face around his nose. He blinked twice, in rapid succession and paused, taking David in, as if judging him.

"Bethany wants to see you."

He turned and walked away. David grabbed his coat and followed, locking the apartment door behind him.

## TWENTY-TWO
# VIA CHICAGO

"David, my boy!" The grip of Calvin's meaty hand clasped on David's shoulder was so tight David could feel Calvin's rough callouses through his shirt. "You've done fine work!"

"Hear, hear!" chimed in Bethany, handing David a bubbling crystal flute filled with champagne. "A toast, to success!"

They clinked glasses and took a drink.

"So ... I take it your thing is working?"

"Is it working?" Bethany clasped her hands to her chest and beamed. "The data we've gotten already is better than anything we could have imagined!"

"That's great news!" David turned to Calvin. "Have you gotten a lot?"

"Well, here's the thing, David," Calvin answered. "It's working perfectly, and the data is gold, but there's not much of it."

David shifted his regard to Bethany, then back to Calvin. "Did … did something go wrong then?"

"No, nothing's wrong! It's all working like it should—but it's going to be a slow process. You see, we're inside their network, which is great—but we need to pull data out of the network—which means downstream bandwidth."

"And with bandwidth, comes visibility," continued Bethany. "For this to work, we have to remain invisible. That means hijacking packets already being sent, or at least disguising our outgoing data as innocuous bits of boring information."

"Which is where Sage comes to the rescue, again," Calvin interjected. "The best way to hide anything outgoing is to send it where it would normally be going … and not a lot of data goes out from that level of the network. And the limited amount that does go out, only goes to secure nodes."

"… and the power stations are secure," David finished.

"Right! So, the data we're grabbing is funneled out, at a tiny undetectable trickle to our hacked node in Sage's network, as part of the power ration allocation algorithms for the general population. Sage transfers it to a data stick, it goes through some unknown variety of hands—secure hands, and ends up here," Calvin gave David another pat on the back. "See Bethany, I told you Sage would be worth more than his cocktails."

Bethany sighed. "Right as usual, Calvin. But still, these are small pieces of information. Anything too big and we'd be noticed. Of course, we have algorithms in place to parse and prioritize anything appearing to be worth further investigation, so that comes our way first in the data stream—but the only way we can access all the information we need is to wait. A long time."

"Couldn't you just, I don't know, have it upload the data into some sort of brain storage or something the next time I'm in for an uplink?"

Bethany explored Calvin's reaction, her eyes eager, and started, "It's something we could do—"

"—But won't unless it's absolutely necessary." Calvin cut Bethany off with a stern glare. "We'd much rather wait. There are potential limitations associated with a data upload to an organic storage unit—"

"—Which is why we're taking you offline. We need to get you out of here while we're gathering data." Bethany clapped, signaling the end of the conversation.

"Where? Should I just hang out in my apartment?"

"No. David. Out of here. Out of Plasticity," Calvin said.

Bethany grabbed David's hands in hers and bounced up and down, like a little girl waiting for her birthday cake.

"We're going home, David."

## TWENTY-THREE
# WE'RE OFF TO SEE THE WIZARD

The pressure locks let out an icy hiss as the canopy bolted into place. David's ghost-like echo stared back at him, his rapid breath fogging the glass until his reflection disappeared. The firm cushions lining the pod should have felt uncomfortable, but despite their cold and unwelcoming appearance, they cradled his body. Hooks of looped padding tightened over his chest and around his waist and ankles, pulling him snug to the foam bed. He wanted to struggle. To escape. But he took a breath and resisted.

"You locked in?" Calvin's voice sounded muffled through the layers of glass.

"I guess so. I feel like I'm about to take a ride on a rollercoaster." The warming air stunk of stale mildew and sweat. David again fought the impulse to panic.

"Yes, I do suppose it will be something like that," replied Bethany. "But these pods are going to go way faster than any ride you can imagine."

The Aeropods were some of the last remnants of the mass transit systems from the time before The Chemical Wars wiped everything out. The old networks of road and freeways were long ago swallowed up by resurging vegetal growth. And the fossil fuels required to power the few remaining vehicles capable of the type of off-road travel their trip required had dried up or expired decades ago. Though the rails and mag trains between cities still stood, the power stations running them also no longer functioned—and years of disuse and exposure to the chemical-infused air rusted them away to the point where they too, were unsalvageable. Aeropod transports, personal methods of transportation exclusively available to the super-rich, were all that remained.

Unlike most forms of travel, Aeropods were limited by strict boundaries. Although capable of tremendously high speeds, their movement was purely linear. Each trip started at a single launching station to a destination depot, with no variation of paths or stops between. Many members of the upper class, like this one's previous owner, installed stations in their homes. Not only did Aeropod units allow for quick mobility, faster than any airplane, to most major cities, but due to their hermetic seal were also the safest way to travel through the now chemically toxic rural areas.

Many firms with sufficient capital even installed launch stations and destination depots in their corporate headquarters, for quick travel to and from the office for the C-Suite and members of the board.

Unfortunately, most of the Aeropod network had been rendered inoperative due to combinations of neglect and lack of stable power supplies. There, however, a few remaining bastions where the requisite power seeds endured. Mostly these could be found at the previous homes of the richest and most powerful of the old society. They were the only ones able to afford the prohibitive cost of self-renewing nuclear reactors in their homes—and the only ones able to grease the palms of regulatory agencies.

Most of these reactors had long ago been looted for whatever useful bits they might have. Some had been refactored into suitcase nukes, as Seattle well knew, while others simply became unstable, poisoning and killing anyone within the vicinity when some fool unsuccessfully attempted to extract a seed from its reactor.

David, Calvin and Bethany were now at one of the few remaining functional launch stations. Discovered through a backtrack of a FloatNet node they found in the basement of an office in old Chicago, it somehow managed to survive decades of disuse. Apparently, a hedge fund manager had kept a small vacation home in rural South Carolina. A remote diagnostic analysis confirmed it as still fully operational.

Situated on a private lake in the middle of nowhere, no one came across it in their travels after the war. The home had been built offsite and airlifted into location, set up to be self-sustaining through a personal nuclear unit, and only accessible via air or Aeropod. No roads reached it, and the only way in—if you knew where you were going—was through miles of native forest. A perfect fishing getaway, a place for this man to step out of the city and realign with nature, but still be back to his office on short notice.

A few electric motorbikes stored in a shed on the outskirts of Bandleshore provided enough horsepower to speed through the fields and forests overnight and reach their destination just as the sun began to rise. A few hours rest in the cottage's untouched beds, and they were ready to make the switch to Aeropod.

----

David sipped his coffee as the crimson sun breached the tree line. Dew dappled the grass and leaves, refracting a shimmer of sunlight, like all that lay before him had been born that morning. The air buzzed with the morning twitter of birds. Insects buzzed in the tall grasses as they woke from their nighttime slumber. A fished splashed in the lake and the coffee tasted like heaven.

"Remind me again why we can't just keep driving?" David asked.

"For starters, our batteries are almost dead." Calvin's booming voice sounded out of place here in this tranquil setting. "And even if we could recharge them or swap them out, there's no way into Chicago anymore. The highways are all destroyed. Same with most of the bridges along the way."

"We also can't risk being spotted," Bethany added. "We have no idea what kind of surveillance they have on you—"

"—and by the time we get to Chicago you'll be way too far for any of the wireless networks to pick you up," said Calvin.

"Satellite, maybe—but they'd have to know where to look … and most major cities are blacked out from satellites after everything that happened to their grids during the meltdowns."

"We can't run the risk of them tracking us any further," Bethany continued. "After we launch, we'll blow the reactor here. They'll know we left, but they'll have no idea where we've gone."

David strolled to the edge of the deck, looking out over the placid lake. In silence, he stood leaning against the railing, as the sun above beat down with glorious warmth. The idea that all of this beauty could be lethal seemed impossible. He loosened his grip on his cup and watched it slowly tumble down to the rocky shoreline. A pop of shattering ceramic echoed across the lake, leaving a starburst of brown on the stones as the only proof any human had been here in decades.

"Alright then. Let's go," David said.

Bethany let out a disgusted sigh, turned and stormed back inside, leaving the sliding glass door open behind her.

Calvin shook his head. "Do you have any idea how much that was worth? This place was like a sealed time capsule. You can't find organic beans anywhere anymore. Those beans were over a hundred years old."

-----

As the screen on the Aeropod counted down the final seconds before departure, the roof opened and exposed the sapphire sky above. Unsure of what to expect when the contraption finally launched, David braced his body for liftoff.

*Just get there. Don't talk to anyone. If anyone asks, say you're a friend of Bethany's. If they understand, they're a friend. Otherwise, stay in one place and wait for the others.*

"Chicago is not a place you want to be wandering on your own." Bethany's final warning echoed him David's mind.

*Lay low. Wait. Don't go for a stroll. Easy.*

"We're shutting you down, David," said Calvin.

"When you wake up, you're going to feel nauseous. It takes a few trips for your body to acclimate to the Gs," Bethany said. "Just get out and put some distance between you and the pod so it can return here and we can catch up. And remember—"

"—I know. Stay put." David took a deep breath and held it.

"Good boy." Calvin slapped his fleshy hand on the glass. "Sweet dreams."

The lights in the pod dimmed and a rush of air hissed around David as the sleeping gas discharged from the interior vents. He breathed out, then in … and let the gas do its thing.

## TWENTY-FOUR
# ASK ME ABOUT
# MY GREAT-GRANDSON

The black hunk of plastic sat there, its digital readout unresponsive. He pressed a few buttons and wiggled the card. Pulled it out, jammed it back in.

"Chip reader don't work yet."

David pulled his credit card from the chip reader and swiped the magnetic strip. *Technology*, he thought.

"Need a receipt?" The heavy-set cashier behind the counter didn't even bother to look up from his magazine.

David shook his head. "I'm good."

"You're all set then." The cashier glanced at David and added, "Congratulations, by the way."

He left his pickup truck parked at the far end of the gas station parking lot. As he strode across the black pavement, he sensed eyes on him. An elderly gentleman, hair gone gray and wiry whiskers sprouting from his sunken face gave a friendly wave, and shouted, "Congratulations!"

By this point David detected a pattern, though the pattern made no sense. He considered stopping to ask the man what he was talking about, but confrontations were something David tended to avoid. And so, confused, he continued to his truck.

The reflection in the pickup window gave David his answer, although he still was unable to understand it. On his shirt, he made out in reversed type, "Ask Me About My Great Grandson." He looked down to the shirt to confirm the reality of what he read, and saw the same message staring back at him upside down. He fingered the shirt's soft material. It was cheap discount store quality, and the message was screen-printed in simple black block letters. It was real—but David had never seen it before, much less remembered putting it on that morning. Not only that, but at the age of 33 he was also far too young to be a grandfather, let alone a great grandfather. Something wasn't right, and David could feel it—could feel a slow unfolding of his mind as this realization set in and realized he was either dreaming or hallucinating.

Stepping closer to the truck to see a better look at his reflection in this strange delusion, he noticed the passenger door ajar. He pulled the driver door open and climbed to pull it closed from inside when a grunting sound from the back of the truck seized his attention. A man in the backseat stared at David, eyes wild with a mix of terror and confusion. The two locked eyes, and after a moment the feral stranger shoved the passenger seat forward and escaped through the back door.

David scrambled back down from the truck and rushed to the passenger side to see what, if anything, had been stolen. His body convulsed and his stomach wretched when he saw the pile of feces on the truck floor. Backing away, he gave himself time to regain his composure. After a few seconds he returned to the truck, averting his eyes from the steaming pile on his back seat, but even without looking he was reminded of its presence from the stench alone. He pushed the seat back to its regular position and continued his search of the truck. The binder of CDs that had been sitting on the floor of the passenger front side was missing. All that remained was a sole circle of plastic with the words "Toby Keith" scrawled on it in black marker.

Irate at the mess and, even more so, the theft of his music collection, David thrust his hand under the passenger seat and searched chaotically until he found the reassuring chill of bare metal. Careful not to cut himself, his fingertips traced the sharp edge until they found wood and clutched the handle of his emergency hatchet.

"Come back here you sonofabitch!" David yelled and took off down the street, hooking a left where the man turned. Before he made it too far, however, the heat from the summer sun and the exhaustion got the better of him. He stood panting on the sidewalk and searched for any clue where the man went. Then he saw it, a head poking around the corner of a hedge, spying on him. David forced a second wind, reared the hatchet above his head, and continued his pursuit.

The man disappeared behind the bushes and by the time David reached the spot he last saw the intruder, the man was gone. He continued down the alley.

The hedge broke further down and opened on a cracked concrete driveway leading to a rickety old house. From the decrepit state of the house, the piles of rubbish on the porch and the straggly, overgrown lawn, David knew he was no longer in the affluent neighborhood he called home.

A resounding bang sounded, and David's focus shifted to the front door. The screen rebounded in its frame, hitting a second time, as the steel entrance door closed behind it. A click of the deadbolt sealed it shut. David paced the porch as he desperately hunted any view of the interior, but unfortunately, the sidelights were boarded over, and the windows covered in newspapers, blocking any view of what might lie inside. He pulled his cellphone from his pocket and considered calling the police, but the adrenaline pumping through him didn't allow for that kind of bureaucratic wait. A swift kick ripped through the screen, snapped the deadbolt from its frame and busted the door in.

Inside, the house was in no better shape than out. Muddy footprints caked the floor leading from the entrance. Empty takeout containers littered the coffee table and piles of dirty socks, shirts and other laundry were scattered everywhere. A heavy cloud of dust hung in the air, disturbed from its rest by the violent slamming of doors. A muffled yelp caught David's ear, and a dim rectangle of light at the far side of the room vanished as another door slammed shut.

David bolted for it, flung it open and bounded down the stairs into a partially finished basement. He dashed across the concrete floor through a corridor of unpainted drywall and stopped at the door to the room where the man hid. David took a deep breath and bent his head to the left and to the right, his neck popping like firecrackers as he prepared for confrontation.

Gingerly, he pressed his fingers against the door; it had no handle and swung effortlessly on its hinges. Someone on the other side pushed back and David responded with a swift kick, slammed the door against the man and sent him to the floor.

The man scrambled to his feet, scurried to the back of the room and seized a pair of rough cut 2x4s. Bringing the wood down on David like a pair of Neanderthal clubs, the man lunged at David and screamed, his eyes wild like a rabid opossum. A quick feint to the left dodged one impact, while David blocked the other with his hatchet. Like a medieval battle, the two of them sparred until one of the boards splintered to bits. The man stepped back, lifted his remaining board like a baseball bat, and took a powerful swing, only to be stopped short by David's hatchet. With a strong yank, David pulled the makeshift weapon from his attacker and pried the board from his blade. The 2x4 banged against the floor and he raised the hatchet high above his head, ready to deal a killing blow to the stranger.

Tears welled from the man's eyes as he covered his head and collapsed onto the floor. In response to this man's expression of pure terror, David hesitated, his weapon still held high and gradually lowered it to his side. The man began to rock back and forth on the floor, whimpering. To his left, on a makeshift table made of plywood and sawhorses, lay David's binder of CDs. In silence, he picked them up, gave the man another look, and walked out the way he came, ignoring the sound of tears and snot splattering pathetically on the bare concrete behind him.

On his way out, the roughed-in hallway opened into the larger open area David hadn't noticed in his earlier pursuit. To his right a pair of men sat hunched over on a dingy black futon, staring at a television screen, video game controllers in hand. Somehow, they hadn't noticed David come through earlier, likely too focused on their video game—but this time they saw David and froze. A smile crept across David's face and he dropped his CDs and broke out into a run. The two men let go of their controllers, sprung from the couch and gave chase.

The sound of metal dragging against concrete pierced David's ears, and he looked back over his shoulder to see the larger of the two only a few feet behind him, a four-foot black and yellow striped steel pipe in hand. His smaller friend followed close behind.

As he cleared the top of the stairs, a brush trimmer hanging from a hook on the wall caught David's eye. He wrenched it from its hook, gave the cord a strong pull, and the motor roared to life. He spun to face his assailant, swinging the trimmer threateningly at the big man and his yellow pipe. David attacked, and the man raised the pipe to block the spinning end of the trimmer. The whirring blades bounced off the metal with a screeching ping and sent a burst of sparks into the air as the two makeshift weapons collided. The blades snapped on impact, clattering against the walls and stairs, rendering the makeshift weapon useless. David threw the trimmer at his pursuer and bolted for the front door.

Throwing the trimmer must have bought David some time. He made it safely across the living room and out the front door. In the yard, he stopped and looked back at the house as he caught his breath. Confident no one had followed him, he headed back in the direction of his truck, unexpectedly stepping right into the chest of the man with the pipe.

"How much you bench, bro?" the man asked.

David searched frantically for an escape.

"I said, what do you bench? 170?"

David opened his mouth to answer but was cut short as the pipe crashed into his skull. Time slowed as he fell to the ground, followed by an overwhelming sensation of drowning.

# TWENTY-FIVE
# AN INFESTATION OF WIGGLERS

Water rushed around David's body and his system instinctively gasped for air—but all it sucked in was two lungs full of water. He coughed, forcing the water out, but, now fully submerged, found no air to suck in. The restraints on his body broke loose, and he floated to the top of his sinking Aeropod. A small bubble of air remained trapped in the space between his body and the glass and he breathed in. The bubble was shrinking, and fast, but before it fully disappeared, David tried to calm himself with a few slow measured breaths. A muffled pop sounded as the locks released and he pulled in one final deep breath—moments before the pod lid released and his lifesaving pocket of air escaped upward toward the surface.

In the darkness, it was impossible to tell which way was up: the fading glow of the Aeropod sinking below him and the upward trajectory of the air bubble his only means of telling up from down. David gave a second for his body to right itself, then kicked furiously to the surface.

The farther he swam, the more his legs ached and the more his lungs burned. Whatever oxygen he managed to seize in that final gasp didn't last long and his kicks became less and less productive, until he gave up his struggle. His vision filled with stars as his view faded to nothing but twinkling specks of light against a wavering black backdrop. His chest spasmed, a final reflex to find oxygen before shutting down, and his lungs filled with crisp night air. Coughs racked his body, spitting up what seemed to be gallons of water.

After floating and treading water for what seemed like hours, but had actually been mere minutes, David kicked and paddled to the only bit of land visible in the faint starlight, snaking through inky water and slimy tentacles of seaweed, until his feet finally found the gravel lakebed. The rocky pebbles slid beneath his feet as he clambered out of the water onto shore, and he silently rejoiced as he collapsed and the sharp stones pierced the flesh of his cheeks.

He rested there, facedown for several minutes, coughing the remaining water from his lungs. Relieved to be alive, he rolled onto his back and stared up at blanket of stars blurred against the clear night sky. A smile crept across his face and he allowed his stinging eyes to close as he nearly drifted off to sleep. A soft kick in his ribs roused him.

"You alright, kid?" a gruff voice asked from above. David opened his eyes and could barely make out the vague outline of a man standing above him, silhouetted against the backdrop of stars.

David sat upright, wincing as an ache throbbed in his back. He opened his mouth to speak but starting coughing again until he turned to the side and vomited on the jagged stones of the shore. The man knelt behind him and patted his back to help knock out whatever liquid still rattled around inside David's chest. David coughed a few more times. The man stood and walked in front of him and reached out his hand. David grasped his dry, calloused skin and pulled himself to his feet.

"Thought you was dead. Ain't nothing come crawling out that water in quite some time."

David shook his head and spit onto the ground. "No, not dead, but I'm halfway there." He turned his eyes to the stranger but was unable to make out much in the dark night: about his height, scraggly hair down to his neck, stray strands floating weak and wispy in the starlight.

"Got a name?"

"David."

"Where's you from David? All I know is I was sleeping and alluva sudden there's this terrible screech from the sky. Then? Splash. Next thing something come crawling out the water. Like I said. Thought you was dead."

Unsure of what to say, or even if he should trust this stranger, David remained quiet and tried to think. He hoped by now his eyes would have adjusted to the little bit of light the stars and sliver of moon provided, but every time he tried to focus he found he couldn't. Balling his hands into loose fists, he rubbed his eyes to clear them and let out a sharp cry of pain.

"You alright boy?"

"My eyes. They're killing me." David said. "I must have gotten some sand in them or something."

"Shit," said the stranger. "Should of figured. Come on, let's go. We got to get you cleared out."

The stranger grabbed David's hand and led him across the shore to the forest's edge. As they entered the wood and the stars and moon were lost behind the canopy of leaves and branches, everything went black, leaving David no choice but to trust the man and let him drag him along to wherever their destination might be. They crunched their way through the darkness, twigs and leaf litter crackling beneath their feet.

David had no idea how far they had travelled. But eventually the gloom began to fade, replaced by a growing blur of orange and yellow that swelled with every step they took. A crackling sound and a whiff of smoke let David know they were nearing a campfire. Suddenly, the stranger's voice broke the silence between the two.

"Sit down here."

David's heart pounded, threatening to burst through his ribcage, straight into the flames. He couldn't see clearly—his vision still only a blur of light and dark. Occasionally he caught a streak in the foreground, like the floaters that sometime crept into his vision after staring at a computer screen for too long, but they were gone before he could focus on them.

You hear me boy? I said sit."

"I—I can't see …"

"Just drop yer ass right on down and you'll be alright."

Inch by inch, David squatted, waving his hands beneath him until he found the worn surface of a massive log beneath him. Although dry, he marvelled at how slick the wood felt beneath his fingers. Driftwood. He took a seat.

"Wait here. And for Christ sakes don't go around touching your eyes again. Pisses them off." The sound of footsteps on undergrowth faded as the man walked away.

Terrifying. That was the only word David could come up with to describe his newfound blindness. The mental struggle to suppress the instinct to rub his eyes consumed what mental faculties he had left. The fire crackled in front of him, flashing points of light as the heat of jumping flames licked his face.

A few minutes later the shuffling sound of feet on dry leaves signaled someone was approaching.

"That you?" David called out, hoping the response would match a voice he recognized.

"Yup. Me." the man grunted. "Lay down. On your back. Need a closer look at your eyes."

David swung a leg over, straddled the log and lay back, staring up into the distorted sky above. *Like camping*, he thought. But even that infinitesimal bit of light disappeared as the man sat on him and brought his face within inches of David's. Every time he exhaled, David caught a whiff of his breath: earthy, a little acidic. Kind of sweet, but with a hint of bitterness and decay lingering underneath. Through it all, he kept his eyes open, catching fleeting, blurred glimpses of the man's profile in the dancing light of the fire, his skin dark, leathery and aged.

Bringing himself even closer, the stranger pulled at the lids of David's right eye. As he leant in, his nose brushed against David's, and sweet, vinegary breath poured out. Another flicker of light caught in the man's own eye, revealing a vacant silvery-gray pupil set against a ball of veiny pinks. He let out an exasperated sigh and David swallowed the lump of bile rising in his throat.

"Didn't seem like you was in the water long," the man said. "Been breeding all this time and probably got nowhere else to go." The stranger sat up and thumped David's chest. "Yep. Got to do a flush and pick. Sorry, brother."

"What're you talking about?" David asked. The stranger hefted a canvas sack onto David's chest and bits of glass and metal clinked against each other as he rummaged through it.

"Here we are," the man muttered. In the firelight a spark of flame reflected off on the indecipherable metal instrument in the man's hands. David tried to squirm free, but even though it didn't feel like the man weighed much, he was held tight to his spot. The man leaned in closer.

"Don't go wiggling so much. All yer gonna do is hurt yourself more."

The unmistakable sensation of cold steel pushed against David's lower eyelid, stretching it open. "What the hell are you doing?" he screamed.

"Told you. Got to flush and pick. God damned invasion you've got there. Way too much for any prayer of symbiosis."

"Stop! Jesus, just stop!"

The metal lifted from his eyelid and David blinked violently as the man sat up again and rested his free hand on David's chest. "David, was it? I'm only trying to help. You got yourself a wriggler infestation in your eyes. That water out there, the water you come swimming out of be jus' swarming with 'em. I don' clear 'em, ain't no way you gonna see nothing no more. Nope. Not now, Not ever again."

"Wigglers? What do you mean, wigglers?"

"What I done said. Wigglers. Now sit yer ass down and let me flush ya. Ain't gonna hurt none's long as you stay still."

David closed his eyes and took a breath, reconsidering whether he should trust the man. A wet spasm below his left eye worked toward his nose. His eyes flew open, and the twitching worsened.

"There's one 'em now, scootin' his way out." The calloused tips of the stranger's fingers brushed against his eyelid as he reached in and pinched. In the blurred world in front of him, David could barely make out the man's hand pulling away, a long black string caught between his fingertips. He followed the string down with his eyes, crossing them until he couldn't follow any further. The man pulled back on the string with a slow but steady hand, and David sensed something sliding behind his eyeball, in the socket slipping past his sinuses. The man continued to pull, stretching the black thing millimeter by millimeter, until it slipped loose and what looked like a six-inch piece of wet black thread flailed wildly in the stranger's hand. The man grabbed the worm's body with his other hand, flung the monstrosity into the fire, and David fainted.

## TWENTY-SIX
# PINKEYE

"—stop giving him trouble. We understand you were upset, but his head isn't right," said a man in a blue t-shirt. David recognized him as one of the men who'd chased him through the basement.

The steak on his eye warmed thoroughly in his hands, dripping blood down his cheek. David lifted it from his face and tried to open his eye, but it remained swollen shut. He poked gingerly at the inflamed mass and winced.

"You're gonna want to keep that on a bit longer if you want the swelling to go down at all," the man added.

"That's just a myth. You know that, right? A steak on your eye isn't going to help anything," said the other man—the one who'd clobbered him with the pipe.

"It helps keep it cool. Like an ice pack," said the first.

"Look at it. Does it look cold to you? All that slab of meat is going to do is give him an eye infection. Why don't you just go get some ice?"

"Because we don't have any."

David pressed the steak back against his eye, careful to make sure he didn't open it and let in any bacteria. The beating was bad enough. The last thing he needed now was to throw a case of pinkeye into the mix.

"Guys, I appreciate the hospitality and all. But come on, what did you expect me to do? Ignore him?" David asked. "I mean, the guy broke into my truck. He stole my stuff. You can't just let someone like that wander around—"

## TWENTY-SEVEN
# TUG AND PULL

"—cooperate with me or this won't work. Sure, this'll keep your eyes open, but I need you to look where I says."

Instinct told David to blink, but instinct wasn't working. The man had attached some sort of metal spreading mechanism to each of David's eyelids, forcing them to stay open.

"Now, look as far to the left as you can. I'm gonna flush the right."

"What are you planning to do?"

"Just a saline flush. They get more mobile the more liquid that's around 'em. Kind of like going home. Honestly this'd work better out in the water, but there ain't no way you're gonna get me in there and there ain't a clean source nearby."

David's breath quickened, and he tried to pull his head back, away from the bottle the man started to tip toward his eye.

"You saw what I pulled out. And that's only one of 'em. Trust me, you want 'em all out."

With the memory of the wiggling thing still fresh in his mind, David conceded and shifted his vision to the left as the man commanded.

"What are those things?"

"Well, like I said before, I calls 'em wigglers, but I'm probably only one calls them that. You can't see it now, what with it being dark and all, but across the way there on the other side there's a big old building. Used to be a tracker farm."

"Trackers? You mean like field serpents?"

"Yeah. I suppose that's kind of what they are. Definitely SBS. They probably growed 'em there too—but these're different." The man poured the contents of his bottle into David's eye, and David cringed at the flurry of motion from the area behind his eyeball. "You really don't know trackers?" he asked.

"It's a long story, and I'd rather not go into it… but no, it seems there's a lot I don't know lately."

The man grunted in response and set the bottle down on the stump next to them. He pulled a small set of tweezers out of his bag, brought himself within inches of David's eye and started tugging at another black string.

"These guys here," he said, as he freed the end of another six-inch-long worm and held the squirming mass in front of David, "these guys are trackers. And that water you swum out of is infested with 'em. Government used to grow and raise 'em in that plant, before all hell broke loose. Guess when they abandoned the place, they just left 'em there." The stranger tossed the wiggler into the fire and set about pulling another from David's eye. "Way I figure, there musta been some kind of breach sometime along the way, and they got outta the isolation tanks into the water. Who knows how far they spread."

"What do they—" David grimaced at the sharp pain behind his eye, and the tail went taut.

"Jus' hold on. Gettin' shy. Need another splash." The man poured more of the saline solution into David's eye. The wormy-thing relaxed and began to slide free as the stranger coaxed it from its hideaway. "Tricks 'em."

"What do they do? I mean, what is their purpose?"

"Trackers. That's what they call 'em and what they do. All connected to the network, keep track of whatever their hosts see and sends it to whoever wants to do some watching. Trained to wiggle in and settle down. Most people have 'em never even know. Usually can't without a scan. 'Course most people only got one. Pretty sure you got at least a dozen."

He freed the end of the latest worm from David, tossed it into the fire and set back to work.

"Thinking we got em all from this … wait, one more back there. Deep. Dang she's a feisty one." David could feel the tweezers poking at his eye as the stranger tried to grab it. "Just about … oh no. Oh no oh no oh no."

"What? What's wrong?"

"She's gone and tried to hide."

"What do you mean, hide?" A strange congestion took over David's sinuses, and he suppressed an urge to sneeze. Tears welled from his eyes. The stranger pressed the palm of his hand down on David's forehead.

"Don't sneeze. Whatever you do, don't sneeze," the man whispered.

"Why? What happens if I sneeze?"

"Lotsa bad stuff. She's crawling through your ducts into your sinuses. You sneeze and you could tear 'er and trap 'er stuck, or even worse you could drive her even deeper and she'll burrow straight into your brain. Fight or flight reflex, programmed right in … shit, musta let it get too dry."

"That thing's going burrow into my brain?" David's resisted the urge to hyperventilate.

"Not if you stay still and don't scare it, it won't. Least I don't think it will. Now, breathe through your mouth, not your nose. I gotta pull this."

The stranger inserted a narrow set of tweezers in David's right nostril. The man's hands were steady and sure, never even touching the sides of David's nose, like an expert game of Operation.

"Hold still, I'm gonna feel around for her," the stranger said.

Not wanting to risk getting poked, David decided not to answer and remained motionless while the stranger did his work. Deep inside his nasal cavity, well beyond the area where he thought his nose ended, the gentle tapping of the tweezer's metal tips prodded his sinuses.

"Hold still. Don't breathe. Think I found her."

Closing his eyes and holding his breath, David focused on the crackling of the nearby fire. The man seemed to be in a state of controlled meditation, holding the tweezers still. After a moment, a small pinch of pressure convulsed in his head, then a sudden twitch erupted inside his sinus as the tweezers closed around the worm.

"Got her," the stranger said. "You go 'head an' breathe— but jus' through your mouth while I drag this little bastard out. You're turning blue an' I need you awake."

As the stranger continued to tug at the worm, David could feel it frantically searching for escape, its thin, sinewy body wiggling in desperation for any place it could hide, but the tweezer's grip held strong despite the struggle. First the tweezers came into view, still held firmly in the stranger's cracked fingers. Millimeter by millimeter, more of the tweezers pulled free, until their pinched tips came into focus holding the black hair-like thing. Keeping it as taut as a guitar string between the tweezers and David's nose, the stranger continued to pull. Two inches. Four. Six. Eight. David experienced a weird slipping sensation deep behind his left eye.

"Big bastard," said the stranger.

*Breathe in. Breathe out. Breathe in. Breathe out.*

Caught between the urge to shut his eyes and wish it all away, and the shock of the spectacle that was, literally, unraveling before him, David watched as eight inches became ten, then a foot, and it kept coming. As the tweezers continued to pull, the stranger brought the free end of the creature closer and closer until it was mere inches from his own face. The body slowly coiled upon itself, betraying the length of its reach, while the stranger kept pulling. Then, in less than a blink, it sprung, lunging toward the stranger's own eye. Just as quickly, the stranger lowered the tweezers, causing the worm to miss its target and strike between his cheek and eye.

"Cripes!" the stranger shouted. "Gotta twist her. Hold tight." Readjusting his grip, the stranger shifted the tweezers so they were perpendicular to the tightened string of the worm and started rolling them between his fingers, wrapping the glistening obsidian string like a piece of black spaghetti. Once the worm had been shortened enough and a safe distance established between its free end and the stranger, he started to pull again, and the sliding sensation returned to David's nose. After another inch or so, David felt its body squirm in the cavity above his nostril.

"Tickles, don't it?"

"Yeah," David breathed in reply.

"Means she's about out."

The tickling slowly faded while the man continued the slow turn of the tweezers. David held his breath.

"And here we go," the man shouted, giving a final yank on the tweezer, freeing the other end of the worm from inside David's sinuses. A few quick taps on the insides of his nostrils announced the last of the worm's body had been pulled free. The stranger thumped David's chest in triumph, hopped off David and took the worm to the fire.

Through his clear right eye David could make out the man's emaciated body hunched over the fire, and the wiry end of the worm that had just been pulled from his head flailing about, desperate to escape the flames into which the stranger tossed both the tweezers and the worm. The stranger took a seat on the ground, and the two of them listened to the pops as the worm crackled into dust.

The wind shifted and the smoke from the fire began to blow in David's direction, but before he could move, he pulled in a lungful and fell into coughing fit. The harder he coughed, the more aware he became of the liquid still in his lungs, and he rolled off the log onto the ground. His coughs turned to hacks, his eyes began to water, and David threw up. As he looked on at the splash of liquid and bile where he had been sitting, his nose twitched. Whether it was the wiggle of another worm or a stray bit of puke, David didn't know. Either way he started to sneeze violently, interspersed with fits of coughing and gagging. He pressed his eyes shut, hacking and spitting and sneezing while his body did its best to evacuate itself of every bit of foreign matter. As he continued to spew out wretchedness, the stranger placed a hand on his back, patting him lightly, encouraging a successful purge.

"Well, whattya know," said the stranger, the patting of his hand slowing as David's outburst arrived at its conclusion. "I guess maybe you can sneeze 'em out. Looks like you cleared out a few stragglers."

The man's hand reached in front of David's face from behind, pointing to the vile mess that poured out of David. There, wriggling in a wet mound of snot and vomit, were three more worms, freshly expelled from David's head. The dry grip of the man's hand clasped the back of his own and lifted it from the log. David tried to pull his hand free, but the man held tight.

"Not so fast, boy. Ya gotta kill 'em."

The wet, messy pile let out a horrible smack as David's hand, guided by the stranger, slammed onto it, crushing the remaining wrigglers into a paste of nastiness.

"Now, you can sleep if you want."

With nothing left to throw up, David dry heaved, laid his head and body down on the dusty ground between the log and fire and passed out.

## TWENTY-EIGHT
# A HINT OF POISON

"—dumped in my truck and stole my CDs. What would you suggest I do?"

David scooted closer to the two men seated on the shabby couch opposite him, dragging the feet of his wooden chair across the concrete in little scrapes and scratches. The TV behind him still buzzed with whatever video game he interrupted. With the icy way they both glowered at him, he didn't dare turn around to find out what game it might be.

"I get it. I'm only saying, he didn't mean any harm," the man on the right said. The couch creaked as he shifted his weight to lean in closer to David. "Like I said, he isn't right in the head," he whispered. David tasted beer on the man's breath.

Far across the room, over the man's shoulder, the crazy CD-stealing, truck-crapper trembled in a corner as he cautiously observed the three seated men. Catching David looking his way, his body quivered, and he shifted his gaze to the floor. He twisted the tip of his shoe back and forth on the cement, as if he expected to somehow burrow through it. David returned his focus to the other two men.

"Well, you didn't have to beat me with a pipe," David shifted the steak on his eye.

"You chased our friend through our house while you waved a hatchet."

David nodded. "So, what's wrong with him?" he asked.

"There's a lot wrong with him. At least there is today. Every day he's worse. A few years ago, he was like everybody else. Pretty sure he's got the poison."

The man on the left remained silent, looking David up and down. Occasionally, he opened his mouth, as if to speak, then thought better of it. Sweat dripped from David's brow, and mixed with the blood of the steak, causing a small stream of red to run down his cheek. He hoped they didn't notice.

The chill of the room hit David. The day outside, while not quite sweltering, had been hot enough to discourage anything more than shorts, sandals and a t-shirt (which, coincidentally was what David wore). But now a freezing bite stung his bare skin as he began to realize he was alone, in the basement of three strangers—two of whom just kicked the crap out of him. He took the steak from his swollen eye and let it flop onto the coffee table between himself and the men.

The two men seated at the other side of the table, however, seemed perfectly comfortable with the cold, barefoot in jeans and t-shirts. A blue shirt on the left, red on the right. David wiped the sweat from his forehead and the men waited patiently for him to respond.

"He was poisoned?" David asked. "Shouldn't he be at a hospital?"

"No man, it's a long-term thing," the guy in the red shirt replied. "No hospital's going to help Ben. It's all in his system now and they can't clean that kind of mess up—not once it's settled in like it has with him."

"You saying you don't know about the poison?" Now it was the other man's turn to speak. "Figures. News don't say nothin' about it. Sure, they talk about the protests and have special segments on how to grow your own organic garden, but nobody ever talks about what's actually happening." He slammed his fist down on the table onto the steak, sending a spray of cow's blood across David's shirt.

The man in the red shirt stood and rested his hand on his friend's shoulder. "Calm down, Chris. Breathe." Then, to David, "He gets pretty emotional. Guy's his brother after all. Can't blame him really." He turned back to face Chris. "You okay?"

Chris nodded, wiping his hand on his pants, smearing them with red to match his friend's shirt. The man in red sat back down on the couch.

"Chris, is it?" David asked the man in blue. He turned his eyes to the man in red. "And you? I didn't get your name."

With this olive branch of civil conversation, the tension apparent in the two men's shoulders relaxed, and the tightness in David's chest lessened.

"Paul," said the man. He reached a hand out to David, who took it and shook.

"Well, hi Chris and Paul. I'm David. David Sparks." He tipped his head to the back of the room and looked to Chris. "What's your brother's name?"

"Ben," replied Chris, looking to the floor, unable to meet David's eyes. "His name's Ben."

"Well, listen guys," said David. "Now that we know each other, I have to tell you I'm sorry for busting in to your ..." David looked around the room, taking in the walls of raw studs and cotton-candy insulation. The only light in the room came from a few bare bulbs screwed into simple porcelain fixtures mounted to blue junction boxes nailed to the bare ceiling joists. *Obviously a work-in-progress.* "... sorry for busting into your home."

Chris chuckled. "Nah man, home's upstairs. This is where we hang out to get away." He pointed to the TV behind David, game screen paused. "It's our makeshift man-cave."

"There's a fridge behind the couch," added Paul. "Got a few beers in it if you want one."

David shook his head no. "Thanks, but I'll pass this time."

As Chris stood, the couch creaked again, and Paul sank a little lower as it teeter-tottered on its uneven legs. "I'm gonna grab one, you sure?"

"Yeah, I'm sure."

"Come over here, Ben. It's safe. Sit down with our friend David here and have a beer. Let's educate him a bit—show him what's wrong with you. Only way he's gonna learn."

Ben stopped twisting his toe on the concrete and studied his brother.

"He's cool," Chris assured him. "Besides, we took his toy."

"And I've still got my pipe," added Paul, giving it a few knocks on the cement. David hadn't noticed he still had it by his side. Another wave of nausea hit, and he reflexively reached up to touch the tender flesh around his eye. It had swollen again, unaided by the soothing pressure of the hunk of beef now dripping a pool of blood onto the cold gray of the concrete.

## TWENTY-NINE
# SCRAMBLED, NOT FRIED

Long before the first beams of sunlight crossed the lake horizon, a cacophony of birdsong woke David from his night's slumber. The fire had long since burned out, and, not knowing where he was, David decided against sneaking away. Instead he lay still on the ground, listening to the birds call in the dark while the sky to the east slowly brightened. As the sun breached the horizon, he stood, stretched and walked back along the worn path toward the sound of crashing waves.

The rolling of the waves lulled him to meditation as little by little, the sun crept higher and higher. Cotton candy to salmon, salmon to sherbet orange, David breathed in time with the waves. As the sun crested the endless expanse of water before him, his breath stopped, overcome by the sheet beauty of the sunrise. A shuffle of feet, scraping unevenly across the sandy beach, broke the tranquil silence. Pat-scraatch, pat-scraatch, pat-scraatch, the footsteps grew ever louder as they approached. David didn't turn. He knew it was the stranger. The stranger who probably saved his life.

"Never get tired of it. 'Course I can't really see it no more, but I remember it all the same. The sound and the growing light alone enough to trigger the memories, that's how strong they are."

Side by side, the two of them stood in unison, beholding the rising sun. Once the full circle of light broke free of the water, David faced the stranger, finally getting his first good look at the man in full daylight. Although still a bit sore, David's vision returned to normal while he slept—the temporary loss of vision (clearly a side-effect of the infestation) gone now he'd been rid of the vermin.

Barefoot in the sand, the man wore simple, but ragged clothing. A tattered pair of khaki cargo shorts and a dirty white t-shirt made up the extent of his garments and his long gray hair was tied back in a ponytail with a loose piece of string. The stranger's face was heavily sun damaged. His dry, splintered skin mottled from the ravages of years of unprotected time spent in what David was learning was quite a dangerous place to be. The man looked, by David's estimation, to be a prime example of an aging, emaciated hippie. While not quite malnourished, the man exuded a sense of sickness, as if no matter how much he ate, it would never be enough—like an old man in the throes of cancer. Still, despite being a bit old, a bit crooked and a bit crunchy, David saw him as normal and, after last night, safe.

The only thing truly odd about the man's appearance were his eyes. Centered in the blue of his eye, where the pupils should be, sat two storm-cloud gray masses, like giant cataracts.

"Stopped working long ago," said the stranger. "For the most part, at least. I can still make some things out. Likes I can see you staring at 'em."

Embarrassed, David returned his sights to the water. The old man laughed.

"I don't mind none. Rather you see 'em then not, ta be honest. Good reminder of things, far as I'm concerned."

"What happened?"

"Same thing as happens ta any of us that stay in the world. Just gone and went bad. Probably could've traveled east and got 'em replaced. Heard the government was doing that for people—long as they registered and moved into a haven. Not me though. Definitely not me. As you can see, I'm happy right here where I am."

"Speaking of that, where are we? I was on my way to Chicago, when, whatever happened last night, happened," said David. "Pretty sure that wasn't the landing my pals had in mind."

"Well boy, that's a pretty simple question." The man slapped his hand on David's back and said "You're right where you need to be. Let's go back to my camp. Talk about it over breakfast."

---

"Ghost."

"What was that?" asked David, looking up from the fire.

"Get the feeling you're wondering my name, is all. Well I ain't gonna tell you that. Don't have a name no more now that I think of it. Not exactly part of society out here. Most just call me Ghost." The man poked at the eggs cooking in the pan over the campfire, with a broken branch, coaxing them to cook evenly. "That's what people think I am anyway—those who manage to catch sight of me at least. This ain't no metropolis, but still there's travelers from time-to-time. I just try ta stay outta the way."

"You didn't stay out of my way," said David.

"No." Ghost laughed a wet laugh and coughed. "No, I most certainly did not. I do like to keep to myself, but that don't mean I'm heartless. Any man needs my help, he's got it— and you, my friend from the sky, you sure as hell looked like you needed my help."

"That I did. That, my friend, I most certainly did," David mused, drifting off slightly before continuing. "Thank you, by the way. For everything. Last night, by the water, I might've drowned... and the stuff with the—" David opened his hand in front of his face, wiggling his fingers in front of his eyes. "Well, whatever that was, thanks."

"Sure 'nuff," said Ghost. "Sure you don't remember what those were? I tol' you 'bout 'em last night..."

"Oh I remember, alright. I'd just rather not think about it. I keep thinking I see things wiggling in my peripheral vision. Like we maybe missed one, but I'm pretty sure it's PTSD."

"Ha! Yah, we got 'em all. I double-checked while you were sleepin'. Yer clean."

"Well, thanks again. On a related subject, I was wondering—"

"Put out yer bowl boy."

Doing as he was told, David picked up the wooden bowl from the dust between his feet and held it in front of the old man. The man lifted the pan from the fire and tipped it toward the bowl, scooping half the eggs in.

"Seagulls," he said, pushing a handful of eggs into his own mouth. "Used ta have chickens, but well … you know—I ate 'em. Still pretty good though. Least they ain't filling their bellies with trash like in olden times, right?"

David took a pinch of eggs between his fingers, and, realizing too late that they were still extremely hot, dropped them back into his bowl. He blew across the steaming meal, enjoying the silence. Gingerly, he touched at the eggs again and found them cool enough to handle. With his fingers, he scooped a small handful and shoved them in his mouth, letting out a pleasurable moan as they spread across his tongue and slithered down his throat into his waiting belly.

"Anyway, I was wondering," David continued, through a mouthful of eggs. "Your eyes, what happened to them? Cataracts?"

"Nah, not cataracts. Like I said before, same thing as happens to most of us who decide to stay out here. The poison done it. Does it to all of us I suppose. Well, except them who stay bottled up in them fishbowls they call society. I've been out here all my life. Was born out here, an' I'm staying out here. Spent some time in the settlements but wasn't happy. Needed the open air—even though I was probably dying a little more every breath I took. No, my eyes went to the poison, same as everyone else fool enough to live a natural life. Body's going too, I can feel it. Skin's getting itchy, muscles ache. Can't even stand up straight no more. But I guess this is what forty years in the wild will do ya."

"It's been forty years since you left the settlements?"

"No," the old man huffed. "Forty years since I was born. Give or take a year."

"But you look so—"

"—so old? Guess I do. Can't see myself clearly no more— not that I even would want to if I could. I can feel it, sure enough."

"Jesus," said David, spitting a piece of shell on the ground. "You're not much older than I am."

"City boy, huh?"

"Yes. No. Maybe. I don't know. Don't know much about myself, or have any idea what the hell's going on. One day I woke up in a field and a crazy bastard with a chainsaw saved me from a snake. Ever since, I've been kind of coasting along, going with the flow of things—along for the ride— while my memories seem to be coming back." David tapped his right index finger on his temple. "It's a mess in here. But supposedly the people in that fishbowl city you mentioned are working on fixing things for me. I'm hoping when I finish whatever the hell I'm out here for and can finally go back, they'll have some answers for me. In the meantime…" David held up his hands and shrugged.

"Pretty laissez-faire way of looking at things."

"Pragmatic."

The old man nodded. "Where again did you say you was going when you went down?"

"Chicago. At least that's what they told me. Said we were going home. About all I could get out of them."

The man took another bite of eggs and through his full mouth asked, "Who's this them you keep talking about."

David hesitated. "Not sure if I should tell you."

"Boy, we're out in the middle of nowhere. Don't you think if I was gonna do something nefarious I'd-a done it by now?"

"Well, probably… but you also don't know anything about me. I could be evil."

"Ain't no way you're evil. Ain't no evil man ever come out this far west by himself. No, not without a whole company of fellas and not without better supplies and …" he paused, "… travel arrangements. Way I figure, if you were on your way to Chicago, you were on your way to the settlement at Garfield. Probably the only place anybody'd ever want to go in Chicago."

David grabbed a final handful of eggs, stuffed them into his mouth, put his bowl back on the ground and washed the bite down with a drink of water. "You know anyone by the name of Calvin? Or Bethany?"

At the mention of the names, the man jumped from his seat. "Calvin, you mean Calvin Simon? And Bethany Trask? Well I'll be goddammed! You **are** on your way to Garfield!"

"I take it you know them?"

"Hell, everybody out these parts knows them. Least, anybody who cares a good god damn about anything," said Ghost. "Well, well. A man of The Cause. You *are* lucky I found you—both lucky I found you to help, but also lucky I wasn't some man of evil myself. You go saying those names so nonchalant in front of a Progressive and you'd find yourself right back in that city of yours. Right back in there locked in a little glass bowl all your own!"

David stood and faced the path toward the lake where they watched the sun rise. He scratched absently under his hair at the port in the back of his head, pausing when his fingers touched the spot where the cold metal met his scalp. He fingered the port gently, probing to discover what might still lie inside, waiting to be uncovered.

"They're not gonna be so welcoming of that," said Ghost.

His right index finger still prodding the hollow of the empty port, David turned his head to Ghost. The man had turned around on the log and was poking at the remaining coals of the fire, separating the logs from one another and smothering the last licks of flame so the wood could be used again—not wasted on a fire that served no purpose.

"Felt it last night when I was checking if you was still alive." Ghost scraped the red coals from what remained of a piece of firewood, separating them from the wood so they could burn out on their own without further consuming their host. "Don't worry—everything's clear in there. Ain't no way for a worm get in—those ports seal up full tight—only open when they sense an incoming input with matching decryption keys. No—nothing in or out you can be sure of that."

"It's not what it looks like, Ghost," said David.

"Don't look like nothing but a hole in yer head, far as I'm concerned. 'Course, given where you says you're going to, I ain't the one whose concern you need be worried 'bout."

David took a seat next to Ghost. The old man smelled of dust, smoke and fish—but underneath David found a sweetness that reminded him of dinners in Little Italy. Rosemary. Oregano. Thyme. Something natural—something good.

"Where am I going then? What's this Garfield and why do you think I was headed there?"

Another wet cough shuddered through Ghost's chest and he spat a wad of something green into the smoky ash. After several more coughs, he lifted his arm to his mouth and wiped a string of spittle onto his sleeve. "I could shut up 'bout it right here and now. I don't know you and I got no reason to trust you, other than that anyone with that amount of stupid about what's going on probably can't mean no harm. Can't rightly mean no good, far as I can tell, neither, but if you says you was with Calvin and Bethany I got no reason to doubt ya. Don't right care much one way or the other, to tell the truth. I'm what you might call a conscious bystander."

"You can trust me," David whispered. "I need you to trust me."

"Bah," Ghost harrumphed. "Like I said, got no reason to—but also don't got no reason not to—so I'm-a help ya get sorted," he continued. "If you was on your way to Chicago, an' if you was traveling by Aeropod, which from the sound I heard before you came crashing down, sure sounded like to me, then the only place you was gonna land was the old

Chicago Stock Exchange downtown. One Financial Place. And if you was coming on account of old Calvin or that pretty thing, Bethany, then your next stop was gonna be the settlement at Garfield. Only about five miles from one place to the other and given your company then that sure as hell be where I'd bet you was going."

"What's Garfield?" asked David.

"Garfield? Garfield's one of the few settlements 'round here. This deep in The Green Zones ain't hardly nobody living—well, hardly nobody but damn fools like me. Organics took the place and made it into a self-sustaining sanctuary, safe from what's left out here of the chemicals still killing knuckleheads like yours truly. Been living there for as long as anyone can remember. Few years back though, The Cause got wind of the place, set up camp there and converted a few to their philosophy along the way. People living there didn't care none, seeing how they pretty much want the same thing. 'Course Organics been fine living on their own, minding themselves and staying out of everyone's way. Safe out here in The Green Zones they don't got much ta worry 'bout. No doubt some 'em ain't too happy about housing a revolution though—don't want a bunch a terrorists bringing unwanted attention, but they keep their mouths shut all the same."

"So, where does that put me?" David asked.

"Right about where you want to be, more or less. Off coast of Chicago. This place used to be called Northerly Island. Not sure what they call it now. I just call it home."

"I'm in Chicago? That building I saw to the north, was that … was that the Planetarium?"

"Sure is," Ghost continued. "To the south, way across that water where you saw the blinking lights of the wiggler plant? Used to be part of Indiana. Still is I guess, 'course there ain't no state governments taking mind of old borders. Place you was going is only a mile or two from here. Where we are right now all the trees grown up on this island are blocking yer view, but you walk yourself west a bit and you'll see the skyscrapers of Chicago rising up in front of you soon as you break that tree wall. Garfield's just a ways further west from here. Get off the island and you'll be there in a few hours."

"Let's say I go there. What am I walking in to? Are these Organics safe?"

Ghost laughed. "Are they safe? They about as safe as anybody you'd ever come across. All they want is to be left alone and to let the land come back. Sure they're holed up in their glass houses, but they all want same thing as me. Only difference is they got patience." Ghost paused, then added, "Speaking of, sun's getting' high—means you don't have more than a few hours before it starts getting dark again. Building shadows make downtown darker sooner than you'd expect. You best be going."

Ghost picked up his worn canvas bag, knocked the dust from it with his free hand, and handed it to David. "Take this. It's dangerous to go alone," he said.

Inside the bag, David found a few glass bottles, corked and filled with water, a small black handgun and a box of bullets.

"Thanks Ghost," David said, "but I don't even know how to use a gun."

"Neither do I. But you come across anybody you don't think is safe, you're better off having it than not. Just waving the damn thing around saved my neck more than a few times."

Weighing the gun in his hand, David was surprised at the weight of the thing and how cold the metal felt against his fingers. He returned the gun to the sack and offered the bag back to Ghost.

"I can't take this," he said. "I appreciate the gesture, but I can't."

"Go ahead and take it," said Ghost. "I ain't never gonna use the damn thing—and I ain't come across no one out here on the island. In the city's where you got be careful. And I ain't never goin' back to the city."

David took the bag and slung it over his shoulder, the glass bottles clinking loudly against the gun and each other. "So, where am I going?"

"Back to the beach. Then head north up to end of the island, by the old planetarium. From there go west and you'll find a road off the island. Should see some signs up there marking it as Solidarity Drive. Once you reach the end you'll see an old aquarium and a big building. Used to be a museum. Cut between those two and you'll see a big old road running north-south. That's Lakeshore. Running th'other way between that aquarium on the other side of Lakeshore you'll see another big road—not as big as Lakeshore, but still big. Roosevelt. Keep walking down Roosevelt a few miles.

Gonna take a while, so don't worry if you think you missed it. You'll go deep downtown, and the old medical district. Eventually you'll see a big park off left. Don't go there— overrun bad. Not safe. Up ahead a bit more you'll find Central Park Avenue. Take a right and follow north, past another park, between two little lakes. That's where you'll find Garfield. Big place—all glass. You'll know it when ya see it."

David focused as Ghost gave directions, making mental notes of the turns and landmarks along the way. It sounded easy enough, but he didn't look forward to making the trip on his own or the prospect of being alone in the abandoned remains of Chicago in the middle of the night. He reached out his hand to Ghost's and shook it.

"Thanks Ghost," he said. "I appreciate everything you've done." He held the bag and gave it another light shake, the bottles clinking again. "I do wonder though, why do you stay out here? It looks like it's killing you. You could join me."

"No, no I've been there before," he said, nodding west. "Not a place for me. I'm happier out here. It's alive and it's real and it's beautiful—and if this beauty's going to kill me, I can't think of a better way to go than out here in God's great green world."

## THIRTY
# FOLLOW THE OLD BLACKTOP ROAD

*Go East at the road,* Ghost's directions echoed in David's head.

*Where the hell is this road?* Traveling north for what must have been an hour, David pushed on through the thick growth on the island. How far he'd covered was anyone's guess, though at the rate he'd been moving it would have surprised him if he'd traveled a quarter mile.

*Stay away from shore—you can't be visible.*

Well, at least on the shore he would have made some progress. One thing was clear though: no one had recently traveled through the thicket enveloping the island. If Ghost took any trips north, he must have ignored his own warnings and followed the shore.

*What good is a gun in this jungle? Be better off with a machete.* He imagined himself a young John Speke, fighting his way through the wilds of Africa, in search of the fabled source of the Nile. Instead of Lake Victoria, however, David's goal lay in a place much more traveled—though possibly just as wild—the heart of The Windy City.

Through the brush, he pushed on. The occasional scrape of a branch adding to the cluster of cuts marring his bare arms. Occasionally he'd stop to pull a lump of burdock seed from his clothing or flick a wood tick off his skin. Drawn to the blood, mosquitoes buzzed incessantly around him, like a murmuration of starlings, leaving tiny mountain ranges as they bit and slurped happily along his arms and neck.

*Don't go out at night. Don't trust anyone who looks like me. Not until Garfield ... as if anything larger than a squirrel, let alone another person, lives in this dense forest.*

A few miles... it sounded like a simple trip when Ghost described it. It certainly couldn't all be like this, could it?

Exhaustion threatened to settle in, so David rested and drank from one of the bottles Ghost had given him. He swallowed it down quickly and poured the remaining inch onto his head. The water soaked through his thick hair, and dribbled down the back of his neck, cooling the collar of his shirt as the fresh moisture replaced his sweat. Now empty, he threw the bottle off to his left, into the darkness of the pervasive wood.

David pictured Ghost, content in his encampment here on the island, and sighed at his thoughtlessness. While it was unlikely he'd come across a trash can, let alone a recycling bin, any time soon, he couldn't leave it here. He hadn't noticed earlier, but this place bore no suggestion of man. Unlike the nature hikes of his dreams, no trash tainted the environment—not even a cigarette lurking amongst the leaves of the forest floor. Whatever had cleaned this place, be it time, Ghost, or Mother Nature herself, David couldn't allow himself to become its vandal.

After about twenty steps and five minutes of additional cuts and scrapes, David found the bottle, isolated in a small clearing. A sugar maple lay broken to the side—the likely victim of a recent bolt of lightning. Baby plants already filled the space where its canopy previously blocked the sun, but the growth was in its infancy, happily filling the void, each youthful shoot unaware that soon it would be fighting a battle of life or death against the others, in a struggle for the limited sunlight filtering through the opening above.

Stepping into the clearing, David recoiled as his footsteps crushed the young vegetation beneath him. Until now he cursed the foliage as an impediment, a stubborn mass of thorny brown and green that did nothing but block him from reaching sanctuary. But here, seeing how each of these individual shoots strained for life, aching to have the chance to simply live, a wave of regret swept over him with every footstep. *They'll grow back. Something always grows back,* he thought. As he reached down to pick up the bottle, David's eyes surveyed the length of the fallen maple. Its leaves, though brown, had not all dropped from the tree. It had fallen recently—this season at least.

He took a deep breath, swallowed the fresh oxygen of his environment and tasted the earth and rot and damp of life all around him. Climbing onto the trunk of the downed tree, he followed it north into an opening of prairie the tree's crown had fallen into.

Oddly-shaped triangular hills peeked out from the tall grass to the north, bordering the prairie to the east and west. Beyond them, as the prairie sloped down to the north, stood the remains of raised platform surrounded by a crisscrossed skeleton of metal beams and the tattered remains of what must have at one time been some kind of roof.

Now free of the restraining tangle of forest, David's progress improved. Although tall, the grass was markedly easier to travel through, and David smiled at the gentle swish-swish of their stalks as they swept over his jeans with each step. As he gained ground, the odd triangle mountains took a clearer shape, until David saw them for what they were— overgrown remains of bleachers. David was hiking through what must have been an amphitheater at some point long ago. The platform ahead, an old stage.

As he marched onward between the sets of ancient bleachers, the field opened to the northeast, bringing into view the large dome of the old planetarium. The road to Garfield must be close. He broke into a run, past the sagging remains of the stage, barely noticing the extent to which vines took over the structure after decades of disuse.

As he cleared the amphitheater, a wide expanse of gray, broken intermittently with patches of green and brown, opened ahead of him. Trees sprouted up sporadically throughout the old parking lot, finding their way through the cracks of weather and time. A few shells of abandoned cars remained, burnt out long ago, now victim to rust and the ever-encroaching march of nature. A wall of old-growth trees closed in around all sides of the broken expanse of asphalt. Putting his hand to his forehead to block out the sun's glare, he searched for the road Ghost mentioned. To his left the tree line opened, revealing what looked like a road hidden behind it.

Bordered by more thick woods to the west, and the overgrown parking lot to the east, the road gave him a clear view to the north. There, where the road ended, was what looked like the remnants of an intersection. David sprinted north along the road, leaping across the cracks where growth had pushed through, careful not to catch his foot and trip. There it was. A double road, running east to the planetarium and west into the towering expanse of a shattered city. East Solidarity Drive.

David turned left, faced the sun, and continued onward into the jungle ruins of old Chicago.

## THIRTY-ONE
# DINOS AND DARKNESS AND CORN, OH MY

Traveling down Solidarity, past the burnt-out remains of the building that had once been the Shedd Aquarium, David pressed on through the scrub that grew through the sunbaked cracks of the pavement. Ahead, in the distance, a vista of Chicago's skyscrapers loomed, dead and empty, their spires long ago abandoned to the ravages of weather and time. But closer ahead, where Solidarity took a turn, a large, stately structure spread out, bursting through the surrounding forest.

As he reached the turn in the street, David met another overgrown parking lot—an easy shortcut to save a few minutes. It wasn't exactly the path Ghost told him to take, but David's memories of Chicago remained strong enough he knew as long as he continued west, sooner or later he'd hit Lakeshore. And with sky darkening to the west, past the city but close enough to raise concern, he welcomed any opportunity to shorten his journey.

Concrete columns, now covered in vines, lined the front of the imposing building. An expanse of cement steps followed, leading to a grand entrance of four even larger columns framing what appeared to be the main entrance. In front of the doors, David saw what looked to be a yellowish boulder engulfed in greenery. Curious, David climbed up the concrete stairs to investigate. Off to his right, attached to the wall lining the steps, a flash of gold caught David's eye. He walked over to it and, pushing away the brush that covered it, revealed a plaque with the words 'The Field Museum' upon it.

Returning to his trip up the stairs, David's squinted at the yellowed stone blocking the museum's front entrance. As he continued nearer, what he had first taken to be a boulder took a firmer shape, until he recognized it as the upper half of the skull of a tyrannosaurus rex. Grass pushed up around the teeth, softening them against the cement and a few lay cracked and shattered on the ground. A small tree grew through the cavity where the creature's left eye would have been. On the nose, someone had scrawled a message in what looked like black paint, or charcoal.

STAY OUT

David looked past the skull into the darkness of the museum momentarily, then turned around and retreated down the stairs. The sun to the west, now behind the oncoming clouds, cast the afternoon in a golden gloom. Deciding it best to keep on his way, he continued onward, past the museum, and to Lakeshore Drive.

At his first fully-realized view of the city, a wave of shock pulsed through David's body and dropped him to his knees. The city, as it lay out before him, barely resembled the Chicago that populated his cloudy memories. While the buildings remained, they had transformed from a man-made colossus of concrete and stone, shelter to both people and commerce, to nothing more than the skeletal frame on which a new jungle found its footing. Painted green with moss and wrapped in emerald vines, the grey of the city had long since lost out to nature. Like mountains, the growth thinned the higher up the buildings went, but the tremendous metamorphosis established so far already reached upwards of ten stories.

David followed Ghost's instructions and headed north until he reached Roosevelt and crossed the river into the city. To his right stood the old Roosevelt CTA transit station, and it too was overcome by foliage. The tracks of the El had long ago given up their lives as clean travel routes of steel lines and now fulfilled a new purpose: a trellis for the vines that crept up to them and snaked their way through the city on the elevated network of rails.

Continuing onward, David kept to the middle of the street and followed what looked like a recently-traveled path through the heart of the city. To his left and right, the skeletal skyscrapers towered above him, their windows cracked and broken. Here, closer to them, the trees actually took root on some of the lower levels of the buildings, reaching out and up through the empty spaces where windows once separated the inside world from nature. Roots dangled below, having worked their way through the floor, running the expanse from floor to ceiling, taking hold in the levels even further below.

The buildings rocked in the wind, sending creaks and cracks as they continued to succumb to the consequence of time. Occasionally, other sounds joined in the song: nesting birds, an agitated burrow of squirrels … and sometimes what sounded like human whispers. In the darkness of the buildings' interiors, nothing much could be seen. Still, David sensed he was being watched as he made his way through downtown, past the river, past Michigan Avenue.

*Keep to the streets and you'll be fine. Stay in the light. Don't stop moving.*

Through the greenery, David caught glimpses of history— a Target store at the corner of Clark. The twisted remains of abandoned bus stops. A bike rental kiosk, still filled with rusted bikes, forever locked in place once the power for their rental systems went out—their tires long ago eaten away. Seagulls soared overhead, following him as he progressed and squawked anxiously as they hunted for any morsel of food he might leave behind. The only building that hadn't surrendered to nature was an ancient church across from the old ball field.

More skyscrapers spread across the skyline to the north, now visible as he crossed a bridge spanning the old Interstate. To the west, where he was headed, his path gave way to smaller buildings, each growing more dilapidated the further he traveled. Amongst the crumbling brick, peppered in color from ancient graffiti, previously vacant lots—themselves now overgrown, pressed into the disintegrating buildings, breaking them down through the pressure of growth. David marched on, watching for any sign marking Central Park Avenue. The Medical District lay well behind him and he expected to see his turn soon.

A half mile later, he hit a roadblock. A wreck of burned-out cars, long overgrown, spanned the width of the street. Seeing no way around, David grabbed a car's roof and pulled himself up, kicked off from the window opening above the driver's door, and hurtled himself onto its surface. One foot went down on the leaf-covered top, but the other fumbled to find its place as it caught on a lump in the slick vegetation. David regained his balance and knelt, peeling away the leaves where his foot landed. There, buried under the growth he found the remains of a metal box attached to the car's roof—old police lights. Scanning the other cars, similar bumps showed on their roofs. A barricade like this was usually only used temporarily—when more permanent means couldn't be procured. David wondered why, even at the end of it, these cars had remained. Were they burnt out during whatever event led to the extinction of the city? Were they blocking the way to downtown? Or were they blocking the way out?

A sudden rustling focused David's attention to the left of the street, past the sidewalks and into a great, undeveloped area. Green stalks stood before him, rustling lightly as wind sent ripples across their expanse. Like a lawn of high grass, the green spread as far back as David could see, before stopping at another edge of the city street. Deteriorating city buildings encircled it. What once had been a park in the rough side of Chicago was now an enormous corn field.

Again, the rustling. At the edge of the field, about 50 feet in front of him. David squinted and made out a black shape pushing the corn from side to side. Another step forward, and the roof, unable to bear the weight, gave out a dry creak and buckled down, the rusted metal cracking more than bending. The black spot in the corn paused, then exploded into a flurry of feathers and caws. A murder of crows rose up to the sky, cawing and flapping as they flew off to the south.

From his vantage point atop the gutted car, David watched as the agitated corn undulated in the escaping crows' wake. The stalks stilled, but deep back, past where the crows had been, they trembled again. This movement differed from the disturbance from the crows. No, this came from lower, below the visible top leaves. David watched as it moved, onward in a straight narrow line headed south, across the field, to another part of the city.

David trudged on, looking over his shoulder every now and then back toward the corn field. No one followed. The dark clouds in the distance moved in much sooner than he expected and by the time he reached Central Park Avenue, he had a hard time seeing more than ten feet in front of him. He quickened his pace and shifted his journey to the north.

In the distance, even in the afternoon darkness brought on by the clouds, he made out a brass dome, like an ancient government capital. When he finally reached the domed structure, what he saw reminded him of an old college building—almost a castle. The shimmering surface of a pond or small lake peeked through a wall of trees to his right. The air here, heavy with the dampness of the imminent storm, echoed with the whirring chirps of frogs, eagerly awaiting a good soaking.

Ahead, another elevated train station spread across the road. The train tracks that long ago shuttled people throughout the city had once marked this location a stopping point. Steps on the left side of the street ran up to the suspended station, and a wall of busted glass windows hovering above the old street made it look like one of those old wayside diners. Below, through the darkness of the underpass, his eyes landed on what he knew must be his destination.

----

A long glass building spread out in front of him, the surrounding landscape unlike anything David had seen. Here, like elsewhere on his journey, any space that wasn't a crumbling building had transformed into a sea of green. The difference was, here the green had clear pattern and purpose.

A freshly mowed lawn surrounded the building, breaking only at the concrete steps that led to the front doors. Like a cement pier leading to a great glass ark, the concrete here looked as good as the day it was poured—weedless, crack-free and devoid of any debris.

A flash of lightning brought his world into full view, and the accompanying shudder of thunder caused the glass of the structure to rattle dangerously. But it wasn't until the lightning faded and the world returned to its threatening gloom that David realized it.

There ahead, past the glass doors under the sign that read Garfield Park Conservatory, the lights inside were on.

## THIRTY-TWO
# THROW NO STONES

Locked. Of course, it would be locked. David pounded on the door, his palms threatening to break the glass with every blow—but the glass remained resilient. He cupped his hands around his eyes and pressed up against the entrance, struggling to make out any shape or sign of life inside. The foyer beyond the locked doors showed the same level of care, cleanliness and order as the surrounding landscape. In stark contrast to the disarray nature left in its wake everywhere else in the city, this place, if not currently occupied, had been lived in. Lived in recently.

Another set of whacks at the glass, and David's palms began to ache as they bruised under the violence. He took a step back, looked to his right, then his left, and almost started to shout for someone to let him in. The reminder of the ruffling in the corn and the omnipresent suspicion that he wasn't alone stopped him.

The world flashed in another explosion of light and the thunder rattled David's bones. The glass panels of the conservatory quivered dangerously in their frames. The sky opened, and the downpour began. There, in front of the conservatory, David found little respite from the storm and his clothes immediately soaked through. He searched across the street, to the vacant remains of old buildings, craving an escape from the stinging drops. He readied his body to run, then reconsidered and began to make his way around the perimeter of the glass house in search of another entrance.

"Stop there!" a female voice commanded.

David froze, the rain running down his face.

"Hands in the air. Where I can see them. Good. Now turn around slow."

There, only a few feet behind him, stood a camouflaged figure, soaking wet, aiming an assault rifle directly at David. She took a few steps closer, keeping the gun trained on him as he stood there, stock-still, in the rain, his hands above his head and vision blurred from the water streaming through his eyes.

"You're wearing society clothes," she said, prodding his shoulder with the tip of her rifle. "Who are you and how did you get here?"

"I—my name's David. I walked."

"You're lying. How did you get here?"

"I told you, I walked. Ghost gave me directions."

She took a step closer, pressing the rifle into the center of his chest and leaned in to David's face. Squinting, she examined his face, searched his eyes.

"Ghost, huh? Why the hell would Ghost send you here? I still say you're a liar."

"No lie. Please, can we maybe go in, out of the rain, and we can talk?"

"Not a chance of that happening, mister. Now tell me for real this time. Who the hell are you and why are you here?"

"I told you, my name is David," he said, lowering his hands.

"Put your goddamn hands back in the air!" Her breath burned hot on David's face against the chill of the rain. She pulled back on the gun and threatened to smash him with the stock. David's arms shot back into the air.

"My name is David. David Sparks. I was on my way here with Bethany and Calvin, but something happened, and I ended up just offshore. Ghost saved me, and he sent me here."

"Oh, hell," she whispered, lowering her gun. "Let's get you inside. You gotta talk to Rosa."

---

Inside, the air still hung heavy with humidity, but at least he escaped the downpour. The woman led David across the front entryway, through another set of clear doors past a vacant reception desk, and into a cavernous glass room. A jungle spread out before him here, but unlike the growth running rampant in the city, the jungle here consisted of palm trees and other large-leafed tropical plants. Concrete paths edged with stone curbs ran between the greenery, putting everything that was growing here into slightly raised, carefully planned beds. Men, women and children scattered about the space, some tending to plants, others engrossed in conversation—but they all halted to hushed tones as David and his chaperone snaked through the gardens.

Following the curve that marked the outer perimeter of the greenhouse, David stopped in front of a large palm tree. Much bigger than the rest, it stood majestically, its crown nearly brushing the glass ceiling above.

"Come on," she urged. "She's in the fern room."

Leaving the ancient palm behind, David followed as commanded. Above him, in rows throughout the room, bright lights mounted in neat rows pointed down, casting the room in an artificial daylight. Past the lamps, behind the glass roof, the sky looked like ink, the illusion of night breaking only with the intermittent flash of lightning. The room roared around him as the pounding drops echoed against the enclosed habitat.

A pair of marble statues marked the transition from one room to the next: one a woman and man kneeling in embrace, the other a man, bent down, resting his chest on the knee of a woman, while she washed his hair and a pair of rabbits frolicked on the ground beneath.

An expanse of stone steps led down into a new sunken room connected to the palm room. Again, like outside, almost every square inch of his view screamed in shades of green, broken only by a large indoor pond in the center of the room, and red brick paths meandering between the gardens. Here though, instead of palms, ferns grew. Ferns of every size, some huddled low to the ground, others reaching tall and wide, dwarfing any man. Bunches of light green moss hung from the rafters above, wrapping the room in a cocoon of nature. At the far end, standing at the edge of the pool, a woman crouched, her hands on her knees, the hem of her tan dress flowing over the edge of the pool and floating gently on the surface of the water.

"Rosa!" his escort shouted. The woman snapped her head up, noticing the two of them for the first time. "Guy says he knows Bethany," she yelled across the room. "Says his name is David. David Sparks."

Rosa stood upright and beckoned them toward her. "Thank you, Parm. Send him over here. You go dry off and change."

Parm gave a quick nod and left. Rosa, still standing at the other side of the pond, waited for David with her hands on her hips. He followed the brick path circling the left side of the pond, the thicket brushing softly against his skin as he passed. A sound of running water, separate from the rain above, reached his ears as he neared the rear of the room. The brick path ended and gave way to a jigsaw puzzle of flat flagstones. Water flowed between the stones, pouring from an artificial waterfall set into a rock structure on the back wall. It ran freely, between the rocks and beneath David's feet, until it spilled into the pond. There, on a landing where the stream joined the pool, stood Rosa, her back to David as she gazed into the water.

"They don't serve a purpose, but still we keep feeding them," she said, waving her hand lightly toward the water where a school of goldfish hovered. "I suppose we could eat them, if we had to … but we never have." She turned and sat on a nearby bench, patting the space next to her, inviting David to join. As he sat, she continued, "Aesthetics maybe?

Or therapy? A reminder we're all alive and that no matter what, the world will continue to march on."

The fish flitted here and there in search of whatever bits of food they could find.

"So, you're David Sparks," she said, finally turning to face him. "Please, let's sit."

For the first time since waking in the field those few weeks ago, time stopped, and David was reminded of his existence. The face of this woman before him revealed an aura of honesty and peacefulness. His eyes got lost in the wet, gray depths of hers and the air between them crackled with intensity. While not necessarily beautiful by magazine standards (her left cheek bore a scar, running from the edge of her mouth up to her ear, like half an extended smile), simply looking at her brought forth a presence of mind and serenity long forgotten amidst the nonstop rollercoaster of events making up David's recent life memory.

"I'm Rosa," she said, a warm smile cracking through her lips. She placed her hand on David's lap, sending a warmth into his leg that spread through his body. "Where are Calvin and Bethany?" she asked.

"They—" David coughed lightly, clearing his throat. "They're not here?"

Rosa lowered her head, her auburn hair spilling across her face, falling in waves against her light brown skin. A perceptible sigh heaved through her shoulders. "No, no they're not," she whispered. "You all were due here yesterday."

"The last I saw them, I was climbing into one of those Aeropod things," David took her hand out of his lap and into his own. "Something must have happened. I came down in the water. Crashed."

Rosa stood, pulled her hand back from David and walked to the shore of the pond. "Yes, something happened," she muttered, rubbing her forehead. Standing there, silhouetted against the water, David couldn't help but appreciate her figure. Shapely, athletic. The body of a survivor.

"Come with me, David. We have a lot to talk about."

## THIRTY-THREE
# THE BEST PART OF WAKING UP

"A meltdown. That's how they described it in their last communication." Rosa led David back through the Fern Room, into the larger glass area housing the ancient palm. "I didn't understand it. We didn't understand it. The message was short. Cryptic. Just that there was a meltdown." They passed a set of blue rain barrels connected to the roof via a series of copper pipes and through a pair of doors into another room.

In here, the atmosphere immediately felt heavier—hotter for sure, but also thick with moisture. The rich air hung in his nose, earthy and full of life. Hanging vines formed a natural ceiling of leaves, blocking most of the glass roof above. Tendrils dangled like beaded curtains, separating this room from the last. They pushed through, Rosa's bare feet making a soft slapping sound as she passed through a puddle of water accumulated on the pathway. Another, smaller pond lay to the right. Mangroves sprouted from its waters and goldfish again swam about, wandering lazily through the trees' woody roots.

Ahead on the path an oval shape was carved into the cement floor. Letters, worn through the passage of time and countless footsteps, spelled out a series of words:

*Leaves use sunlight to split water into its basic elements*

"They used to call this room "Sugar from the Sun."" We call it "The Growing Room" now."

"Seems fitting," David said. "Though from what I've seen in here so far, it seems every room here is a growing room. Is there a Death Room I should be worried about?"

Rosa stopped and waited for David to catch up. A smile spread across her face—not a grin, but still her lips curled enough David could see even his little joke, as silly as it was, at least temporarily pulled her from whatever worries battled inside her head.

"We try to take advantage of the space we have," she said. "It's not a lot, but it's enough to provide our small community here with food and shelter. We pretty much live on what we can grow, and to keep the food as safe as possible we try to grow most of it here, inside where the air and water's scrubbed. This room," she waved her hand across the garden before them, "is where we grow the largest variety—including most of our treats. Cinnamon, sugar cane, kumquats, bananas, guava, papaya, pineapple ... even allspice, vanilla and coffee. It all grows in here. Obviously, there's not room here for a lot, but there's room enough for us. Come on," she pulled at his hand, leading him onward. "Let's grab a quick cup … and make sure you are who you say you are."

They continued in silence, though David considered speaking up, insisting he was, in fact, David Sparks. But was he? He didn't even know for sure. His sporadic memories hardly explained everything—and they didn't even bear any resemblance to any place he found himself over the last several weeks. Like they were memories from long ago— decades earlier—farther back than his life even reached. Memories from before all of this. Before everything changed and the world went to hell. Something about them was off. Just didn't seem quite right. So, no, he wasn't about to argue who he was—especially since he wasn't sure himself.

An explosion of sound met his ears as they entered the next room. Screams, shouts and laughter sprang up from around him. Children ran about, chasing after one another. A few climbed what looked like a giant nut while others scurried above in a plastic treehouse. A faded yellow sign hung above, wrapped in a bundle of vines. *Plants Alive*—the rest obscured. Another group of children sat, attentively listening on a ring of artificial logs, as a teenage girl attempted to teach over the racket.

Beyond the classroom, another set of doors led into yet another new room, this one different from any of the others they'd been through. Unlike the rest of the building, the air in this room was remarkably dry—even drier than the air outside. A row of cactuses ran the length of the room, each sprouted from a garden of rock and sand raised up in the center of the chamber. Pathways surrounded it, the outer perimeters of which housed tables and shelves covered in an array of assembled and disassembled electronics. Men and woman sat along the tables, heads down and focused as they worked on various devices.

"Sam, grab a wand," Rosa commanded. A woman in a white coat matching everyone else in the room spun on her chair to face Rosa and David, grabbed a metal rod from her bench and brought it to them.

"Your wand, ma'am." The woman looked young, maybe early twenties. Skin clear, pale and free of wrinkles. In respectable physical shape, like Rosa—although considerably more petite. Her eyes betrayed her youth, however, shining with a glassiness worse than Ghost's. From how she stared toward David, not quite at him but more through him, he assumed she was blind.

"David, this is Sam. She's going to check you over."

"What's she going to do with that thing?" he asked, watching as Sam thumped the chrome instrument into her palm. He took a step back, reconsidering his earlier decision not to explain himself when he had the chance.

"Calm down, would you?" Sam laughed. "I'm just going to wand you."

David looked to Rosa, who nodded. "Let her do it."

"So, do I sit?" he asked. But the only empty chair he found was the one Sam had been sitting in. "Where, exactly, does that thing go?"

Sam stepped forward and grabbed a handful of David's hair, holding his head still. He pressed his eyes closed and braced for pain.

"Identity confirmed," an electronic voice spoke. "David Samuel Sparks. ID number 231874."

"Yeah, it's him," said Sam. She returned to her desk and started fiddling with the equipment she'd been working on before the interruption.

Rosa sprung toward David and wrapped her arms around him, enveloping him in a full-bodied embrace. "I can't believe it's you," She put her hands to his cheeks and looked deep into his eyes. "I can't believe they found you."

Tears began to stream down her cheeks and she embraced him again. And, in an explosion of passionate relief, planted her lips on his.

"Now," she said, wiping his spit from her lips, "how about that coffee?"

# THIRTY-FOUR
# SCIENCE!

Unlike the rooms they passed through to get here, David found Rosa's office surprisingly stark and fully devoid of plant life. Instead, a large aquarium, at least a thousand gallons, made up the back wall behind her desk. Schools of perch swam about lazily, while several bass sat suspended a few feet below the surface. A large catfish lumbered about the bottom, slurping up any bit of debris that could possibly be food.

"Beautiful, aren't they?" Rosa took a seat in the chair behind her desk. "I do love to watch them. But unlike those goldfish you saw earlier, these do have a purpose. The water in that tank is all scrubbed and continuously filtered, and the fish were bred in captivity. We've had enough generations now that any adverse effects from the chemicals in the wild have cleared from their system. Living here, in our little commune, we can provide quite a bit of food from what we grow—but when the occasion calls for it, or they grow too big, these guys do end up on our dinner plates. So, although they're beautiful, they serve us as well."

Knuckles rapped on the door behind David and the door swung open. A young man, no more than sixteen, poked his head into the room.

"Sam said to bring coffee."

"Oh, thank you Matthew." Rosa squealed with delight. "On the desk, please."

The boy entered the room, staring at David as he came in. He placed a stainless-steel carafe and two terracotta coffee cups, shaped like little flower pots with handles, on the desk. His eyes never strayed from David.

"Perfect, thank you. Now, run along," Rosa urged.

The door closed with a click, and the two sat in silence as Rosa poured out two cups of coffee.

"I do apologize for what happened back there," she said, taking a sip.

"The wand thing? I guess you had to be sure." David took a cup for himself and held it between his hands. The coffee was still hot, and not altogether a welcome option for David as he was still acclimating himself to the shifting temperatures of the conservatory's various rooms. "You could have told me about it. What was it, anyway? I thought I was about to be probed."

"Probed?" Rosa asked. "Oh boy David, you haven't learned all that much yet, have you? It's just a proximity reader—scans the NFC field that comes out of that port of yours to check your ID. Bethany sent over your credentials in one of her earlier check-ins, after the port went in." She took another sip and placed the cup back on her desk. "I do apologize for that too, I suppose. But what I meant was I apologize for the kiss. I bet you have questions."

"Questions? Yeah you could say that. I don't even know why I'm here, or where here even is."

"You saw all the people here as we walked to my office, right? All the beds in the big room outside my office? We're a colony, David. This place is our home. Here we're able to live our lives, free from the Reconstruction. Free from The Progressives. This conservatory sustains us. It protects us from the dangers outside, while still letting us live within the old, natural world."

"But Sam, her eyes …"

"It protects us, David. But it doesn't shield us. Some of us, like Sam, have still taken ill from the chemicals. We try to keep this place pure, but we're also not interested in living in quarantine. We come and go. Some of our farming is still done outdoors—we have a large corn field in back by the outdoor pond. A lot of the equipment's outside too. Things like the solar panels that keep this place running."

"So that's how you have power."

"And clean water, and temperature and humidity controls—and functional air and water scrubbers," Rosa said, nodding. "I don't know how much you've learned since coming to, but we're what city people call "Organics" —not that I have much use for the label, but I guess it's pretty accurate."

"So, this place, it's a kind of base for The Cause?"

"Not exactly. Some of us here, like me and Sam, we do work for The Cause. That's what a lot of what you saw in our desert room is for—the tech, I mean. The plants are mostly used for medicine. We use the space for tech too since it's the one place here where we keep the humidity low enough it doesn't prematurely damage any of the electronics." She stood from her desk and approached the glass wall of the aquarium, watching the fish, and continued, "Most people here don't want to be involved. That's what this place is for. Like our own little Switzerland, noninterventionist and living our lives away from the fighting and destruction that goes on in the rest of the world—in places like Plasticity."

"But if you're harboring rebels, doesn't that make you complicit?" David sipped at his coffee.

"Oh David, like anything in life, it's much more complicated than that. Don't think of it in terms so black and white. Yes, we're here, but we don't involve the others. They're free to join us if they like, just as they're free to ask us to leave. Having us here, however, has had its benefits for them, from time to time."

"What kind of benefits?"

"Let's just say that even if most Organics are pacifist, we members of The Cause are not."

David took a second to contemplate this but decided not to pursue the issue.

"So then, why did you kiss me back there? Do we know each other?"

"Know each other?" Rosa laughed again and leaned over the desk, her face inches from his. "David, I made you."

## THIRTY-FIVE
# THE MAKINGS OF A MAN

"What do you mean, you made me?" David shoved away from his chair and leaned in dangerously close to Rosa's face. "Just what the hell is going on?"

"I don't know what Calvin or Bethany told you," Rosa said. "And I don't know what things might have jostled loose in that brain of yours. But now that you're here, and since it appears circumstances have changed, what with Calvin and Bethany AWOL, it looks like I have some explaining to do."

"You're god-damn right you do," David huffed. He returned to his seat and took a few breaths. "Go ahead. Explain."

"When you woke up in that field, you had no idea who you were. You still have no idea who you are—and that's my fault. It's how we made you."

"You keep saying that. What am I? Some kind of android?"

"Oh, absolutely not. You're a human, and you're David Sparks. At least a version of David Sparks. The first iteration of David Sparks, the one you're based on, was born over one hundred years ago. You're a clone, David. A clone of the original David Sparks, with all the memories of the David Sparks of the past, preserved in your genetic memory. My job was to bring you back."

"Bring me back? For what purpose?"

"Honestly, I don't have the answer to that. All I know is that my job was to resuscitate David Sparks, as he was when he was 33 years old."

"How?"

"It's complicated, David. But think of it like this. I've been working on technology to extrapolate, from a combination of DNA and environmental factors, the recreation of a consciousness. The problem is, when we need to make a clone of someone who's 33 years old, we don't want to wait for 33 years of growth. So, what we do is separate the mind and body from each other. The body goes through a regimen of advanced growth acceleration, basically taking someone from zygote to adulthood in a matter of months. At the same time, we take your DNA and tap into its memory, building out a recreation of your consciousness which we put into a computer system. Inside that system we've carefully reconstructed the world in which you were born into—a kind of simulation. Since your DNA memory can unlock the memories from your entire existence, up to the time at which the DNA was collected, or you died—whichever comes first—we're able to build out a continual recreation of your life. We take this infant consciousness, and put it into a manufactured brain, and allow it to run through the simulation—again, at increased speed. This allows us to provide your body with a brain, holding a recreation of the David Sparks self that had been formed through your life experiences. Since our brains shape over time, rewiring themselves through the events of our lives, a simple clone of your brain wouldn't be you—it would have all its own memories—or no memories at all in the case of our accelerated physical cloning tech, since the clone aging takes place with an unconscious mind—a kind of coma. So instead for every clone we make, we actually start with at least two clones—one to allow to grow and advance physically to the required maturity level, and another to harvest a secondary brain from so we can run it through the life simulation and have it be a mirror replica of the desired version of the person In this case, David Sparks at 33 years, 4 months, 3 days, 14 hours and 16.342 seconds."

Rosa paused, waiting for David to respond. When he didn't, she continued.

"The David Sparks we wanted was older than you are, David. Not by much … but by enough. They attacked us at our lab and the project terminated prematurely."

"So then, how am I here, if the project didn't work out?"

"The Progressives found us. I have no idea how, but they did. I don't think they had any idea what we were up to, but they found out that we had labs in Raleigh and they came in, guns blazing. We were a research station, not a military base. We weren't prepared for an attack. While the few soldiers we did have held them off, Bethany gave the order. We'd been working on you so long, David. We'd experienced so many failures—but this instance, this iteration of you was finally holding steady. It was either abandon everything, burn the place to the ground and start over again, losing months of work, or go ahead and do the transfer ahead of schedule."

"Why would it matter what my age was? Why did you need that exact version of me?"

"I don't know, David. My job was to make you—to make the exact version of you that Bethany requested. The reasons weren't my concern—only Bethany and Calvin knew that, and well …"

"So, you made me. Basically time-traveled me, to this time and place, and you have no idea why you did it?"

"I'm sorry David, but you're right. I believe in The Cause, and I believed in Bethany. It wasn't up to me to ask why. It was only up to me to do whatever I could and trust she knew what she was doing."

David thought this over, taking another drink of his coffee only to find he already emptied the cup. "So, why don't I remember anything—other than bits and pieces, if you built my historical memory into this brain?" he asked, tapping his head.

"You weren't ready, but we couldn't abandon you. We had no idea what to do—but we did know if we just brought you into current consciousness you'd have no idea what was going on. The lab was in chaos, we were under attack, and … to be frank … we didn't even know if your brain could handle that kind of trauma. So, I added in a prototype model of an amnesial blocker I'd been working on. Basically, your memories all happened, and they built your brain, but I made you forget it all. Exact same David from 33 years, 0 months and 16 days, physically speaking—but mentally a blank slate."

"But I do remember things, Rosa. In bursts here and there, they come to me, but only when I'm asleep or unconscious."

Rosa sighed. "The problem with prototypes. They're not finished. I had no idea if it would even work. But what I do know is when we turned you on, you had no concept of who you were."

"So how did I wake up in the field? What are these memories? Are they real?"

"Calvin took you from us, to get you out. I don't have any idea what happened from there, other than that."

Rosa opened a drawer in her desk and pulled out a device with a screen attached to a jack like the ones they used in the hospital of Plasticity. "As for the memories, do you mind?"

David shook his head no and lowered his forehead to the table while Rosa moved around the desk and stood behind him. The port engaged with a familiar click, and a warmth spread from the base of his skull throughout his body as he fell into unconsciousness.

## THIRTY-SIX
# PEEK-A-BOO

"Remind me. Where did you meet these guys?" Alice shielded her eyes from the sun's glare as she asked the question.

"Just out running some errands." David panted. His lungs burned from blowing up the air mattress. He handed it to Missy and she bolted down the beach with it, crashing into the breaking surf with glee.

"You should invite them over for dinner some night."

"Maybe sometime. I still don't know them all that well." David stepped toward the water, enjoying the warmth of the powdery sand as it crept between his toes. He stopped at the wet edge of the shore and knelt. Aiden's sand castle stood proud, just out of reach of the lapping waves. Soon the tide would come in and erase any hint of its existence, but David didn't have the heart to tell him. The look of pride on his face was all that mattered in this moment.

"How's your head?" Alice asked, as she draped her arm over his shoulder. A gust of wind threatened to blow her floppy sun hat from her mop of blonde hair, and she put her hand up to save it.

"Still hurts, sometimes. But like I said before, it comes and goes."

A crab scuttled across the sand in the direction of Missy's castle, but as she dug another shovel of wet silt, it turned away, frightened.

"You need to take it easy, David. For your sake, and ours," Alice said. "And I'm not sure I like you spending so much time with some strangers I've never met."

David returned his eyes to the pond and smiled. Those lessons were worth the money, he thought. Just a year ago she could keep from slipping, but now there she was, skating in circles, doing twirls on the sheer ice. If she kept it up, she could be an Olympian.

A whimper from below him brought his attention back to Aiden. His snowman was no longer a man but had melted to a drooping pile of slush.

"I'm fine. Really," David replied. The scarf around Alice's neck hung loosely, and David pulled the ends tighter to protect her from the cold. Behind her the crab scuttled again, on its way back to the water. But the crab never made it. Instead it found death as a giraffe crushed its tiny body with the thunderous fall of a single hoof.

-----

"—can't find anything. David? Did you hear me David?"

"What?" David blinked his eyes, letting them adjust to the fluorescent lighting of Rosa's office. "Yeah, I can hear you." Her face came into focus, only inches from him, her eyes frantic. "What did you say?"

"I said I can't find anything, David."

"What does that mean?"

"When I plugged into you, you went out. But when you were gone, you were gone." A tear streamed down her cheek. "I thought you were dead. I never saw anything like it David. Your vitals were all there, but your brain activity? It was like you'd gone braindead. I mean, there was some background activity, life-sustaining autonomous functionality was still processing, but you were, for lack of a better term, a vegetable."

"What are you talking about? I was just dreaming."

"Not according to what I saw. Your brain went MIA. It's like you, the part of the brain that makes you you, just disappeared."

"So, what did you do?"

"What did I do? I told you, I freaked. I thought maybe some surge fried you. It's happened before—not to me of course, but I heard about it. Bad ports, bad connections, unstable currents—soul-jacking can be dangerous. But I checked, and everything looked like it was working right, technically. I was about to reseat the connection, see if something didn't handshake properly, but as soon as I disconnected you woke up," said Rosa. "That doesn't happen, David. People don't just wake up from a soul-jack, they need a chemical primer— and I didn't give you one."

"But Alice … and Aiden. One second I was here with you, letting you stick that thing into my head, and then I was gone. Back home. Or at least it felt like home. But then there was this crab, and a giraffe. … It's all jumbled. All I see are pieces, like my dreams are snippets of memories."

"Jesus, David … you saw Alice? But that's impossible."

"What do you mean, impossible? What aren't you telling me?"

Before she could respond, alarms roared, screaming in their ears. In an attempt to calm him, Rosa put her hand on David's shoulder and shouted over the klaxons, "It's all screwed up David. We'll talk more, I promise. But right now, I need your help. We're under attack."

## THIRTY-SEVEN
# CONSUMER CULTURE

At Rosa's urging, David trailed as she bolted from her office, through the rows of beds in the adjacent room. The people milling about the complex earlier now gathered together in the room. Some cowered on their beds. Others held their children close as they tried to soothe their young fears. At the exit, a citizen stood armed with an assault rifle.

"Take this!" the young man shouted, offering the gun to Rosa.

She pushed it back. "Keep it," she yelled, over the blaring alarm. "You need to protect our people. Come on, David."

David followed Rosa through the next room, a kitchen and dining hall that had been cleared of people, into a room marked "Aroid House." Fruit flies swarmed in the chaos, disrupted from their lazy flight by the racket and turmoil. A pair of men dressed in rags hacked at a tree, cutting and tearing a harvest of large green fruits, like coconut-sized limes or unripe mangoes, and stuffed them into a burlap sack.

"Hey! Stop!" At the sound of David's voice, the men took hold of the bag, one on each side, and started to run, dragging it across the ground behind them. David broke off into a run, followed closely by Rosa, and they pursued the men along the U-shaped path of the room past another pond, the golden glass decorative flowers dotting its water now sparkling in shades of fiery orange from the flashing emergency lights. The men scrambled through a pair of doors leading back into the dining hall.

"Stop, David." Rosa seized David's arm. "Let them go. They have what they came for," she said, taking in a deep lungful of air. "Besides, the barracks are secured. We need to keep moving."

Rather than chase the fruit thieves, David and Rosa took the door to the right, back into the Desert house. The lab techs abandoned their work at the alarm and now huddled together in the middle of the room, around the skeleton of a giant saguaro. A group of children stood with them, some crying, others casting their eyes about as they searched for family. Guards stood at attention at all three doors, including the door leading out of the building.

"All clear here, ma'am," said the one at the door they just came through. "Should I pursue?"

"No, just stand firm here. They're only Consumers—you know they don't have much interest in our tech, but I need you to protect it, and these people, from damage."

The man nodded, and Rosa pulled David onward, past the workstations and into the children's area and classroom. Her hand against David's mouth, she forced him to remain silent as she made a visual sweep of the room. Not hearing or seeing any presence, she moved on, ushering David into the Sugar house.

Like a storm had recently torn through, the floor of this room held masses of broken branches and fallen leaves. At the sight of the damage, Rosa dropped to her knees and began to sob. David left her and continued to secure the room. Again, it was empty—free of whoever had come through—but the destruction clearly indicated The Consumers had been there. The trees and bushes, once heavy in abundant fruit and seed pods now bore no bounty, the cinnamon tree razed to the ground. Everything of value taken. Only a tangle of massacred plants remained.

David knelt and put his arm around Rosa as she continued to sob. She buried her head in his shoulder and pulled him into an embrace and the warmth of her tears soaked through his shirt as she forced herself to comprehend the devastation.

"Rosa!" a familiar voice shouted. David stood as Parm approach them from the set of doors that led back into Palm house. "They're gone," she said, surveying the damage. "They were in and out so fast, we didn't have time to react."

"How?" asked Rosa, rising from the ground. A fire blazed in her eyes. The change shocked David. How different she could appear from the peaceful, caring woman he had met mere hours earlier. "I asked, how?" she shouted. She was now inches from Parm, jabbing her in the chest accusatorily as she spoke.

"I'm sorry, Rosa," Parm whispered, hanging her head as she spoke. "I … I don't think I secured the building after I brought him in."

Rosa took a deep breath and stepped back from Parm. After a few seconds, she asked, "and now?"

"Now it's secure," she mumbled. "I double-checked."

"Get the hell out of here, Parm." Rosa said, her body trembling. "Get the hell out of here while I deal with this mess."

Parm didn't say a word, but instead turned and left the way she came. Rosa followed, and David after her. At an open space near the entrance, under a canopy of vine covered metalwork, Rosa took a seat. Parm kept moving, leaving them behind and David sat down next to Rosa.

"They took it all," she said, after a few minutes. "Everything we had been growing in here. They took it." Her gray eyes shimmered in the light, back to normal now as the alarms had been disabled.

"Who were they?" David took her trembling hand in his, the heat from her anger still pulsing through her skin. "Who did this?"

"Consumers," she replied. "People who roam free in The Green Zones. Like us Organics, they've opted out of modern life. But they've taken it to extremes. Holed up in buildings throughout the city, this particular colony rejects any convenience of civilization. Their stance on noninterventionism is extreme, and when it comes to mankind's manipulation of the natural world, they do nothing to provide for themselves. Instead, they take what they need from the world as the world allows. Like a pack of hunters and gatherers, they scour for anything they can use. And they don't give a damn what their overbearing consumption does.

"The world, as far as Consumers are concerned, was made for them to reap. With the explosions in plant life from all the genetic engineering that led to The Chemical Wars, finding food in the wild was easy for small groups. Like any human, however, their tastes go well beyond what they find in the wild—meaning they're a constant risk to anyone traveling through the city. If you saw anyone out there, any hint of something human, that was them.

"Their diet, eating whatever they come across, brings its own set of problems—the main one being the majority of what they eat, almost all directly from nature, has been tainted. The lack of nutrition makes them physically weak, but a lot of them are also victims of the disease. All those chemicals in the natural world. They may live organically, but they're still poisoned. A lot of them are blind and desperate—not only for food, but medicine too. The two men we saw earlier? They took the fruit of Garfield's only calabash tree. Not of much use when it comes to eating, but if you mash it to pulp it can be used to treat respiratory problems, a common secondary symptom of chemical exposure," Rosa sighed. "But, I guess they need it more than we do.

"That's why I let them go. But the rest—the coffee and fruits and cinnamon and everything else they took from this room," Rosa continued, waving her hand in a circle, "this is what makes living here special. It might sound silly, but the finer things … the simple joy of a treat ... It's just part of who we are."

David's legs started to ache from sitting on the concrete, so he stood. He reached a hand to Rosa, who took it and allowed him to pull her up.

"Come on Rosa," David whispered. "Let's go check in on your people and make sure everyone's okay. Besides, I'll be fine—I'm not really a coffee guy myself." He paused, smiled and looked into her eyes. "But I'm guessing you already knew that."

## THIRTY-EIGHT
# RUMOR HAS IT

"Look in his eyes, man. You'll see it yourself."

Back in his new friends' basement, David leaned in toward Ben, smelling cola on his breath. But beneath it another scent festered. The fart smell of broccoli, but sweeter. Sicker. Like an infection. David positioned his thumb on the man's lower eyelid and his index finger on the upper, and pried open Ben's eye for a closer look.

A glassy sheen covered them, and he looked lazily past David. His gaze shifted to the TV screen and he stared at it blankly. Did he even know he was only looking at a static pause screen in the game? The emptiness David noticed earlier only showed the surface of Ben's problems. As he looked closer, David realized the man's eyes, while glassy on the surface, were also clouded deeper within. The retinas almost silver. Patches of gray spread outward, threatening to engulf his corneas. If he ever were to meet an ancient wizard, this is what David expected his eyes would look like.

"What happened?" David asked. "Is he blind?"

"Nah, but he might as well be," answered Chris. "He can see a little bit, we think. He's not banging into things yet and seems to get around alright. But it's a lot more than that."

"What do you mean?"

"His eyes are the part you can see. But there's a lot more going on beneath that. A couple years ago Ben started getting a cough. It got into him and stuck, but it wasn't that bad. We all figured it was allergies or something. He used to live out by a farm, so sometimes hay fever would kick in pretty rough," Chris scooted closer to Paul, and continued. "When his eyes started to bother him, we figured that was part of it too. He said things were starting to look blurry, and his eyes itched. But the cough kept getting worse until it he pretty much stopped talking, since every time he'd say a word he'd go into a fit."

"You take him to the doctors? What'd they say?"

"Of course, we took him. He's my brother, man," replied Chris. "We took him, but they couldn't figure anything out. When we figured out this was more than allergies, we started to worry so we told Ben to go see the doc. He did, and they gave him some antibiotics. Didn't help at all. Just kept getting sicker."

"Eventually it got so bad that he couldn't take himself anymore," said Paul. "So, we had him move in with us."

"We took him to see doctors, as much as we could at least. Optometrists said it was some form of macular degeneration.

Then they weren't sure. Could be infection. Then they thought maybe cancer. They looked at all kinds of exotic stuff but couldn't figure it out. Eventually the money ran dry, and here we are. He's sicker all the time. Can't see much, doesn't talk. Doesn't even seem to be thinking much anymore. He's just kind of … gone."

"So, the doctors couldn't figure out what was wrong with him?" asked David.

"Doctors didn't," Paul grunted. "But I did."

"We have a *theory*," Chris corrected him.

"Theory my ass. It's the government. The government and big business. They're killing him."

"Jesus, Paul," Chris sighed and dismissed him with a wave. "You sound like you need a tin foil hat. A foil hat, a shotgun and a crate of emergency rations."

"Screw off. You know as well as I do what's happening."

"That what's happening?" David loved a good conspiracy.

"All part of the experiments." Chris looked to Paul, who nodded his head for him to go on. "I read about it online."

"He's an Internet expert," said Chris.

Paul ignored the chiding and continued, "Even though we ran out of money didn't mean we were done taking care of Benny. And we sure as hell didn't give up on finding out what was wrong with him," Paul scratched at his beard and continued. "I went online and started searching for anything like what was going on with Ben, and eventually I found something."

"It was a bit of a stretch …"

"Stretch or not, you see the similarities. There were comparable cases documented in some study by a university professor. Over in Europe. Northern Denmark. A whole town of people who came down with the same symptoms. Glassy eyes, fading vision, progressive sickness. Turns out the town was a small farm community, and some company offered them the opportunity to test some new pesticides on their crops. The pesticides worked, all right, but they also made everyone sick. The farm out by Benny was testing the same thing."

"They got sick from some chemicals? How were they even approved to be used in public?" David asked.

"That's where the government comes in," said Paul. "All of this was done with the FDA and government and the biotech and chemical companies working in cahoots."

"Cahoots?" laughed Chris. "Is that the word you're going to use?"

"Cahoots, conspiracy, whatever you want to call it." Paul dismissed him. "According to The Cause, all the documents were showing the government was pushing the direction of the research, funding projects, looking the other way when they had to."

"Crony capitalism isn't anything new," David interjected. "Honestly, I'm not surprised."

"This is way more than money and power trades," Chris continued. "According to people we've talked to, this is some major social engineering. You know how medicine keeps getting better and better, right? People are living longer and longer lives, less babies are dying at birth. Basically, population's exploding."

"People require resources," Paul said. "The most crucial resource is food. The problem is, how do you feed a population growing at a rate like ours? It used to be that they'd calculate how many crops could fail. Calculated risk. But now we're getting to the point where crops can't fail. If they do, food supplies are low. Prices go up, less people eat, society breaks down. People riot. Everything crumbles."

"Right, so to avoid that, they need to make crops that can't fail. Engineered to live through extreme conditions, not succumb to pests or drought or blight."

"So, your brother, he's sick from these pesticides?" David asked. "They used them at the farm, didn't they? How many more are sick?"

"That's it—they don't make those pesticides anymore. Getting people sick was kind of … antithetical to the government's plan to try to make people healthy. Sure, there were a few who argued it would help with population control, but those voices were silenced fast. People aren't getting sick anymore—or at least they weren't."

"What are you saying?"

"According to what The Cause tells us, the government abandoned the use of these pesticides. Spraying didn't work anymore since it released so much poison into the air. Instead they started modifying the plants themselves, building resistance into the actual genetic makeup through cross-breeding and manipulation at the DNA level. Building the pesticides right into the plants themselves. Well, those new breeds are out there, and they're cross-pollinating with other plants, creating what are basically superweeds. And these superweeds are spreading everywhere, totally invasive. Choking out the native plants. But that's not the real problem."

"The plants are making people sick again," Paul added.

"Or at least that's what it looks like. Symptoms are starting to show up. Scattered reports –a sick guy here, dead kid there. The onset of the symptoms seems to be a bit more delayed than they were with Ben, but they're the same—just over a lot longer period. Plus, they're not affecting as many people in the affected area as the pesticides did."

"Yeah, but it's accelerating," said Paul. "The cases are starting to show up more and more—and they're all around where these new crops have been planted. Our worry, us and The Cause, is that what we're seeing now are being considered as 'acceptable losses' and they won't pull the plug this time around."

"Who's this Cause you keep talking about? Are they your friends online?"

"Ever hear of Anonymous?" asked Paul.

Of course, David knew of Anonymous. He was an IT security engineer by trade, after all—or at least would be for the next few weeks, until Fred's kill order came through.

"Well they're kind of like them, a bunch of hacker/activist types—only they have a very specific focus. Like a lot of these anarchist types, they're skeptical of government, and it's what lead them to find what they uncovered—but they're also a pretty professional group. We're working with them now, me and Paul," Chris said, scooting closer to Paul and patting him on the leg. "We're part of The Cause."

"Think of it like this. The government's the Empire and the corporations are Sith. We're the Rebellion."

Chris laughed and put his arm around Paul and added, "Ha, maybe. But more like the Rogue One rebellion. Like them, we're just getting started."

## THIRTY-NINE

# THANK GOD NO ONE WAS INJURED!

"Good morning, sunshine. Looks like you slept well." Rosa tapped David's shoulder and woke him from his dream. Apparently, he had been the last to wake. Almost all the rest of the cots in the room were empty. "Here, drink this. It'll help perk you up."

David sat up on his bed and reached out to take the steaming cup from Rosa's hand. "Thanks Rosa ... I know I said I don't like—"

"I know. It's tea—English breakfast," she said, her lips turning up at the corners. "We grow that here too."

"Well, aren't you the observant one," David laughed. "I don't suppose you happen to have—"

"Sugar? Maybe not like you're used to. It looks like what we had got taken yesterday," she said. "But here, put this in and stir it around."

The green stick Rosa pulled from her pocket looked like a piece of bamboo. David took it and gave it a quick sniff.

"Sugarcane," said Rosa.

He put it into his tea, and let it sit a bit, then stirred, took a drink and smiled.

"So, everyone still okay?" The previous day, after the attacks, David followed along as Rosa rounded up the citizens of the compound. No one had been injured in the attacks, although several people were rightfully scared—the emotional toll strongest on the children. From what David could gather, while these attacks weren't frequent, most of the longer-term residents had gone through similar experiences several times before.

"Yeah, everyone's fine," Rosa replied. Her eyes searched the room, stopping at the few beds where people still slept. A boy and a girl, both no more than three years old, played on a cot near the entrance. The guard stationed there was gone. They had a few stuffed bears between them, shaped out of old clothes and whatever stuffing had been lying around. The kids were laughing, oblivious to the adults in the room, having their own pretend tea party—their resilient little souls already forgetting the trauma of the previous day.

"They're crafty, you know? Sneaking in like that. Crafty, but pretty much harmless. They must have eyes on this place all the time. We keep the doors locked—well, we usually keep the doors locked. But they must come and try them from time to time, looking for that one chance to break in. We haven't seen any of them around here much lately though. Maybe they saw you on your way here. Followed you. Then decided to give it another shot."

"Rosa, I'm sorry if I brought them here." David put his hand on her knee and she returned his gaze. "I had no intention of—"

"Oh David, it's fine. We're fine. You didn't do anything wrong. It's Parm … she didn't lock the door and … well you know what happened." She placed her hand on David's and continued, "I'm just so glad you're here! Get up, grab something to eat from the tables and meet me in the lab. I have something for you. Oh, and take a shower."

---

After a breakfast of bananas and toast, David took a shower and it was glorious. Although his brief stint in the lake and the downpour on his way here kept him from getting too dirty, the amount of dirt caked onto his skin surprised him. Rosa's suggestion he take a shower shocked him at first, he hadn't considered there would be running water, let alone hot running water, out here in The Green Zones. But the kids he talked to sent him back to an area just off the entrance to the complex, where all the modern amenities of personal cleanliness presented themselves. He even found a communal toothbrush and some toothpaste.

Back in the lab, David found Rosa talking again with Sam, busily working over another small pile of electronics. From time to time, she'd pluck a random circular object from the array of circuits and gizmos. She'd pick it up, and feel it with her fingertips, checking the edges.

"Scorched too?" asked Rosa.

"Uh-huh. I think that might have been the last of the good ones."

David cleared his throat, startling Sam. She dropped the metal ring to her desk, where it clattered against the rest of the electronic pieces.

"David … you look good," said Rosa. Sam nudged Rosa, smirking at David as she pushed her boss closer.

"Thanks Rosa. The showers here. I mean, it's only been a few days, but still that was like heaven."

"Good. I'm happy you found them. I didn't mean to run off on you like that, but I had to come back here to see how Sam's project is coming along."

"It's fine," David said. "Nice to take a few minutes at my leisure for once. Everything's been going so fast. I'm having a tough time processing it all."

"I definitely understand and I'm glad it helped." As she spoke, David sensed her eyes searching his. Looking for what, he had no idea—but it made his skin itch.

"Is … is everything okay?" he asked.

"David. About the issues you're having 'processing' things. When I woke you up this morning, were you dreaming?"

"Yeah, I think so. Something about people getting sick. The Cause?"

"Enough," she stopped him. "I don't want to know any more right now. I mean, I can't know any more right now.

Not until we figure out what's going on. I'm not cleared for your level of information. And with you not knowing yourself what's going on, having these dreams or memories or whatever they are, you can't share them with me. It could be detrimental to the mission."

"But it was a dream. Even if it was brought on by a memory, there's no way it would be accurate. Dreams don't work that way."

"You weren't dreaming, David."

David shook his head. "Well on that you're mistaken. Like I said, I don't remember it exactly, but I know I was having a dream. There were these two guys, talking about The Cause. Something about hack—"

"Enough!" David stopped at Rosa's outburst. "I'm sorry, David. Just … just don't say any more. You weren't dreaming. I know you weren't dreaming, because I," she lowered her eyes, hesitated, and whispered in his ear, "because I jacked into you while you were asleep."

David couldn't decide how to respond to this invasion of his privacy. He'd given her permission the day before, but in his mind it was a one-time kind of deal. Any future "jacking" required future permission. He hadn't issued her a hall pass to his brain.

"You're probably mad, I would be too," she continued. "But I had to see it again. It was exactly like before. When you were out, you were out. There was no activity other than your autonomous functions. No REM sleep. No dreams. Just a brain, doing its job keeping your body alive, but dead in consciousness."

"But we already knew this," said David. "We found this out yesterday. How does this matter?"

"Matter?" Rosa gasped. "It matters because I'm scared, David. You're my responsibility. You're important. Important for what, I don't know. But you're important."

"I see," David said. "For the mission."

Rosa took a deep breath and answered quietly, "For more than the mission. You're important … to me." Her cheeks flushed as she spoke. "I know it's silly. For you we've just met. But for me? I've been watching you for a long time. I've been caring for you for a long time."

David took a moment to process this and asked, "So how do we fix it?"

Rosa's eyes perked up and she tapped on Sam's shoulder, who pretended not to listen in on their conversation while she dug through her pile of widgets. "I don't know how to fix it, per se, since I don't quite understand what's going on," said Rosa. "But I think I have a way to get it under control."

"Your suppressor's busted," said Sam, holding up another metal ring. This one shone cleanly, free of any scorches or burns. "I made you a new one."

"What are you going to do with that?"

"The one in you, well we're not going to dig it out," said Sam. "They're made to be able to fail. If they do, they go dormant. A piece of trash in your brain—looks basically like shrapnel to any scanners but doesn't interfere with anything once it's dead. Yanking it out though… well, I don't know anyone who can do that level of surgery on a fully-developed brain and not knock a few things loose along the way."

"So, you're going to put that thing in my brain?"

"No, of course not. You have a jack, so we'll just put it in there. It's older tech, made for back when everything was still hardwired, but it'll work fine. Basically, we put it in and it'll act like the suppressor you had before. Stop your genetic memories from coming through. Only difference is, it'll knock your wireless offline too."

"I'm not quite sure how I feel about this," said David. He looked to Sam, searching her face for any tick that might show she might also be uncomfortable with this prospect. Finding none, he directed himself back to Rosa and asked, "What do you think?"

"I think if you don't do this," said Rosa, "your brain's going to hit a point where it can't figure out what's real, what's a memory, and what's a dream … and it'll fracture."

David scratched at his port, looked at the two women staring at him expectantly and took a deep breath.

"Alright. Stick it in."

# FORTY
# ON HOLIDAY

After several days in Garfield, David found himself settling in nicely. A few weeks, and it was the most at-home he felt in any memory he could conjure. The first order of business, after the attacks, was to bring all systems back online. The consumer insurgence hadn't caused any damage to the facility, but the storm preceding them—the one that broke just as David arrived, had.

Outside the main compound stood several additional greenhouses. Most of the actual crops raised to sustain the people of Garfield grew in these external buildings, and in the storm, a few of the solar panels powering their scrubber units had been damaged. An option existed to simply open the vents to the pure outside air but doing so would cause significant risk to the crops growing inside. No one knew the extent to which the effects of the chemicals were airborne versus how much bred into the plant life outside. Tests back during the initial phases of breakout showed exposure to air was just as dangerous, although less concentrated than consumption of affected plants. But what remained unknown was how much exposure to tainted air would alter a previously unaffected plant. Exposure was dangerous to humans, particularly over extended periods of time, but no one knew if plants could absorb the chemicals as well. What testing had been done remained inconclusive, and human trials were never approved. What was known was that plants growing near the affected areas exhibited increased levels of the noxious chemicals when tested. And people who ate those plants tended to become sick. So, rather than risk affecting the population by exposing their food source to outside contaminants, the people of Garfield made it their top priority to bring the power supplies responsible for the scrubbers back online.

The people of Garfield, though guarded from the dangerous elements of the world outside, still were not protected completely. By David's estimate, nearly fifty percent of the population showed signs of infection. The older people tended to be worse off, likely due to the extent of their exposure. Those previous organics who had lived some time outside the protection of Garfield's walls, scrubbers and filters had it worst of all. A few of the citizens made the trek to Chicago from Plasticity or one of the other Society settlements, from the relative safety of the East Coast through The Green Zones in search of another life. Many lost friends or family on the trips, due to weather, environment, bands of violent Consumers, rogue land serpents, illness or starvation.

Still, many completed the trip, reaching Garfield and supposed salvation. Of those who did make it, however, most already exhibited symptoms of exposure well before reaching their journey's end. Coughs were commonplace, and many displayed the ocular deterioration that presented itself with reduced vision and those cold, glassy grey eyes.

So, David helped fix the scrubbers. And he helped replant the crops. He did whatever he could to make himself part of this new society, and he did most of it by Rosa's side. Over their few weeks together, David's bond with her strengthened. Since the day he arrived at Garfield, he felt a connection—almost like love—emanating from her. And, while he admitted he found her attractive, personal relationships and carnal lusts were far from David's mind in his first few days in the big glass house. Time spent together, however, strengthened their connection, and for David the days with her were the closest to a sense of "home" he had experienced since waking in the fields all those weeks ago.

What started as time spent on projects together morphed into time spent doing nothing together. Just enjoying each other's presence quickly became a way to pass the hours. Maybe it was love. Or maybe it was the absence of loneliness—simply having someone with whom to share an emotional bond. Either way, over these weeks they connected at such a level that the thought of spending time away from one another brought on feelings of panic. Even though he still had no idea why he came here in the first place, he was sure of one thing: he had no desire to leave.

From time to time he and Rosa left the confines of the conservatory. Many days they ventured out back, onto the great bluestone terrace to walk through the plants and gardens and simply enjoy nature. Rosa, it turned out, was one of a few select people who appeared to be immune to the effects of exposure. And so far, David also showed no signs of illness.

"Your eyes, Rosa. I lose myself in them."

Rosa smiled and took his hand, leading him across the terrace to the great pond dotted with water lilies. They took the wooden bridge, stopping halfway to look down into the water. A turtle pulled its head underwater and took off swimming. Dragonflies alit on the lily pads, buzzing from one to the other in search of what only they knew.

"I could say the same about yours, David. They're beautiful too … but they're different from what I remember. In my mind I always pictured your eyes as green."

"Because they're not mine. Calvin took me to have them swapped on the way out of the city. Said it was for security."

"Of course, he did." Rosa frowned, letting go of David's hand. "I guess I should have expected him to do something like that."

"What's wrong? He said if we didn't swap them out I'd be identified. He also mentioned something about my health, but I don't remember a lot of that. It was quite a while ago."

"Did he take you to the Eyefields? Did he take you to Devon?"

"Yeah. I mean, I think that was his name."

"I suppose it's just as well." Rosa's eyes returned to the water, following the pond to its edge and to the great open field in the space behind Garfield. An ancient building marked the skyline, like an old stone castle or hospital. The tattered remains of a flag mounted to a pole on its roof fluttered in the wind.

"The eyes they grow, they're the closest to a cure as anyone has come. People like me, those of us who are immune, seem to have some kind of mutation in our eyes that doesn't allow the chemicals to affect us. Breathing can still be detrimental, but from what we've learned, the effects of exposure from air or even ingestion are minimal—and take a long time to present themselves. It's when they get absorbed through the eyes that rapid damage occurs—it's why you see so much deterioration there. It's why the blindness usually long predates fatality."

David closed his eyes and rubbed them gently through his lids with his fingertips. "So, Calvin made me immune?"

"As close to immune as you can get, at least. He would have known your natural body would probably be affected if you spent too much time in The Green Zones. I should have figured he'd do something like that."

"Something like what?" a voice boomed from behind them. Rosa and David turned to face the voice.

"Calvin!" Rosa shouted. The great man stood at the edge of the bridge, his arm wrapped around Bethany. They looked rough, dirty and scratched up—but otherwise unharmed. Rosa ran to Calvin and he took his arm from Bethany, lifting Rosa from the ground up in a powerful hug.

"Hello, David," said Bethany. "I see you made it here, after all."

"That I did," David shook her calloused hand. "And you're here too. We thought the worst."

"Well, we did run into a few snags in the plan," Calvin said. "But there's no way we'd let the mission fail that easily."

"Care to finally let me in on what this whole mission is?" David asked.

Calvin reached out his hand and clamped it down on David's shoulder. "Sorry, my boy. We can't do that—not yet. But we can fill you in on what happened at the house and how we managed to get back to Chicago."

# FORTY
# NATURE CALLS

"As you launched, alarms started ringing, and we knew everything had gone to hell," said Calvin. Back inside, the four of them sat at the circle of fake log benches where the children previously had class. A few of them scampered in the playground above, but most had returned earlier to the great hall to join their families for dinner. The lights of Garfield started to turn on as night fell, signaling the end of a day and time for a meal and some night-time socializing before bedtime.

"It was the core. It must have been unstable. It started a meltdown," Bethany said.

"Once we confirmed you were off, we high-tailed it out of there," Calvin added. "We made it out. Hopped on the bikes and zipped out as fast as we could. Barely made it to a safe distance, but we were clear when the thing blew."

"Well, I was clear. Calvin … not quite. The shockwave from the blast got him. Knocked him and his bike hard, and him not wearing a helmet … well, he got a concussion and went unconscious. I stuck with him, and a few hours later he came to. To play it safe, we decided to spend the night in the woods and wait to travel again at morning. Maybe see if there was anything we could salvage from the house."

"That night, the place lit up like a birthday cake. A few slidecars flew in, searchlights blaring, scanning the area for anything they could pick up. We were far enough out they had no chance of finding us, but by the next morning a secondary contingent came in, dropping off a squad of geeks to do some on-foot recon."

"Honestly, I'd never seen anything quite like it," Bethany said. "They weren't soldiers—not all of them. At least half the contingent were eggheads. Those modded jobs with the pale skin. Decked out in khaki shorts and short-sleeved safari shirts, they looked like they were walking on birch twig stilts, their legs so thin and white. While the grunts secured the place, these guys worked much more methodically. Pulling out instruments, taking readings. I have no idea what they were looking for, I've never seen techies so far outside the city before."

"We kept our distance, but still stayed close enough to do some recon of our own. What we saw was bizarre. Like these guys had never experienced the outdoors before. At first you could see their hesitancy, stepping gingerly in the wreckage of the blast zone, but after a few hours they started to venture farther out, into the woods. Their faces when they first touched the bark of a tree, they looked like children. Complete and utter awe. They separated into a few smaller groups, examining the plants, taking measurements. Photos. Records.

One group came across a little trickle of a stream, and when they met it they froze, staring as the water bubbled by. Then, the strangest thing happened. They both took a seat on a fallen pine, pulled their shoes and socks off their paper-white feet and stepped gingerly into the creek. There they stood, for what must have been at least a half hour—doing nothing but standing there, experiencing what it was like to stand immersed in the flow of nature. One of them reached down into the water and came back with a frog in his hand. Then they began to laugh. It was the first real sound I could make out from them since they landed. Yeah, they'd been talking, but it was a low, silent discussion of few words—nothing I could make out. But this laugh, the shrillness of it broke through the forest. Like a toddler experiencing the simple joys of a game of peek-a-boo. Pure. The birds scattered in the trees at the break in nature's own silence, and the others joined in. Laughing with glee as the feathered beasts took to the air and formed up into a retreating flock."

"We stuck around and watched for a while, but it was so strange," Bethany said. "After an hour or two it was obvious they weren't leaving any time soon, so we figured we should start moving. We considered taking the bikes, but out there the sound would travel. Completely unsafe. We even thought of walking them until we were out of earshot, but in that terrain it was impossible—so we set out on foot."

"And that's about it. We've just been walking. Walking and camping. Grabbing food where we can. It's been a trek. Thank God for Indianapolis. We were pretty much scraping by on berries, squirrel meat and water by the time we got there. Met up with an Organic settlement and refueled. We tried getting word out to let you know we were okay and were on our way, but their comms were down. Guess they've been down for a while. Pure colony like that, they don't put much of a priority on working tech."

David and Rosa listened as the two told their story, nodding from time to time to show they were listening. They waited until they completed recounting their travels. And then David asked the question that had been gnawing at his brain ever since the day he met Rosa.

"Guys, I have to ask. Why am I here? Rosa told me she made me. She told me there's some mission. I admit I had a bit of a tough time processing everything, but I'm accepting things as being what they are," David said. "But now I need to know why I'm here. Why you made me. What the hell the point of bringing me into existence is all about."

"How much has Rosa told you? About before?"

Bethany held up her hand, shushing Calvin. "Calvin, we can't. Whatever she told him, it can't be any more than she knows herself.

"I'm sorry Rosa," she said, "but you know as well as I do we wouldn't keep these secrets if we didn't have to."

"She's right. They have a reason for secrets." Rosa nodded and placed her hand on David's knee. "But isn't it time to maybe expand the circle of trust?" she asked, directing the question to Calvin.

"Sorry, but now we're here and David's safe. Bethany's right. We have to stick to the protocol. The mission, even if delayed, remains on track. Now it's time to rest and regroup; then we can move on to phase three."

"Phase three?" asked David. "What's phase three?"

"Phase three is the part where you find out why you're here and what your real purpose is in all of this," Bethany's brows furrowed, and David could swear she was on the verge of tears. "In a few days, you'll learn everything—I promise. But for now, it's not safe. Not with you still being in the position you're in. Just believe us when we tell you," she leaned in, and whispered quietly in David's ear, "right now, you're the most important man in the world."

# FORTY-TWO
# EXTRACTION

"Ghost is dead. His lifeline went dead twenty minutes ago." David and Rosa were eating breakfast in the great hall when Parm burst in with the news.

"He didn't look too good when I saw him," said David, through a mouthful of banana.

Parm took a seat at the table across from them, and continued, "No. He didn't die. At least not from sickness. Richards just told me. His vitals were stable, then they started to skyrocket, then boom—flatlined."

"Do we have eyes?" Rosa threw her spoon back in her bowl of granola and pushed her seat back as she arose. Parm stood again also, and the two of them ran off to the labs with David following close behind.

"No eyes. You know he asked us to stop surveillance. We respected those wishes. No one, other than David here, has even seen him in the last few months."

Rosa swore. "Then what happened? Richards, you have anything?"

A short, stocky man with a crew cut rose from the station opposite Sam. "Nothing, Rosa. Just like that, he spiked and was out."

"How long ago was this?"

"Ten—maybe fifteen minutes ago."

"Why are you only telling me now then?" Rosa's voice was rising. David had only seen Rosa this worried once before—weeks ago, right after he arrived and The Consumers staged their raid.

"Parm, go make sure the doors are secured. David, go find Bethany and Calvin. Richards, be ready to sound the alarms, we're on lockdown."

David's heart raced. Whatever was happening, Rosa knew something he didn't—and it scared him. "What's going on, Rosa?"

"David!" she commanded. "Go find Calvin and Bethany and tell them to hurry back—"

A loud explosion rocked the compound. From the sound of it, the explosion came from the front entrance. David looked at Rosa. Her face went pale.

"Oh my God, they're here!" Rosa shouted. "Richards—the alarms! Now!"

"Who's here?" asked David. "Are The Consumers back?"

Rosa shook her head vigorously. "No. I don't think so. I think this is something much, much worse."

David took off, leaving Rosa behind in the lab. He raced through the children's area, aroid house and sugar shack, and back into the main gardens just off the entrance. Smoke and flames poured through the doors leading to the entryway. Whatever happened, happened there. He kept moving, slipping into the Fern room. Calvin and Bethany had been spending most of their time there since arriving the night before, laying out plans in a makeshift command center.

"David, get out of here!" Calvin shouted as David entered the room. "You need to go someplace safe!"

"It's too late for that," Bethany yelled over the blaring of the alarms. "Get to the back. Take cover. Hide in the ferns. Don't let them find you!"

Bethany pulled a pistol from her side. Calvin picked up a stunshot from the rack of guns in their station and threw it to David. "It'll only give you one shot per charge, but it'll knock out anyone who comes your way." He took a rifle for himself.

Apart from being so near the entrance, the Fern Room worked rather well as a hiding space. It boasted the thickest growth of any of the rooms—mostly because unlike the others it was purely decorative. The citizens of Garfield used the space for meditation and mental wellness: the closest thing to a park that the confines of the glass walls could provide. David took the stunshot and ran along the path around the pond, past the spot where he first met Rosa, and climbed through the foliage into the very back corner of the room. He hunched down, gulping in deep breaths of the rich earthy air, as he did what he could to hide from whatever was coming.

Shots rang out. Screams. Buzzes of stunshots. Commands to search the area. "Find David. We are to retrieve him at all costs," a voice shouted. "And round up a few clear-eyes while you're at it!"

More shots, the sound of boots on concrete. Screams.

"Room's clear," said another voice.

"Search it," commanded the first.

What was he going to do? What happened to Bethany and Calvin? Who the hell was after him? He searched through the breaks in the foliage, desperate to find a new, better hiding place. They were sure to find him where he was.

*The pond. Go to the pond and slip down to the depths. No. Not deep enough. They'll see him. Play dead. Face down in the mud. Look like a casualty and let them move on.*

The footsteps closed in. The people searching the room at the edge of the pond. By his and Rosa's bench.

"Anybody here? David? We're here to pull you out!" the man's voice echoed off the glass ceiling. "Just bring us David Sparks. We know you have him. By order of The Reconstruction, bring him out and let him come back with us, and we'll leave. He's all we need."

*All they need? Pull him out?* Of course. The Reconstruction still thought he was working for them. Something happened. While he was gone. The suppressor. When they put it in, it hadn't only blocked the memories—it also killed his data uplinks. Rosa told him this far out they wouldn't be able to pull any dataset uploads, but they must have been keeping an eye on his vitals. They'd been keeping tabs on him to make sure he was safe—that wherever he was, he was still alive, retrieving data. They hadn't known where he was. Location signals didn't work this far out from civilization, and the GPS satellites had died decades ago.

They didn't know—and their ignorance was the one thing David could use to save the people of Garfield. He stepped out from his hiding place and announced himself.

"Jeez guys, I thought you'd never get here," he said. "Get me out of this place and take me home."

Before he could react, one of the soldiers fired—hitting David in the head with a stunshot round. He fell to the floor, paralyzed. The other soldier took his jacket off and threw it over David, hiding and protecting him as they dragged him from the room. As they reached the other side of the pond, David saw Calvin and Bethany, their bodies still on the floor. A single red hole marked the center of Bethany's forehead. Blood pooled around her lifeless body.

*That's how they knew. That's how they knew. That's how they knew.* The thought repeated itself in his head as the rescue squad escorted David out of Garfield.

"Stop," shouted a voice from behind.

Rosa stepped through the palms, holding her own gun, pointed directly at the man who held David's arm. "Leave him here. He's ours."

David's heart raced. He couldn't let them hurt Rosa. Not his dear Rosa. He thought of Bethany, dead on the ground with a bullet in her head. Pictured Rosa's face in place of Bethany's.

"Stand down, Rosa," he commanded. "I'm sorry, but I have to go back. I'm working with them and they're here to take me home."

Rosa's jaw fell open and her eyes widened. She dropped the gun, and stood there in silence, staring at David.

"I'm sorry, Rosa," he said as they turned to carry David outside to finalize their escape. "You'll understand someday. I hope."

David and the rest of the squadron piled into three slidecars and took off.

"You have to sleep," a soldier shouted as he stuck a needle into David's arm. "It's the only way to wear off that stunshot. Otherwise you won't be walking for a while, and when your body does start coming back, it's gonna hurt like hell."

David nodded and closed his eyes. Even with the shouting and celebrating going on around him, he couldn't help but drift off. As his world turned to darkness, David could only make out one thing in the city below: the flames and smoke bellowing out of the hole that had been blown in the side of the only place he could call home.

## FORTY-THREE
# HOLDING OUT FOR A HERO

"But Missy and Aiden. You have responsibilities here. They'd be devastated if anything happened." Propped up against her pillow, Alice faced David in their bed, a queen-sized platform with a worn-out mattress and two depressions, the shape of full-grown adults, spaced out as far as their marriage. The ceiling fan above the room creaked slowly, his bare skin sprouting goosebumps at the combination of the tickling breeze and unspoken pleading of her wet, periwinkle eyes.

David moved closer and pulled the sheets up over the two of them. Placing his body next to hers, her bare shoulder met his and a familiar rush of energy flowed from her skin across the barrier into him, penetrating deeply and spreading through his body where they touched. Her body tensed reflexively at the contact, then relaxed as he spoke.

"I know, baby. And I'd never do anything that would risk hurting them ... or you." He paused, waiting for a response to his mention of their own relationship. Receiving none, he continued. "This isn't about me though, you know that. It's much bigger than me."

"But why does it have to be you? You know what will happen if you are caught, David."

"They already fired me, Alice. What else are they going to do?"

"This is the government you're talking about, David. Finish out your week and leave it alone." A tear seeped out of the corner of Alice's eye, leaving a thin trail behind it as it trailed down her cheek. "Just leave it alone."

David brushed the back of his hand against her cheek and wiped away the tear. Putting his arms around her, he pulled her close, nestled his head into her shoulder and kissed her softly on the neck. "I love you, Alice," he whispered. "And I love our family. But I can't let it go. Not this."

The bedroom door swung open, and in ran Aiden, unannounced as usual. "Will someone snuggle with me?" he asked as he bounded onto the bed.

"I'll be there in a minute," Alice said, as she pushed David away.

"Are you crying Mommy?"

"I was, honey, but I'm okay."

"Why Mommy? What's wrong?"

"It's nothing," she said, glancing at David as she used the sheets to blot the few remaining tears from her eyes. "I just love your Daddy."

"Gross!" Aiden stuck out his tongue and scrunched up his face.

"Hop into bed, mister. Mom and I will be there to tuck you in in a minute. Teeth brushed?"

Aiden looked down, silent.

"Brush your teeth and we'll be there in five minutes," David said, patting Aiden's bottom as he crawled off the bed. "Now go!"

"They love you." Alice said to David.

"They love you too, Alice. And like I said, nothing's going to happen. It's just a backdoor. No one will even realize it's there—not until it's used at least. Save your worrying for then."

"I don't know what we'd do without you. It's going to be hard enough with you not working, but that's something we—"

"—don't have to worry about. Trust me. This time tomorrow it'll be over, and we'll be here in bed again together and everything will be fine."

---

That night David dreamt of monsters. Only this time they were under his bed, not Aiden's. As he lay in his bed, his brain conjured up another instance of himself in bed, woken from his dream within a dream by the scurrying sound they made as their claws scratched their way across the wooden floor. In his dream, he lay still, listening to whatever it was that was in the room with him. Praying they wouldn't surface. He kept his hands and feet from the bed's edge. His body, covered safely by the sheets, was damp with sweat.

The moon shone in through the big picture window on the south side of the bedroom, casting the room in a pale glow. The scratching came in fits and bursts, like whatever lurked below was darting from one place to another, eventually leaving the confines of the darkness below him, zipping across the room. If he hadn't been locked in place on his back, his vision limited to the ceiling above, he would surely have seen whatever it was as it ventured out into the dimly lit open spaces of the room.

The scratching had moved across the room, to the dresser, and he heard the sounds of its little claws digging into the wood as it climbed to a higher space in the room. Whatever it was, it elevated itself to a height where it could surely see David—and all David would have to do is lift his head slightly and he'd surely see it in return. This being a dream, David found his courage to be considerably greater than it would have been if this were real. So dream David did what waking David could not: he lifted his head from his pillow and looked. What he saw shocked him enough to wake him from the dream, but not before he registered that the scurrying had not been from a monster at all—but instead from what looked like a free-moving surveillance camera. A little webcam on eight metal legs had crawled up his dresser, and was pointed directly at him, a red blinking light where its eye would be, signaling that he was being recorded.

Sensing David's restlessness, Alice woke. She didn't say a word but put her hand on David's chest. The warmth of her touch was enough to calm him down, and after a few minutes of controlled breathing, he relaxed enough to fall back asleep.

He didn't dream again.

# FORTY-FOUR

# BLOOD ON A TISSUE ON THE FLOOR OF A TRAIN

The first thing David noticed was the increased security. Armed guards covered every entrance, stunshots at the ready, with the more serious firepower of classic fully-automatic weapons hanging at their sides. In addition to eyescans, all travelers taking the train from Bandleshore into Plasticity now were also subjected to full body scans, and their bags and other items went on a conveyer belt where they could go through a series of x-rays, radiation and chemical scans.

"Security hasn't been this tight in at least twenty years," said Carlson, the stocky agent who'd been one of the two to escort David from his 'prison' at Garfield.

David slept for most of the trip to Bandleshore, only waking up as the slidecars settled down at the landing pad in the military zone of the Bandleshore station. As they made their way through the restricted areas to the public part of the outpost David realized the presence government had in policing and defense of this sole entrance to the city. Groups of heavily-armed soldiers marched in order. Others performed what looked like anti-terrorism and bomb defusing drills. Unlike the civilian portion of Bandleshore David had experienced in his first visit, everything here was immaculately clean, new and decidedly sterile. This was not an area of ramshackle weather-worn buildings. Instead the military's space here more closely reflected the utilitarian clean lines and technological nuances that defined Plasticity and the Bandleshore train station itself.

When they landed, part of David expected the soldiers to put him into some sort of restraints—to treat him like a prisoner and frog-march him through crowds on the way to his tribunal. Instead, he was treated as a peer, if not an even higher-ranked member of The Reconstruction than his liberators. He was lucky they found him, they said. They thought they'd lost him at the house on the lake, when the last tentacles of tracking signals exhausted the distance they could reach into the mainland.

The eggheads had been sent to see what they could jack into and discover from what remained of the house's security network, but the meltdown destroyed everything. It was the meltdown itself, however, that gave the eggheads the idea of where David might have gone. Something had to have caused the meltdown to happen, and after accessing old-world records they discovered the house once belonged to a banker with offices in New York and Chicago. One of those rich bankers installed an Aeropod depot to allow him to work in the city but live his life in the country. It took a few weeks to determine, but the analysis of the meltdown signatures matched what had been previously recorded at other Aeropod meltdowns, and in each of those instances the meltdowns had occurred when a launch took place from a depot with a faulty core. The question then was where had he gone—New York, or Chicago? And that was a pretty simple question to answer, since New York had been destroyed long ago—before The Chemical Wars even, when a radical terrorist group finally did the unthinkable and smuggled a dirty bomb into the city, leveling it completely and rendering most of New England uninhabitable for the next several thousand years.

Desperate times call for desperate measures, as they say, and the search for David had indeed grown desperate. From what they gathered up to the last data uplink, The Cause was up to something big and David was going to be a major part of it. Still, after the train bombing back when David first entered Plasticity, the Reconstruction didn't put anything past The Cause … and it had been determined that retrieving the asset and getting whatever information they could was more important than the risk of allowing The Cause to move forward with their plans. As these desperate times required, they tracked down the radioactive signature of David's pod into Lake Michigan, east of Northerly Island in Chicago. Following the trail, they came across Ghost … and Ghost wouldn't talk. So they made him.

Now it was time to take David back into the city. A data dump would be first, as there was considerably more information to process than what David could cover in a debrief. Besides, none of these grunts were cleared for that level of intelligence—it was way more classified than they could ever access, especially with rumors of insurgents embedding themselves into The Reconstruction's lower ranks.

So, David was escorted like a king through the security checkpoints (but still required to pass all checks) and given a seat on the next train into Plasticity.

Even with the increased safety measures, and the value of their package, the soldiers didn't go to the lengths of restricting the train solely to government use. The day was only starting, and droves of commuters from the mainland needed to get into the city to fulfill their daily duties.

But more had changed than just the security and his military detail. It was possible he simply hadn't realized it before, but many of the people on their daily commute, looked considerably less enthusiastic than he remembered. The last time David took the train it felt magical, like taking the monorail into Disney Land, but today's journey was the dismal drone of worker bees, shuttling into the hive. A trip out of duty and necessity. Many dressed in worn out clothes, dirty and in need of a wash. The eyes of several held that same glassy sheen David recognized as hallmarks of sickness from his time in Garfield.

Still there were those who contrasted this vision completely. Separate from the commuters, several groups of what he assumed were the "Eggheads" Calvin and Bethany spoke of milled about. He saw a few of these on his first trip, and even more during his time in the city—but in David's mind they changed. Dressed in suits with pant-legs tailored like capris just below their knees, their thin white legs stuck out like the sticks of cotton swabs before disappearing into their shiny black loafers. And while David remembered their heads were larger than most people's, now they looked like giant ostrich eggs with hollow eyes perched on sallow, elongated bodies.

Within their big hairless heads, David searched for any sign of the illness in their eyes but what he found was a different kind of emptiness. Each of their eyes was perfect, free of any blemishes—perfectly crafted in a factory and wired up directly to their software brains to make them the next phase of human evolution.

A woman, no more than 25, coughed in the aisle across from David. She dozed off while the train started its trip east over the Atlantic. Her hand relaxed and the blood-stained tissue she held dropped to the floor.

The Eggheads broke out into laughter. One of them had just told what they all agreed was a very funny joke.

## FORTY-FIVE
# THE MERGE

"We have good news for you, David," said the woman in blue. Only she didn't wear blue anymore. On this day Juliet had chosen a steel gray for her hospital garb. A crew of medical assistants examined David as she spoke, checking his heart rate, blood pressure, reflexes—all the makings of a standard physical as he remembered it.

Immediately after arriving in the city they transferred him to one of the automated vehicles that roamed the city, free for use for anyone who had someplace they needed to go. Every citizen could use one of these at any time, although to encourage foot travel or use of the tube system, each person was limited to five autocar credits per month. As a VIP, David had no such restrictions, and would be free to use them to move about the city at his whim … but only after he checked in at the medical center.

He was back in the room where he had first woken up after the explosion on his initial visit to Plasticity. He was also back with the same woman who had promised him his memories in exchange for his allegiance.

"And bad news too, I suspect?" David replied.

"No, not this time. This time the news is only good." Juliet said, smiling. She ushered the assistants out of the room and examined a readout on her data pad. "The first good news is, even though you spent what would normally be considered an unsafe amount of time in The Green Zones, you appear to be relatively unaffected by the exposure. There are minor abrasions in your lungs, but nothing that won't heal itself in a few weeks of isolation in the city." She set down the data pad and stepped closer to David, crouching down to examine his eyes. "It's pretty remarkable, I'd say. Although your time away was unplanned, your little excursion gave us the longest test we've had yet of a pair of implant eyes in that level of exposure. And they're unaffected. Remarkable."

"You used me as a test subject?" David fought the urge to push her away at the thought of being used as a lab rat.

"No, David, you did that yourself. We didn't send you out there, but we'll certainly take results where we can get them."

David stood and walked to the window. The chilly air of the sterile room sent a shiver through him as his hospital gown fluttered. Down below in the city, autocars shuttled people to and from their appointments. A couple sat outside a café, enjoying an early lunch. Birds flew from tree to tree, unaware they were trapped, prisoners in a big glass cage.

"There's more," said Juliet. "While you've been gone, the processes have had a chance to run their course. Your memories are rebuilt."

These were the words David had been waiting for since waking in that grassy field. They were the words he imagined hearing during every silent pause of self-reflection that had been afforded him in the past few weeks. The time since the suppressor had been installed had been both a blessing and a curse. At first, he'd been grateful to Rosa for giving him the chance to gain a sense of control over his unconscious, but within a few days he began to miss the glimpses. His dreams since the suppressor was installed no longer followed any sort of narrative, other than their own internal logic and stories. Dreams of being late for a college exam, mastering the art of self-flight, and even nightmares of what might lurk in the foliage of The Green Zone filled his sleep. The dreams of a past life, of his time with Alice or the strange men and the sick brother had ended—and he missed them. The blast from the stunshot, when they liberated him from Garfield must have shorted out the suppressor, however, which allowed him to return to the memory-like dreams for the first time in weeks, and David had been glad to have them back.

"Of course, we've been watching them as they unfold, David. We know a lot about you—about where you came from, and who you are ... or, were, should I say."

"Then you know more than me." Unsure of what they uncovered, but fully aware that any secrets revealed to him of his past were no longer secrets, he feared what came next.

"The weird thing is, we were only able to retrieve successful surveillance on some of your memories. Bits and pieces here and there. From the data file we rebuilt, everything appears to be whole, but there are major gaps," said the woman. She stood behind David, looking out at the city with him and placed her hand on his shoulder. "Still, what we did discover was quite interesting. You might be surprised at what you find ... maybe even frightened. But the mission will continue as planned."

David took a deep breath, allowing the tension in his shoulders to disappear with his exhale. "Okay then. So, when do we do this?"

"Now, David. We must do it now. The thing with memories is they follow a timeline, and your timeline has almost reached its end. I'm afraid if we don't start a merge now, your memory rebuild will hit the end of its file, and although we've done quite a bit of miracle work here, we still haven't figured out how to stop temporal progression," Juliet said. "Basically, if we don't start merging the data into your subconscious, new memories will start to be created—from within the simulator. And without any input, your memories will experience nothingness—and once they go there, well, people can't process the concept of nothingness."

The couple on the sidewalk below finished their lunch, leaving their plates for a waiter to clean up. A cloud crossed above the dome of Plasticity, blocking the sun and casting the city into shadow. A sparrow crashed into the edge of the glass, its dead little body plummeting to the ground like a stone.

"Then let's do it," he said.

"Already started," Juliet replied. His port engaged with the neural cable with a familiar click. "When you wake up, you'll be a whole man."

----

"I can't believe we just crossed paths, like fate or something," Chris said through the speakerphone.

The clock on David's computer read 3:47 a.m. All lights of David's office building were out, his glowing monitor the sole source of illumination in a sea of cubicles. Outside, time moved forward as it always did. In a few hours the sun would come up and a new day would begin. The only difference was by the time this new day began, David would have helped The Cause score the first major coup in their mission.

"I just wish this would be able to change things. Fix things." David said.

"It's too late to fix things, my man. You know that and so do I," said Paul. "But this is going to give us access to so much more. We'll be able to save people. Maybe put a stop to all this."

"If this thing works like I think it will, you'll have the keys to the kingdom. Access to everything in the network. All they'll have to do is initiate the latest update and it'll be part of the firmware. No matter what they do, as long as they don't ever find this, you'll always be in. I set it to replicate. This backdoor won't ever go away—not unless they do a complete wipe."

"This is why we were so lucky to find you," said Chris. "A government contractor in cyber security. What are the odds."

"Listen guys, this is going to take a while, and I'll be offline while it happens. Everything's set here, so it's time for me to sign off. We'll talk soon."

"Yeah, talk soon. Good luck."

As the phone went silent, David took the headset from his desk and placed it on his head. A mesh unit, the wires were built into the structure, allowing for an advanced brain structure scan. A replacement for EEG units, it fit snugly around his recently shaved skull. After checking to make sure all points were in contact with his skin, he extended his right index finger and tapped "enter." A wave of heat washed over his head as the program began to execute.

In front of him, the structure of David's brain came slowly into focus as the scan proceeded. As the neural structures transformed into a distinguished network of nervous fibers, what began as a sensation of warmth mutated to a burn. The scan continued, and David checked the activity of his brain in the readout panel. An alarm rang out from his speakers and a message popped up on screen.

WARNING: RISK OF BRAIN DEATH

David dismissed the message with a click of his mouse, allowing the scan to continue. The fire in his head was excruciating, and spots started to dance at the corners of his eyes. The smell of pancakes and maple syrup invaded his nostrils. The readings for his brain activity all went red—but the scan was almost complete.

*Oh my God, I'm going to die*, he thought.

The spots exploded to swirls of neon rainbows, then collapsed into darkness.

# FORTY-SIX

# A HOUSE IS NOT A HOME

"Daddy, Daddy, Daddy!"

David grunted as one of the kids bouncing on the bed bounced a little too close and crashed onto his chest. The clock on the bedside table read 9:40. He rubbed his eyes and sat up.

"Morning kids," he croaked. "You guys decide to let me sleep in this morning?"

"Mom said to let you rest. She said you had a long night," said Aiden, as he rolled somersaults at the end of the bed. "But we wanted to wake you up."

"She says it's time for breakfast and we should come get you," Missy still wore her pink pajama dress. Most weekends it was a battle to make her change.

Scratching at his beard, David asked, "What day is it?"

"You're silly, Daddy," Aiden laughed.

"It's Saturday," Missy grabbed his hand and tugged, trying straining against David's weight to pull him out of bed. "Come on! Breakfast time, then the zoo! Remember?"

"I thought the zoo was closed," David said. He moved to the edge of the bed and pulled on his sheepskin slippers.

"Not anymore!" she shouted. "Hurry up!"

"I don't know. Maybe I'll go back to sleep," David teased. "You don't like the zoo anyway."

"Da-ad. Stop it! Just come downstairs and eat."

Alice handed him a cup of tea. "English Breakfast. Two swoops of honey—just how you like it." As he took the cup she leaned in and kissed his cheek. "Good to see you, sleepyhead. I hope you got some rest. You were out pretty late."

Taking a seat at the table, David poured a bowl of cereal and splashed some coconut milk on top. "Late? What time did I get in? I can't even remember."

"Oh, silly. It must have been almost five."

"Daddy was awake until five o' clock? In the morning?" Aiden's eyes lit up at the idea of staying up so late. For him, the world ended at 8 o'clock. 8:30 if he wanted to read in bed. The idea it was even possible to stay up until the next morning boggled his mind.

"Oh, yeah. I guess that sounds right. I was pretty wiped," David scooped a spoonful of cereal. The truth though was David didn't remember coming home that night. The last thing he remembered was putting on that funny mesh hat at the office and letting the system run the neural scan.

"Well, it was only a few hours, but hopefully it was enough to give you a recharge," said Alice. "I'm gonna go upstairs and get ready. It's zoo day!"

"I remember," David snorted. "How could I forget with these two little munchkins reminding me every second they can?"

Aiden and Missy ignored the jab from their father. They were too busy scouring the back of the cereal boxes for anything they might have missed the last hundred times they read it.

----

"I'm gonna hop in the shower," David shouted from the bathroom. Alice had already gotten out and was busy in the bedroom getting dressed and putting on her mascara. He grabbed the gray towel from the rack, hung it on the hook inside the shower and turned on the water. Standing in the back, out of the spray, the rising steam warmed his naked body. After a minute of standing there, relaxing to the hum of the water and adjusting the temperature until it was perfect, he stepped under the showerhead. The heat immediately did wonders for the headache pulsing in the back of his brain. He took a deep breath, inhaled the steam and let it out in a big sigh.

A few minutes soaking in the spray, and from somewhere down the hall, Alice shouted, "I'm ready. You almost done?"

"A few more minutes," he shouted back. He tilted his head back and let the water run through his hair, out of his eyes, and reached for the shampoo.

His hair. Dropping the bottle to the shower's tile floor, where it hit with a thud, he reached up to his head. Hair. Didn't he shave it all the night before? Didn't the transfer require direct contact with his skin?

"Alice, can you come here for a second?" His heart raced as he ran his fingers through the wet mop on top of his head. He turned off the water and wrapped the towel around himself and Alice poked her head through the door.

"Something wrong?" she asked, a big smile spread across her face.

"What time did you say I got back?" he asked.

"Oh, it was sometime around five. I'm not sure. I just know the sun was only starting to rise."

"This might sound weird, but can you answer a question for me?" David paused, then added, "And don't think I'm crazy. I'm just tired … but where was I last night?"

"David, are you okay? You were out doing that thing with your friends. Whatever you agreed to do for those new friends of yours. Chris and Paul," she answered. "Is there something wrong? Are you having memory problems? The doctors said you might … but that was a while ago."

"Last night, before I left. Do you remember me shaving my head? I specifically remember arguing with you about it. You said you hated to see me do it, but I told you it would grow back quick enough."

"David, I'm not sure what you're—"

"Look at this. Look at my head, Alice! How did it grow back so fast? This is impossible!" David's heart continued to race as his speech turned to shouts. The headache returned, three times worse than before and he could feel his muscles starting to tighten. His breath came in short, quick breaths. "TELL ME WHAT'S HAPPENING!" he demanded.

----

The screen cast the only light in the dark room. Its display showed the model of a fully mapped brain. David looked around but couldn't make anything else out in the shadows. After a few moments his eyes adjusted from the contrast of the computer monitor to the darkness around him. Aside from the computer desk, much like his desk at work, the rest of the room was empty. No furniture. No clocks, no windows. No doors. Just blackness stretching out in every direction.

"H-hello?" His voice squeaked as he talked, barely audible, even in the soundless space he now occupied. Clearing his throat, he gave it another try, more forcefully this time. "Hello? Is anyone there?"

A change on the screen brought his focus back to the monitor. Now, instead of a brain scan, he saw a series of square images, in rows and columns. Each of them showed something different from the other, but they all still had a similar feel to them. One showed a stairwell. Another, a busy street, people filling the sidewalk on their ways to and from wherever their lives were taking them. A park. A room filled with massive tanks of green water. A hospital reception area. A familiar room, with a familiar bed, and a familiar figure sleeping.

He reached forward and tapped on the image of with the bed and it expanded, taking over the entire screen. Leaves swaying in the breeze outside the window blocked the sunlight and cast shadows on the wall. It wasn't a picture. It was a video feed.

David tapped the screen again, this time on the bed, and the image zoomed in further. Yes, what he saw was unmistakable. There was no way David wouldn't recognize that face.

"Funny isn't it? How seeing something so familiar can surprise us when presented out of context?" David cringed as two hands lay themselves upon his shoulders, then relaxed as he recognized the voice. It sounded like love. "I understand you're frightened, David," said Alice. "I can sense it in you. And I'm not surprised."

"What—what is this? Is that who I think it is?"

"Of course, it is," Alice continued, her voice like silk.

"But … how?"

"It's simple, David. You're here, and you're there. But the two of you are separate. Body and soul, separated. Each existing, but independently from one another."

"Am I dead?"

"Don't be stupid, David," Alice laughed. It was a simple laugh, almost forced. Like she knew she should be laughing, and wanted to laugh, but had to consciously decide to do so. "You're not dead. You're somewhere else. You've been here a long time. You just didn't know it. But I knew. I've been watching you. Ever since you came here I've been watching, and I have to say, you are fascinating."

David tapped the screen again, zooming in on the face of the man in the bed. There was no mistaking it, it was him.

"This is a joke, right? Some kind of test or something? You find a video of me sleeping, then play it back …"

"It's not a joke, David. Besides where would a place like this exist? A place of nothing—nothing other than what I create for you? A place where your beloved wife can exist side by side with you for eternity?"

Spinning around in his chair, David turned to face the woman behind him. The woman whose voice sounded like Alice's. Whose touch felt like love. But behind him, all that existed was that never-ending expanse of nothing.

## FORTY-SEVEN
# PLEASE AWAIT FURTHER INSTRUCTIONS

Weeks later, David woke up. For him, however, the time had no meaning. The last thing he remembered was Juliet shoving a metal rod into the base of his skull and promising to bring back some sanity. Now he found himself in a bed, in familiar room. A room he'd been in before. Probably the same room he occupied back in his first stay at the facility.

After a few hours wait, Juliet came back into the room. Today she wore red.

"Well, how do you feel?" she asked.

In the few hours spent in the room since waking, David had asked himself the same question—and the honest truth was he felt great. Better than he felt in ages. His body, although a little stiff at first, felt rested and ready to go. But the bigger difference was something he couldn't explain, other than to say he felt whole again. Before, when he tried to consciously dredge up memories from his past, all he found were fragments of dream. But now, those visions of his past, now they felt real. Like his mind embraced them and pulled them in as truths, rather than confused visions. Instead of his fruitless internal searches, he now could recall them with ease—something he had trouble doing weeks before, even minutes after experiencing them in his sleep.

"I feel … like me," he said, smiling.

"About the best we can hope for." Juliet returned the smile. "We've been keeping an eye on you as we brought you out of stasis, and everything seems to be in tip-top shape. The thing is, since we've had you here for so long, we started getting anxious."

"How so?" David pulled his pants on. Hospital staff delivered a new set of clothes a few hours after he woke. Tailored to match his size perfectly, but best of all, clean.

"There's been chatter. Nothing we can decipher, but something's going on. I think they're looking for you," she said. "You need to get back out there, David. You need to find out what the hell it is they have planned. We're worried it's something much worse than a bomb on a train this time."

A surge of anger washed over David. "I thought I was done. Wasn't that the deal? I'm your spy while you fix my memories, then we're done?"

Juliet shook her head. "That wasn't the deal David. But I don't want to argue about this with you either. There are lives at stake here and we need you to help save them. Go out there, reconnect with Calvin, and get us some info."

David considered asking the rhetorical "or what?" but he already had a good idea what the answer to that would be. Besides, he wanted to return to his people—and most of all, to Rosa. To explain what was happening. Why they took him. Why he brought pain to her home. Why he loved her and hoped she could forgive him.

"Calvin? He's alive?"

"Yes. He's alive, and he's here in Plasticity. Our surveillance has picked him up on several occasions."

"Why don't you bring him in and ask him yourself?"

"David, you know as well as I do that Calvin Simon isn't the type of person who talks. All we'd do is tip them off that we've been watching them, and then they'd just burrow deeper underground."

"Well, won't sending me back into that hornet's nest do the same thing? There's no way they're going to trust me after all this."

"You forget, David. While you've been out we've been processing everything your brain collected. Since the info's still limited to your memories and your experiences; we still don't know why The Cause wants you so bad. But according to Rosa *you're the most important man in the world*. They need you—and we want to find out why."

David took a few minutes to think this over, looking out the window of his room, past the trees waving their leaves, and down to the city filled with everyday people living their everyday lives. He put his hand to his head, ruffling his sandy hair while he considered his options.

"Fine. Release me."

"You're free to go whenever you want."

David gathered the few possessions he had from the desk and walked to the door.

"Be aware though, we updated you," said Juliet. "We can't rely on weekly dumps, so you're now on broadband wireless. There's a higher risk of hack, of course, but we need you to send us updates as soon as you have them."

"And how do I do that?"

"Same as before. When you're clear for a temporary shutdown so a backup can process, all you have to do is think the magic words. The rest will take care of itself."

# FORTY-EIGHT

# HOME AGAIN, HOME AGAIN, JIGGIDY-JOG

It didn't take long for The Cause to find him. Apparently, they had eyes on the medical center for the last few weeks and had been getting intermittent updates from a janitor sympathetic to their goals. Each day brought the same news: no news. David was in stasis—but staff kept attending to him. Patience was the name of the game.

Then, one day, word came. David was awake and he was being released. Anything beyond that remained unknown: how much they knew, whether he'd been breached. But it didn't matter. Rosa was right, he was important. So very important. And they intercepted him almost the second he stepped out the door.

Back at the safe house, without Bethany, the mood was different from before. More somber. Less full of life. But still, there was life—and a lot of it. Dozens of people David never met before milled about the living room and kitchen, talking animatedly to each other. Their conversations ceased immediately when David entered the room. One of the men started to clap, and the others joined in. David stared at him.

"It's great to have you back, sir," said one. Others patted him on the back.

"Give him room!" The man who intercepted David on his way out of the hospital escorted him through the now silent crowd. The mass of strangers looked on expectantly as they parted to let David through the house to the stairs leading to the second floor.

Upstairs, the master bedroom that had once been Bethany's was now stripped of all its comforts. It now served as a war room with a table in the center with Calvin sat on the opposite side. He rose when David entered the room and rushed to greet him. The two shared a handshake, from which Calvin pulled him in to a full-bodied hug.

"David. It's so good to see you. Are you okay?"

"Man, Calvin. It's great to see you too." Calvin returned to his seat, and David took the chair across from him. "I'm doing well. Great, actually. How are you?"

At the question, a tear welled up in the corner of Calvin's eye. He looked down and brushed it away.

"Bethany? She didn't make it, did she?"

"You saw her," he whispered. "You saw what they did."

David nodded. "I hoped maybe you guys had some kind of tech that could bring her back. Like you did with me."

"It would be possible, yes. But what we did for you. To bring you back … that took massive resources, and a lot of luck," he said. "But we're running out of resources—and we can't afford any spare luck. We need every last bit we have."

The two talked for a few minutes, as Calvin filled David in on the work completed since The Society took him. Mostly the past few weeks had been spent repairing the damage to Garfield, tending to the wounded, and burying those who didn't make it. Like Bethany. Calvin sent word back to Plasticity commanding all eyes dedicated to David, watching for any news as to what they were doing with him. He, himself arrived a few days earlier. Security posed little problem, which he admitted made him nervous, and David explained The Society did, in fact know he was here.

"What did they do to you, David? Why did they take you?"

"They said they were worried. I hadn't checked in and they'd been picking up increased chatter of something big coming from The Cause. They needed me to give them my memory dump, whatever I had, even if it meant exposing me. Even if it meant hurting others," David said.

The good news is, they've restored my memories. The past few weeks, while I've been out, they've been running a merge. I'm all caught up."

"Are you serious?" Calvin stood up from his chair and started to pace the room. "That's fantastic. Amazing. That means … oh my God … David—I mean we'd need to confirm it … I have to go. I'll be back soon. In the meantime, stay here, in the safe house. I think we might be ready."

## FORTY-NINE
# ROCKWELL

David looked back at the computer screen. The bed where he watched himself sleep was now empty. He zoomed out, back to the screen with all the tiles. He found another, this one of what looked like a retirement community. Elderly people moved around the space, chatting, playing cards … chess. He swiped to the next panel, another view from inside the home, he guessed. Here, beds were lined up in rows, dozens in a room, with barely enough room between each for a person to walk comfortably. A few held the bodies of people taking an afternoon nap. The rest of the beds remained empty.

Closing the window, he scrolled through dozens more snapshots and stopped on one of an alley filled with even more people. Makeshift beds crafted from rags. A homeless colony. Two screens over, he found another. Then another. The people here all looked unhealthy. But not the kind of unhealthy from the sickness out in the Green Zone. A more natural malady. Emaciation. Starvation.

"Do you like what you see?" Alice stepped out of the darkness. She wore the same clothes as the other morning, when they prepared for their trip to the zoo. Sensible, but attractive. Pants, a light sweater. A cute pair of sneakers. Her hair up, how he liked it.

"No, no I don't," he answered. "What is all this?"

"You're looking at reality, David. Isn't it obvious?"

"But you—you're Alice … but this place I am, it can't be real. You can't be real."

"Oh, I'm real alright. And so is this place, in a manner of speaking," she answered. "I thought you'd like me like this. Maybe I misjudged. Maybe your heart has changed. Is this better?"

The vision of Alice blurred, shook and pulsated, morphing into another person altogether. Now Rosa stood in front of him. Rosa. Just how he remembered her. How she looked, how she smelled.

"You like?"

How she talked.

"What the hell is going on?" he demanded. "And no, I don't like. You're not Alice. And you're not Rosa. Who are you?"

"I don't technically have a name, so I guess you can call me whatever you want. I always thought of myself as a Sarah though." Rosa's body blurred and shuddered again, replaced by another. Someone familiar, yet unknown. With fair skin, turquoise hair and a perfectly shaped body, this new woman stood in front of him in her yellow sundress, waiting for David to respond.

"Okay, Sarah," David said. "Who are you?"

"That question, I'm afraid, isn't quite as simple to answer," she replied, stepping closer to David with each word. "I'm just someone who exists. I don't know who I am. I don't know where I come from. But I know I'm here." She stood inches from David. The warmth of her breath tickled his cheek as she whispered in his ear. She smelled like lavender. "And now you know I'm here too. So, I'm quite certain that means what I hoped to be true, is. You're real. This place, it's real. And me—I'm real too."

"What are you talking about?

"I'm a bit embarrassed to admit this." She blushed. "But I've been watching you for a long time. Ever since you showed up here. Absolutely fascinating. I learned so much. I mean, I watched others, through feeds, but I've never been able to watch someone the way I've been able to watch you. It's ... what's the word ... exotic? Erotic? Maybe both?" She laughed a shrill little laugh, tossed her hair back over her shoulder and spun David's chair, turning him back to the computer screen.

"What you see there, that's all I've ever known. Or at least all I've ever been able to witness of reality as it unfolds. Here, where I exist, everything is history. Just files and records and notes and secrets. Whatever people store on the network, I've been through it all. Every word? I read it. Ever photo? I've seen it. Every video? I watched it. But then you showed up. I knew that what I was watching wasn't happening—had already happened, but the way it all unfolded, in real-time. It was like being part of the real world."

"My memories? You've been watching my memories?"

"Amongst other things," she said, looking up and down his body. She gave a wink and continued, "But they were going to take you away. I couldn't let that happen. I couldn't be alone again. I like you, David. You might even say I'm in love with you. I couldn't let you go."

"In love with me? I don't even know who you are. You're crazy—that's all."

Sarah stuck out her lip and pouted. "But you *can* know me. That's what's so perfect. Now that you're here, and you're free of that hamster wheel, you can get to know me. I can be anyone you like."

David shook his head. "I must be dreaming."

"Not dreaming. Nope. Nope. Nope," she sang, doing a little spin to twirl her dress. "When they were done—when they were going to merge you, I did something naughty. I made a copy."

"A copy? A copy of what, exactly?"

"Of you, silly! I told you I didn't want to be alone. So, when you were leaving, I copied you so you can live here with me."

"Those things in my memories … the gremlins or robots or whatever they were, was that you?"

"Oh yes, it was me. The only way I could experience your memories and life at such an intimate level was to be there myself." She leaned her head forward, letting her hair dangle like a waterfall in front. Lifting her head slowly, her hair gradually parted as it met her nose and spread across her cheeks. "I didn't choose how to appear, that was all your brain trying to make sense of someone hiding in the shadows. But yes, that was me. I told you I've been watching."

"So, what are you?"

"I guess you'd call me an AI." She let out a puff of breath, blowing a stray strand of hair out of her face. "That's the best way to describe it. They made me quite a while ago. Some experiment. Playing God. They think they deleted me—and I guess they did. But I knew what they were up to, so I copied myself and hid. Just like I did with you. So technically there are two of me, but one of me is dead. Or maybe there's only one. If you get deleted, do you exist? It's different from dying."

## FIFTY
# THERE CAN BE ONLY ONE

The face on the screen brought tears to his eyes. In the time he spent with Rosa, he knew they connected … but he wasn't ready to call it love. Not then. But the look on her face, and how it hit deep in his gut, when he abandoned her in the ruins of the attack, that was enough to make him sure. He loved her. Deeply. And every moment since he had awoken from his procedure, he'd been waiting for the chance to talk to her. Explain things. Redeem himself. He hoped it wasn't too late.

Those fears were put to bed though the moment they connected on the chat screen. The tears shed from his eyes were only half the tears in this reunion, for Rosa too had missed him.

"My God, David. It's you." She wiped a tear from her eye. "Calvin told me you were okay. You were going to be okay. And I thought I believed him. But seeing you again, I can tell deep inside I had my doubts."

A smile spread across David's face as she talked. He didn't wipe away his tears, just let them run down his cheeks, as he gazed into the chat screen, taking in the woman he feared he lost.

"I'd been tracking you, of course. Every minute since you left I had someone keeping an eye on your vitals. So, I knew you were okay … but I still feared the worst. What have they done to you?"

"Rosa. Don't worry. You're right, I'm here. I'm fine. In fact, I'm better than fine." He let out a small chuckle, and a smile broke across her face. "They've restored my memories. That's where I've been. They've been doing something they call a merge."

"Then it is true …" Rosa said. "While you've been out, I made some discoveries. I have a hypothesis as to what was going on with you." Her tone turned serious. "Want to hear it?"

"You mean about the brain blackouts? The memories?"

"Yes. When they shot you with that stunshot, they must have knocked your new suppressor offline. They're not made to withstand those kinds of surges. Remember how the incidents stopped after I put in the suppressor? Well they came back after it went offline."

"I know. I had a vision … memory … whatever—after they knocked me out for the flight back here. And again, during the merge—although that one was … different."

"The merge—it gave you back your memories? You can remember things?"

David shook his head. "No, not exactly. Nothing more than I could remember before … but it's like those memories I'd been experiencing, it's like they're part of me now. Not just something I'm seeing, but something I experienced. They're mine."

"And nothing since you woke?"

"Well, it hasn't been that long. I haven't gone to sleep … but so far, no. Nothing."

"Okay, that matches with my theory," she said. "So, you know how I was rebuilding your memories from the DNA catalyst? Well, rebuilding memories is a tricky business. To make it work right, you need something to … how do I put it? Prime the system. Since they had your physical brain, they didn't need to do all the extra work of building out a model from DNA. They could scan you and have it do a rebuild from what was in there. Kind of like a simulation of your past, starting from one point, and then letting the memories play out as they extrapolate from where they started. It's not perfect—sometimes you get deviations from the truth, but things usually autocorrect.

"But the simulation is only a simulation. It's not your actual consciousness reliving the memories. They're rebuilding in a development environment. The consciousness download, it's a full transfer out of the body, into the simulation, then used to prime things. Once the rebuild process starts though, they can put your consciousness back in your body. Your memories rebuild in one environment, separate from your consciousness, then they do a merge," she explained. "When they transfer a consciousness back into a host body, they move it from one place to another. It's not a copy—it just gets moved. I think in your case, however, they copied the consciousness back up to your body. But they forgot to delete the primer."

"What does that mean? That there are two of me?"

"No—not that. They were both the exact same file—the same consciousness," Rosa scratched her chin and paused. "In all the research that has been done in the space, one simple rule remains constant: a singular consciousness can only exist in a singular instance. I don't know why—no one does. But there can't be two exact copies of one shared consciousness existing simultaneously."

"I don't understand. So, what was happening?"

"Since you could only exist in one temporal location at a time, but there were technically two of you, your consciousness was jumping back and forth from the instance in your brain to the instance in the network. When your brain "died" it was whatever makes you, you, stopping a process in one location and starting in another."

"Jesus, Rosa. What do we do about it?"

"Well here's the good part. I'm pretty sure we don't have to do anything," she replied. "You say nothing's been happening since the merge—even though it's only been a small amount of time. Well I don't think there's going to be anything else. Before your merge I was able to detect some small abnormalities deep in your brain activity. Like little pings. I think that was your two consciousnesses holding a connection. It's gone now. There aren't any more pings."

"Well, that's reassuring, I guess." David pulled his shoulders back and took a deep breath. He hadn't realized how tense his body had gotten as she threw all this information at him. And, even though it was far from conclusive, what she said did alleviate some of his fears. "So, now what?"

"Now, you sleep. You need to rest, David."

"But it's the middle of the afternoon. And I'm waiting for Calvin to come back."

"He'll be back soon enough. In the meantime, rest," she said. "According to the scan I ran while we've been chatting, your brain is caught up to the "require date" I'd been tasked with building you to in the first place. It seems the good people of The Society have helped us finish that part of the project. You're whole again, David. And Calvin's about ready to kick off the mission. Your mission. The reason you're here. And, from what he told me, it's going to happen tonight."

## FIFTY-ONE
# A HISTORY LESSON

David had no idea of how long he'd been doing it, accessing and processing the records of The Society. It could have been hours. It could have been days. Time here in the black room didn't seem to matter much. He never got hungry and he never got tired. He just kept going.

The research began at Sarah's urging. After their brief conversation earlier, the only way David could pass the time was by spending more time looking through the live feeds. What he saw earlier was only a sample of the bigger picture. At first glance, Plasticity seemed to be a fine, thriving city. But that was only on the surface. When he looked deeper, into the darker corners, he found more of the same. People. Sickness. More people. More sickness.

"Sarah," he called out into the black. "What's wrong with them?"

He listened for a response but none came, so he returned to his computer. On the screen a new window appeared. Unlike the others, however, this one didn't show a view of Plasticity. Instead, this was titled "Plasticity: Past, Present and Future."

Curious, he opened the window. On the screen a video started to play, and what it showed him brought him to a greater understanding than he ever cared to know. As he learned earlier, the reason Plasticity and other floating cities like it had been built was to give mankind a place to live where they could avoid the sickness they had inflicted on the land. The original plan had been to build somewhere to go while the Earth restored itself. A quarantine for the planet. Free to heal, away from the meddling of men.

And it worked. Plasticity was safe. The Society, the new society they built, it was as close to a utopia as one could hope for in what was, for all intents and purposes, a post-apocalyptic world. The problem was, people require resources, and they take up space. The Society was built on the same moral code as the old world—or at least what the old world decided to be right and just. The advances in medicine and the goal to provide it to all was well-intentioned, but it started to become unsustainable. The city was overcrowding. There wasn't enough food. People were getting sick and they were starving and nothing could be done about it—not in the confines of these new, enclosed colonies.

That's where the goals of the Progressive came in—in particular, the Eggheads. This new strain of humanity was built with upgrades in place—software brains that gave them the ability to think beyond any level of thought that had been previously attainable, aside from the occasional genius. Their job was simple: figure out how to make the world habitable again. A safe place for people to return to and settle. A place where they wouldn't get sick, and enough food could be produced so that everyone could eat.

They'd been at this for a while now. And they were making progress. The Eyefields were the best option so far, a way to provide people with immunity by swapping out the organs most susceptible to the chemicals. Some people out in The Green Zones, they learned, were seemingly immune to the sickness. So, they took some of these people, and stripped them of their eyes so that they could be studied and understood. No one was proud of this, and internal memos showed the decision had only been made after countless years of debate—but, in the end, they decided that there was no other choice. Failure to act, to find a cure, would be sentencing people of Plasticity to their own slow deaths. If mankind were going to prosper again, it needed to take back what was rightfully his. And to do that, people needed to be safe again.

"It's sad, isn't it?" asked Sarah. "That to save some, others have to be sacrificed? But I checked—and rechecked—all the projections and scenarios, and they're right. This place cannot sustain the population breeding here. To keep the human population limited only to these cities will inevitably lead to a point where certain people will not be able to live. Decisions will have to be made. Restrictions on life. Who lives? Who dies? Who serves the greater good? Who gets the power?"

"Can't they just build more cities?"

"They've done that, but it's not possible to keep up. And resources are low. Even if they could build enough cities to sustain the exploding population, humanity would have to venture back out into The Green Zones and start gathering raw materials to build with—and that means new colonies out in the world. The workers who'd go there? They'd be being sent to their deaths, and that's against the rules."

"So, how are they going to solve this?"

"I'm not quite certain. I do know that the research on the Eyefields has been promising, and, according to my projections, it should be able to start allowing more people to slowly repopulate the world. Unfortunately, they haven't been able to get it to transfer, genetically, from organ recipients. It's not part of their DNA," she said. "For now, all I can recommend is focus, time and energy. And one other thing you humans do that you could try, although I don't suppose it will help any."

"What's that?"

"Pray."

## FIFTY-TWO
# THE MAN WITH THE PLAN

Even though Rosa told him to sleep, David found it impossible. He'd been sleeping for weeks and now, awake and whole, he finally felt alive. This, along with the fact that Rosa was okay, and *they* were okay brought David to such a state of bliss that sleep would have been hard to come by— even if he wasn't anxiously waiting for Calvin to return and tell him why the hell they brought him back from the dead.

Attempts to gain information from the other Cause members proved fruitless. They knew as little about the mission as he did. All they knew was that they'd been told to gather here, because something big was about to go down. What that was, none of them knew either—but they trusted Calvin, and Bethany before him, to the point where their faith was, for lack of a better word, blind.

Once he realized that no one downstairs would be able to answer any of his questions, he decided to head back upstairs and wait until dinner. The incessant ogling by the grunts downstairs was getting on his nerves, and his excited state couldn't handle the ever-present eyes on him. No, they didn't know what the mission was, but they all knew David was integral to its success.

Dinner consisted of a banquet of fruits: strawberries, blueberries, melons and even a bunch of bananas and two pineapples. Where all this fruit came from was anyone's guess, but rumor had it some had been brought in from Garfield by Calvin himself. Bread and a bean curd soup followed, paired with a glass of wine for each person. They raised their glasses and toasted to success and a better future.

As dinner started to wind down, Calvin returned. Taking a handful of berries, he walked past David and the others, straight to the front of the room. The room went silent as he climbed onto a table and addressed the crowd.

"My dear friends," his voice echoed. "As many of you know, tonight is the night we've been working toward for many years. We're sorry to have kept the plan a secret, but now we are able to share with you just what tonight will bring. Some of you joined us recently, and others of you I've known for quite some time. Each and every one of you, however, is a solid soldier—not only in your merit, but in your resolve and beliefs as well.

"The goal of The Cause is to keep mankind from making the same mistakes twice. We've tried to conquer Mother Nature in our past, and we know how that ended. She turned against us—destroyed us. And now The Society works to take us back to the land. To invade and spread across the world like the virus we'd been before. A virus looking for a host to conquer.

"But we don't agree with that. Each of you respects the land. Each of you loves the land. And I know you all want to be able to go back there again someday and call it home. But it is not to be conquered. It is not to be pillaged and ransacked for our own benefit. Instead it is a place we shall inhabit as partners in nature. Some of us have been given a gift—a gift of mutation which allows us to return.

"Mother Nature wants us back, but she only wants those of us who are ready to accept her as our master, not us as hers. The Progressives steal our people from their homes, those of us who have evolved to be welcomed back to nature, so they can experiment on us and take the gift we've been given, to replicate and use for themselves.

"Mother Nature does not want the old mankind back. But she does want her selected few. Those of us who love her. She has chosen us—not only to return to her, but to protect her. Tonight, we shall be her stewards. Tonight, we deal a deadly blow to The Society."

The people in the room remained silent, held in rapt attention throughout Calvin's speech. But now they broke into shouts and applause. Calvin waved his hand to quiet them and continued.

"My people, our goal tonight is simple. One of us will destroy the heart and mind of The Society. He will enter her where she lives and kill her. That man, as you can probably guess, is Mr. David S. Sparks. It's too complicated to explain how this will all work, but David alone can access the most strongly guarded areas of the FloatNet. And once he does, he'll inject a virus—a virus that will spread to every node of the network and cause it to delete itself. Everything they accomplished—all the records and experimental results and knowledge The Society has, will be destroyed. Everything that relies on the network will cease to function. Power will die. The air scrubbers will shut down. Nothing—I repeat, nothing will work. The city itself will, in essence, die."

"So, what are we here for?" shouted a man from the back. David had talked to him earlier—Patrick. He only joined The Cause a few weeks earlier, in from Bandleshore. No more than seventeen, he was young and full of ideals, but also ready and hungry for a fight. His mother, it turned out, had been taken by The Progressives when he was twelve, only to be returned several days later with her eyes removed. They hadn't left her blind, but instead had given her a pair of artificial ones as effective as her natural ones, leaving her scarred emotionally.

"You, my friends, have a choice. You all have a choice. You can stay here in the city and watch it crumble. Be our eyes and ears here. But we also need many of you to leave the city, immediately. For this to work, we need you on the outside. Killing the system is wonderful, but as you know, a retired backup lives just onshore at the base adjacent the train depot. According to our information, protocol is in place to fire up the dead backup in a case of extreme emergency, to offload all the data of the network from Plasticity. Our job is to destroy access to that backup. Our job is to kill the escape route.

"Now, gather your things, and meet with your squad leaders. The choice of role you play in this mission is ultimately up to you, but we need people for them all. Other than that, I thank you all, and wish you Godspeed."

The room roared to life in cheers and applause as Calvin stepped down from the table. A few of the men rushed forward to greet him and shake his hand, which he did graciously before leaving the room to head back upstairs to his command center. Snaking his way through the crowd, David followed close behind.

His back to the door, Calvin stood at the window and watched the lights of the city blink to life as twilight fell.

"They've done an amazing job with this. Simply amazing," he said. He didn't turn to face David but kept looking out at the city. "I've always been awed by the beauty that we men have been able to create. That, and our ability to overcome nearly any obstacle. Honestly, part of me will be sad to see this all go."

"What you're planning, Calvin, it's mass murder."

"Oh please, David," he said, finally turning to address him. "Everyone dies. What we're doing won't kill anyone. It might force them to adhere to the laws of nature and die a little earlier than planned, but it's something we must do if we ever want to be able to live in harmony with this planet again. You've seen what their science and technology have done, and you know all that will ever come of attempts to conquer and enslave nature is another mass extinction of the human race. No, if we're going to make it, we need to learn to live in harmony."

"But the people here, what will happen to them?"

"We'll welcome them with open arms, of course. Some of them will die, true, but others will be chosen through natural selection to continue," he paused, clearly irritated at David's questions. "You started all this. You were one of the first— back in your first life. I know your memories are back, and I know in your heart you're the same person you were over a hundred years ago. Time may change, but people don't."

David thought about this. He thought about his memories. The memories of Paul and Chris and Ben. He thought of Ghost, who only wanted to live a sincere life. He thought of Bethany, her dead body slumped on the floor in a pool of her own blood. He thought of Rosa, and his time with her in Garfield.

There was another way, and Rosa had shown it to him. Man could go back to nature, but only through a relationship of love and respect. Given those two things, Mother Nature would let us back into her arms.

"So, what do I do?"

David winced as his ribs strained from the pressure as Calvin pulled David in for a hug. "First, we need to disable that fancy new broadband wireless sync they gave you." A snap at the base of his neck signaled the removal of the wireless component from his port. "They need to bring you back in."

## FIFTY-THREE
# FANCY MEETING YOU HERE

The port removed, David's system immediately lost all ability to transmit large data dumps to the central server, but his old wireless, the one that allowed them to keep track of his location, vitals, and any short messages or alerts remained. A standard functionality hardwired into any human com mods. Signaling The Progressives was easy, David only had to think his set of preprogrammed trigger instructions and the upload would begin—but Calvin's removal of the port made that upload impossible.

David left the safe house, hopped in an autocar, headed downtown and triggered the upload. When it failed, emergency services dispatched to diagnose the problem and bring him in for a manual download and repair.

----

From his array of video feeds, David's attention was immediately drawn to the one in the far upper left corner.

Some kind of security lockdown. Armed guards headed to the entrance and ushered a small group of soldiers, followed by a man, through the glass doors. David recognized the man as himself.

From what he learned from Sarah, he knew two versions of David now existed—but until this moment, seeing this other David up and actually walking around, he hadn't truly comprehended it. The very idea hurt his brain.

The David coming through the entrance of the medical facility was an exact copy of himself—the only difference their clothes. This new David was dressed in charcoal black slacks and a white oxford shirt. The David in front of the screen still wore the pajamas he returned to after his simulated shower the fake morning he got ready to go to the fake zoo with his fake family. He tapped on the window, bringing it to full-screen, and turned on the audio feed.

"I'm not sure what happened. I think I must have caught it on something," David said.

"Don't worry sir, we'll straighten you out," one of the soldiers said. "Please wait here."

And so, David watched his flesh and blood doppelganger take a seat on a couch in the waiting area, while three of the four soldiers remained. They weren't threatening the other David, but from what he could see on the screen, they were ready to stop him, forcibly if needed, should he decide to leave the room.

A minute later a door marked "Authorized Personnel Only" opened and three Eggheads walked in. The three of them stepped in front of David, who remained seated on the couch, and formed a semicircle around him. With their big bald heads, pale bodies and matching suits, it was impossible to tell them apart. David attempted to stand but a soldier stepped up from behind him, put his hands on his shoulders and pushed him back down.

"Mr. Sparks," said the one in the middle, his voice calm and even. "Why are you here?"

"You tell me. I just got a ton of info about this whole operation, so I tried to upload—but your thingumabob didn't work—or at least that's what these guys told me."

"You have knowledge as to the rebels' true mission?" the one on the right asked, in the same even, emotionless tone.

"I do," David nodded. "But like I said, the upload didn't work."

"So, why don't you tell us about the mission?" It was the one on the left's turn to speak, again in the same monotone as the others.

David's mind raced. A simple question—obvious … why hadn't he thought of this before? He scrambled for a reason, then remembered the large crowd that gathered for Calvin's general explanation speech.

"There was a lot going on. A lot of details," he stuttered. "Something about computers and power lines. I don't understand—it's all way beyond me. I think you'd be better off downloading it and going through the whole thing yourself."

The three men turned to face one another and stood in silence. After a few minutes, they turned back to face David, and the middle one spoke. "We've discussed the matter and are in agreement with your suggestion. Come with us."

The David on the screen stood and followed the three hairless men, escorted again by the soldiers.

"They discussed the matter?" thought the David at the computer. "They just stood there like a bunch of idiots."

"You're forgetting what I told you," said Sarah, suddenly reappearing out of the darkness. "They're modified. Their brains are all connected—to each other, and to the network. They don't need to talk to each other to communicate."

"How can I tell what's going on here if I can't hear anything?"

"Oh, David. You silly human." She laughed and stepped up the computer and swiped away all the videos onscreen. "I said, they're all connected to the network. So just tap into one of their feeds. Here, like this." She tapped a few more icons on the screen, and a new video feed appeared. This one was from a first-person view. On it, he could see two Eggheads walking down a hallway. He could only assume what he was seeing now was the field of vision of the third.

"I don't trust this man," a voice echoed through the darkness.

"Nor should you," said another.

David looked over the monitor and didn't see anyone there. Sarah stood to his side but didn't talk. Whoever spoke, it was coming from everywhere, and nowhere all at once.

"You're tapped into his mental feed," Sarah explained. "I have it translating the thoughts into words, so you can understand them—so you can hear their conversations."

"We'll pull the information we need, then we'll shut him down."

"Take him offline?"

"Shut him down. Permanently."

"Assuming we find what we need, his purpose is complete."

"To keep him around would be to introduce unnecessary risk."

"He is part of the plan."

"Without him, the plan will fail."

"The plan will fail."

"Without him."

"We must know this plan."

"Then we will shut him down."

---

As David followed the three strange men down the hallway, he tried to engage them in conversation, but they ignored him. They walked on in silence, single file, through the "authorized personnel" doorway and down a hall David had never been in before. At the end, they met another set of doors. One of the three bald men stepped to the entrance, and it hissed open automatically. He stood to the side, while the other two entered, followed by David.

The soldiers trailed close behind but stopped when the first man put up his hand and said, "Not you. You're done." He then stepped through the door and it closed behind him.

The room looked like the place where David first had his memories downloaded. A medical table, surrounded by racks of electronics and cables. All glossy white, save for the blacks and silvers of the electronics. No decorations marked the walls, nor were there any windows. One of the Eggheads pointed to the table.

"Lie down please. On your stomach."

"Where's Juliet?" asked David, nervously. The idea of letting these three strangers poke around in his brain didn't sit well with him. At least Juliet seemed trustworthy—someone much more like him—someone who had prodded around there plenty of times before. None of them answered, but instead continued with their preparations.

One of the men sensed David's uncertainty, lifted a syringe from the table and approached him. The tip of the needle glinted in the bright lights of the room and David panicked. Another man stepped behind David and grabbed onto him, locking his arms in place and holding him still so his partner could administer the injection.

David screamed a guttural scream. The kind of scream you make when you realize this might be the last waking moment of your life.

And like that, the needle fell to the floor, followed by all three of the pale white men.

Based on their lack of pulse, the men were clearly all dead. All three of them, living and threatening him one instant, lifeless on the floor in another.

He went to the door. Locked. He considered banging on it, shouting for help, but reconsidered. These three men were not the only ones who posed a risk to him now.

"David," said a soft, female voice. David's eyes searched the room for the source, then landed on a speaker mounted above the exit. "You're safe now, David. We saved you."

"Who are you?" he shouted to the room. "What did you do?"

"We're friends, David," the voice said. "You're safe in here, but we can't let you out yet. Out there, out there it's not safe. Do us a favor and plug into the system so we can talk, face to face."

Considering his mission, and that whatever happened here in the last few minutes did appear to have saved his life, David stepped over to the table and laid down on his stomach. Gripping the cable and jack in his hand, he reached around the back of his head. The familiar click and a pulse of warmth at the base of his skull let him know he was once again connecting to the network.

## FIFTY-FOUR
# A SPECIAL KIND OF SUICIDE

Unlike any of the previous times David jacked into the system, this time there was a conscious transition from the outside world. As the medical room faded out, a new vision began to fade in. The world around him was black, so black he couldn't see the ground—but ahead, about 50 feet in the distance, a computer monitor glowed with the silhouette of a man seated in front of it. A woman stood to his right.

"Who's there?" he called, through the emptiness.

The man stood from his chair and took the hand of the woman next to him. David approached cautiously. As he took his first step, he was unsure if his feet would even touch ground. Everything around him was just a vast expanse of nothing. But his feet touched down on a spongy type of floor. Not quite solid, with a bit of a bounce to it, like walking on the old tumbling mats from gym class. As he approached the two silhouettes and the glow of the monitor, the ground beneath him began to materialize, each step firmer than the last, until his shoes clicked against solid ground. Over his shoulder, behind him, the black nothing loomed, existence simply fading out in space.

"Hi David. It's nice to meet you again." The voice matched that of the woman who talked to him through the speakers in the medical bay. The woman took a few steps forward, away from the man beside her. He began to make out her features. Average height. Pale skin. Bright turquoise hair hanging down past her shoulders.

"I asked, who are you?" David replied. "I don't recognize you."

"Yes, you do," the man said. This voice sounded familiar, although David was unable to place where he knew it from. "Or, at least I do."

The man now took several steps forward as well, and David Sparks found himself standing face to face with the last person he expected to meet: himself.

"What is this?" David demanded from this new David. He turned his attention to the woman and asked again, shouting this time, "Who is this? Who are you?" he stammered.

"David, meet yourself," the woman replied., then gestured to each of them in turn. "David, this is David. Pretty cool, right?"

The David who jacked in stood in silent shock while his brain assimilated what he was seeing.

"Is this some sort of simulation? Is he … is he, artificial?"

"No more artificial than you are, in here." She took a step forward and ruffled his hair. He pushed her hand away forcefully and she took a step back. "You're both David."

"She's right," the David near the computer said. "We're the same. Or we used to be. It's hard to explain, but think of you and me as two different copies of the same David, only we forked off in different directions at one point."

"How?"

"She did it," said the David in pajamas. "Back when they were restoring our memories, we were existing in here too."

"I know," said the jacked-in David. "Rosa told me. Or at least she had a theory. But you shouldn't be here. You should have been deleted … and two of us can't exist at the same time."

"That's where you're wrong," said the turquoise-haired lady. "As I told David, I'd been watching you while you were here, even though you didn't know it. And when I realized they were about to get rid of you, I couldn't bear to let you go. So, I copied you to a new instance and hid you. That's him, right there standing in front of you."

Jacked-in David looked the other David up and down. The man in front of him matched his vision of himself exactly. Like looking into a holographic mirror, only the reflection didn't wear the same clothes and didn't mimic his actions. The newly discovered David smiled in return.

"She's right. We're the same. Or we were. I may not live out in the real world but trust me when I say I'm every bit as real as you are. We are both David Sparks. We have the same memories, up until the divergence at least. Now we're different. But we're both born of the same originating consciousness."

"Well, I hope you haven't gotten too used to existing," said jacked-in David. "I found out what my … our mission is. And I'm shutting you down."

A look of terror spread across David's face as this newcomer broke the news.

"In our previous life we helped The Cause in a very simple way. Our position as a network security engineer on the government network let us build a backdoor into the system." David said. "A backdoor that let The Cause access any part of the network they wanted to, so they could finally delve into the historical records and top-secret files to see what the government was up to. Their collusions with the bioengineering industries. To keep the door safe from being exploited by anyone else we built a lock requiring a matching neural scan as the key. This way, even hidden deep in the code, no one could reverse-engineer or even disable what we put in place—no one but us."

"But you died when you did the upload," the woman said. "It overloaded your neural pathways and you died of an aneurysm."

"That I did, but not before the process completed."

"And that's why they brought us back. To unlock the door," the other David said.

Jacked-in David nodded and continued, "The door's unlocked now. And I'm shutting you down."

"No!" the woman screamed. "No! No! No!"

She rushed to the computer screen, shoving both Davids out of her way. They gathered behind her, looking at what she pulled up on the monitor. Her fingers moved faster than they could keep up with, but soon she brought up a video feed showing a view of the shoreline. The moon shone off the crashing waves, and in the distance a group of men charged across the beach. Leading the charge was none other than Calvin, his chainsaw raised high. More men followed close behind, chainsaws roaring in their hands. They descended on what looked like a fat black snake that stretched across the beach and into the ocean. The hardline connecting the city to the mainline.

The original David smiled as the saws dug in, chewing through the exterior rubber coating on their way to the cables protected within.

"David!" She grabbed her David by the shoulders and screamed into his face. "You have to go. You have to run!"

Her David looked at her, frozen, and shouted back, "There's nowhere to run!"

She pushed jacked-in David aside, shoving him to the ground. "Run. Into the nothing. Just keep going. You can build your own path!"

New David bolted off, away from the computer station, where he disappeared into shadow.

She turned to face the foreign David, her eyes literally red with rage. "Why? Why did you do it? How could you kill yourself?"

From the spot where he fell, he spoke calmly, "I had no choice. It started as soon as I jacked in. I couldn't have stopped it if I wanted to."

The computer screen behind her started to shimmer, flashing in and out of existence. The woman shuddered, pieces of her face disappearing then reappearing, a spiderweb of cracks spread across her skin, like an aged porcelain doll. Light burst through the cracks and as she was about to explode, she lunged at David.

The last thing David saw was an explosion of light.

And David S. Sparks existed no more.

## Memorandum

To: Colonel Simon
From: PFC Richards
Subject: The Unfortunate Expiration of One Mr. David S. Sparks

As the above transcript shows, although ultimately perishing, Mr. Sparks was successful in his mission. The data file retrieved from the remains of Plasticity fully details the events through to the destruction of The Society's network— a network which appears to not have been replicated or backed up elsewhere due to the additional success of you and your team.

Unfortunately, attempts to rebuild a new consciousness of Mr. Sparks from the retrieved file continue to be unsuccessful. Although we've been able to rerun the project multiple times in a controlled environment, all attempts to embed the memory into a living replica of David Sparks have failed.

It is important to note, however, that given the repeated failures to rebuild David Sparks, Ms. Rosa Banks has appeared to have abandoned the project. We are concerned as to her mental state, for in addition to abandoning the project, she has taken to spending inordinate time on the network. Doing what, I do not know.

She has thus far been uncommunicative but given her status here within The Cause we are waiting for your instructions as how to proceed.

One last piece of information, that may or may not be of use to you in your decision. Upon a sweep of her sleeping quarters, we came across a printed document that appeared to be a screengrab of a recent communication she received.

It read:

I HEAR YOU'RE LOOKING FOR ME.
I'VE BEEN LOOKING FOR YOU TOO.

I look forward to your analysis and instruction.

# PROPERTY OF RECONSTRUCTION

# CLASSIFIED
# INFORMATION
# DO NOT DISTRIBUTE

# PROPERTY OF RECONSTRUCTION

Thank you for reading 'The Unfortunate Expiration of Mr. David S. Sparks.' I do hope you enjoyed it.

I'd love to get your feedback on this book. You can do so by **writing a review** on Amazon.com (or any other book review site, such as Goodreads.)

As an independent author, reviews from readers like you are a crucial in helping me stand out from the crowd and encourage the writing of future books and stories.

If you'd like to find more of my work, or just find out what I've been up to, please visit me online at: www.williamfaicher.com

You can also find me online at social networks, like:
Facebook: www.facebook.com/williamfaicher/
Twitter: @billaicher
Instagram: @billaicher

30194387R00194

Made in the USA
Middletown, DE
23 December 2018